Be Careful What You Kiss For

Jane Lynne Daniels

"This novel dazzles."
—*Long and Short Romance Reviews*

TAKE IT...

When Tensley Tanner-Starbrook gets the chance for one life "do-over" from a well-intentioned but bumbling psychic, she goes for it. But that change turns everything else upside down. Instead of a buttoned-up corporate executive, she's now an entirely unbuttoned exotic dancer. And she's face to...face with the one man she's never been able to get over.

TO THE MAX

Detective Max Hunter has come a long way from high-school bad boy, and with everything on the line, nothing can stop him...except seeing his first love dancing in the club he's been assigned to investigate. Torn between getting her far away from the place and needing her help as an insider, he knows only two things for sure: Tensley's stirring feelings he thought long ago buried, and a relationship with her would be career suicide. Yet, maybe, just maybe, this was a love meant to overcome the past.

Be Careful What You Kiss For

Jane Lynne Daniels

To Diane,
Jane L. Daniels

www.BOROUGHSPUBLISHINGGROUP.com

BE CAREFUL WHAT YOU KISS FOR

Digital edition created by Maureen Cutajar
www.gopublished.com

ISBN 978-1-941260-8-21

For P.G.G., with love

CONTENTS

Be Careful What You Kiss For

CHAPTER ONE

The sidewalk sign, scuffed at each corner, teetered on three legs in the breeze. *Madame Claire, Psychic. Predictions with a 95 percent success rate.*

Great. Tensley could see the follow-up survey now. *On a scale of 1 to 10, how accurate was the prediction that you would continue to fall for lying, cheating bastards...?*

Still, she'd promised her best friend Kate she'd drive clear across town to see Madame Claire. And a promise was a promise. She squared her shoulders and marched up the stairs.

Once inside, she jammed her sunglasses on her head and looked around, letting her eyes adjust to the change in light. The room was small, with wood floors, an overstuffed sofa, two straight-backed chairs and candles scattered on a tray atop a black table. The smell of incense floated through the air as soft music played.

A door opened and out stepped a woman whose face was a good fifteen years younger than her neck, around which hung a necklace with a large ruby-colored pendant. She wore a shade of lipstick so bright that it drained most of the color from her cheeks, and on her feet, red heels.

The woman clasped her hands together. "So you have come." An unfamiliar accent hovered around the edges of her words. Russian? Transylvanian?

"Madame Claire?"

"Indeed." A deep nod. "I have been waiting for you." She stepped aside to motion Tensley through the door into a room lit only by a small lamp with crystals dangling from its shade.

Once they were seated on opposite sides of a table, Madame Claire closed her eyes and bent her head. After a moment, she opened her eyes and reached across the table to take Tensley's hands. "You have regrets."

Tensley's laugh burst like a popped balloon. "Me and every other human being on the planet."

Madame Claire's brows formed a deep V.

"Sorry." The woman deserved a chance, at least. "Go ahead. Please tell me what you see in my future."

Dark eyes met hers. "Your regrets concern a man."

"They do not." Her swift answer carried a warning.

"I see him."

Perfect. A psychic who didn't have the sense to back away from a cement wall when she smacked into it. "Doesn't matter," Tensley said, teeth clenched. "I've moved on—"

"He hurt you."

"I don't want to talk about it."

"Like the sharpest knife, this hurt."

Tensley pressed a fist against her stomach. If it weren't for the promise to Kate, she would have put money on the table and left without saying another word. Instead, she made a conscious effort to keep her butt in the chair and her mind clear of emotional derailments. "Tell me what you see in my future."

"You did not understand what he was trying to do."

Ha. She *understood*, all right. Bryan-with-a-y-not-an-i had wanted sex, over and over, before returning to the wife and baby he hadn't thought to mention. Only Tensley had thought it was something else.

"He was young. So young," the psychic went on.

He was a player. A freaking French-speaking player. He was—*wait*. So young? Not that young. Thirty-two, same as her.

"His name..." said Madame Claire. "It begins with M. Martin. Matt...No..."

Hold on. This woman did not know—she couldn't. "Stop. Talk about me!" Tensley's voice hit the high-pitched tremble that gave her away when she was nervous. She hated when that happened. "I'm going to get a fabulous new job."

"No."

"I'll get my same job back. With a raise."

"No."

Bet you don't get many repeat customers. Tensley tried to pull one hand away, but the psychic kept it locked in hers, rings pressing into Tensley's skin.

"Ahhh," breathed Madame Claire. "Yes. His eyes are blue. An unusual blue. Dark. Like the depths of the ocean."

Tensley froze. Not possible. She couldn't know about Max. It had been years ago. A lifetime ago.

Once again, the psychic's eyes met hers. "Your first love."

Tensley stopped breathing. The feel of Max's warm, strong fingers stroking her body, cupping her breasts with fierce tenderness and moving slowly downward...came rushing back. The moon shining down on them. Max's body, muscles rippling, ready to take her places she'd never been. The smell of the grass that cradled them, mingling with the clean Tide smell of the blanket they lay on. Max's blue eyes darkening with passion.

Heat flowed through her at the remembered imprint of his body on hers. How it had felt to have him inside her. Filling an emptiness she hadn't known existed until then. Like nothing she'd ever known before. Or since.

Tensley's eyes squeezed shut. "Next topic," she managed to say.

"A woman, she never fully lets go of her first," Madame Claire said.

He'd whispered how beautiful she was, how she took his breath away, how there was no one else like her. She'd believed him. "Not true. I let go of my first." Her voice broke, betraying her.

"This may be what you believe."

Tensley's eyes flew open. If she were prone to violence, this woman would be in trouble. "So I made a mistake. A big one. Lucky me. *He* had to be my first." She'd caught Max kissing another girl.

"I tell you this, with love comes mistakes."

"Not like this one." Tensley yanked her hands away. "I should have known better. Should have known someone like him wouldn't care about someone like me." Even after all these years, it still hurt to say, to think.

"Ah, but he did. You trusted your eyes instead of your heart. You did not understand."

"I should have stood around waiting to ask?" Tensley leaned forward, her voice rising. "When he came up for air?"

Seconds ticked by as Tensley swallowed the memories. Instead of going down, they caught in her throat, making it ache. *Damn it.*

"Every woman, she knows her worst mistake. Yours has to do with this man."

Tensley arched a brow. "Really."

"Tell me, please," said Madame Claire, "if you could have…" She gestured with her hands, as if they could help her find the right word, "a do-over…yes, that is it, what would it be?"

"This isn't Nordstrom. You can't return parts of your life."

"In your world, perhaps. However, in mine, it is different. It is possible once. But only once."

Ohh-kay. Maybe Kate had been inhaling the anesthesia in her vet office when she'd sworn Madame Claire could help Tensley move on from Bryan. "A do-over." Tensley eased her fist from her stomach and threw out the first thing she could think of. "I guess I would have punched Rhonda the Skank when I had the chance." *Instead of running away in tears.*

"Rhonda...the Skank?" Madame Claire's lips pursed.

"Rhonda Reardon. From high school." Tensley could still picture Max's hand on the tight jeans that covered Rhonda's ass, his mouth on the lips of the girl who allegedly carried a knife and boasted about a tattoo most of the football team had seen.

Rhonda the bad girl and Max the bad boy. It made a hell of a lot more sense than Tensley the awkward girl and Max the bad boy.

Tensley started to tell Madame Claire to forget she'd brought up something so stupid, but stopped before the words came out. She'd always regretted not letting Rhonda have it. Awkward girls had their dark sides, too.

"I see," said Madame Claire. "If this is what you choose, then it shall be so." She sounded relieved.

Tensley straightened. What did she mean by that?

"All of us, we have regrets," the psychic went on. "Yours, however, run deeper than many. It was the same with your friend Kate." A pause. "Before."

"Before what?" A bad feeling crept up Tensley's spine.

"She was at one time in a very different place. But this regret she carries no longer and that is why she sent you here."

"But—"

"When you leave here, you will have punched Rhonda...the *Skank*, as you call her, when you had the chance."

"That's—not possible." Then Tensley pictured her fist connecting with Rhonda Reardon's nose. Saw the blood mix with layers of Cover Girl makeup to form a globby mess that ran down the front of Rhonda's tight shirt and made suicide leaps off the ledge of her gigantic boobs.

Tensley smiled, surprising her face muscles, which had been as good as frozen for days. What was the harm in pretending? She got it now. Why Kate had sent her here.

With a glance at the clock, Madame Claire said, "But you are to tell no one. This promise you must make."

Tell them what exactly, that a psychic had told her she could do the impossible? Then her mind made another leap, imagining Max's stunned expression if she *had* decked Rhonda. She saw herself walking away from them both, chin held high, while Rhonda wailed. While Max left Rhonda to cry into her giant boobs-slash flotation-devices and instead followed Tensley.

"You are to promise," the psychic repeated, louder this time. "If you speak of this, events would unravel most unpredictably." She shook her head and muttered something under her breath.

Tensley leaned forward. She'd only caught a few of the words, but they'd sounded like all hell would... "Excuse me?"

"Make. This. Promise."

Tensley sat back, folding her hands in her lap. "Even Kate? She's the one who sent me here. If I don't report back, she's going to wonder."

"Only her. No one else must know."

Sure, she'd play along. "Fine. I promise."

Madame Claire stood. "Our time has ended. You will go now."

Not a moment too soon. Tensley's chair screeched as she pushed it back to also stand. She hesitated, though, before turning to leave. "You do also see good things ahead for me?" She hated how much she wanted the answer to be "yes."

For the first time, the shadow of a smile curved around Madame Claire's lips. "That is up to you and how you look at your journey."

Her journey. So far Tensley's journey had veered from her internal GPS at least a dozen times. Any more route recalculations and she'd be watching *Jeopardy* in a nursing home before she decided whether or not she wanted to have kids.

"Right." As though it would have been so hard for the woman to throw her a crumb, like hearing from an old friend, getting unexpected good news. Something.

Sometimes Kate had great intentions, but really bad ideas. Tensley lifted her hand in goodbye and power-walked toward the door to the shop. As her foot crossed the jamb, she heard a noise behind her and turned to see Madame Claire raising her arms slowly, silent lips moving. A white light flashed over the psychic's head and sparks rained down, obscuring the woman.

Holy shit. Tensley stumbled and had to put a hand out to catch herself. When she looked back, the psychic had gone. So had the light. If…it had ever been there in the first place.

Seriously. Tensley needed to filter her best friend's ideas a little better.

Feet squarely beneath her this time, Tensley stepped outside, the bright sunlight such a painful contrast to the dark shop that her eyes squeezed shut. She barely had time to take a breath before there was a whoosh that whipped her hair straight back from her head. When she managed to open her eyes again, the light was muted, different. Not sunlight.

No. Not sunlight at all.

***

Tensley peered into the dim light. As soon as her vision adjusted, she snapped her eyes shut, unable to believe what she had seen. She was standing on a stage in a large, dimly lit room that smelled of sweat and alcohol.

Hungry-looking men, drinks in hand, stared up at a woman to her left, bathed in blue light and writhing to the beat. The woman was working her bare boobs and ass for all she was worth, her gaze fixed on an open-mouthed man in a business suit. With one hand, he reached inside his jacket, drawing out bills. The fingers of his other hand curled, as though longing to grab a handful of her. Or himself.

A spotlight jumped to life, nailing Tensley. She flinched, looking down to see her body glowing at center stage, one hand gripping a brass pole. It was her body, all right. Minus the five pounds she'd put on since the Bryan incident and at least fifteen more. Her nipples stood at attention, pointed toward the ceiling. She wore a tiny red thong, plexiglass stilettos and nothing else.

Ohhhh. M-m-m-m. G.

Think, Tensley. Madame Claire. That flash above her head. Like a sparkler, on the Fourth of July. The offer of a do-over. A do—Oh God. It couldn't be—

Goose bumps crawled up her arms at the same moment sweat broke out on her forehead. The room began to bob and weave. Her other hand moved to the pole, holding on tight.

Footsteps shook the stage. A minute later, fingers tipped with crimson daggers closed over Tensley's death grip on the pole. "What's going on?" a female voice demanded in her ear.

For the second time that day, Tensley jerked her hand away from a stranger, this time hunching her shoulders inward and folding her free arm across her breasts.

"You've got back house rent to pay, Starbrook," the woman hissed. "So you'd better start shakin' your ass."

Tensley owned an upscale one-bedroom condo she'd barely furnished because she wasn't sure what went with a paint color called Butterscotch Tempest. And her ass hadn't shaken since—um. Ever.

The woman released her and took a step forward, holding her hands up for the audience's attention. The music slid into the background and even the transfixed man and the dancing girl in the corner turned to look.

"It's okay," the woman on stage announced. Her voice dropped to a purr that carried all the way to the back wall. "Lila Delightful's just feeling a little shy tonight. Guess you're all going to have to show her how friendly I know you can be."

Lila Delightful?

The male voices roared encouragement in whoops and hollers and the woman, in a black leather dress so tight that most of her pale skin spilled over the top, spun back toward Tensley, her smile glittering a warning. As she passed by, she paused long enough to lay a hand on Tensley's arm and say in her ear, "If you're loaded, I swear I'm going to throw you and all your shit out on the street." She turned to give the crowd a broad wink and then half-walked, half-danced off the stage, blowing a kiss before she disappeared into the darkness.

Tensley's body began to move of its own accord. Hips thrusting from one side to the other in time with the music. Before her brain could catch up with the rest of her, she'd straddled the pole, spinning in one fluid motion, head down, hair brushing the floor. Her legs spread until they were parallel to the floor, her toes pointed.

Then she pulled herself upright, legs still in a straight line, as effortlessly as someone who actually had been able to get the hang of the monkey bars in first grade.

She spun again and dropped to the floor in a perfect split. The audience, all ten—or a hundred—of them, shouted its appreciation. Tensley heard herself join in, as surprised as anyone. If she'd known she could do this, she would have tried out for high school cheerleading instead of hiding her envy as she watched other girls flip, leap and bounce.

Then she was down on her knees, thrusting her crotch toward the audience, her back bending like Gumby and her hands traveling upward to cup her...*whoa*...much bigger...breasts. They had either finally grown in or she'd had a surgery she didn't remember.

She tipped her head, raking her fingers through her hair in one agonizingly long and slow motion. A collective intake of breath from the audience sent a thrill of excitement through her. This was, well, she wouldn't go so far as to say fun, but *damn*. No one had ever looked at her quite like this.

When her fingers flashed by on their way back down, she realized she had her own crimson daggers. And toned, slender arms. She must have found time to work out. Not to mention motivation to work out.

Look at the guy with the striped shirt. And the one wearing the baseball cap. Neither one can take his eyes off me.

One by one, her arms snaked along the stage, her ass in the air and hair falling around her shoulders as her nipples brushed the floor, sending waves of an I-can't-believe-I'm-doing-this thrill through her. The man in the striped shirt gripped his drink and leaned forward. Tensley made straight for him, the tip of her tongue working a lazy, seductive journey around her mouth.

His face lit up in anticipation, which turned to raw desire as she reached the end of the stage and rose on her knees to stroke herself while watching him through her lashes. Then she beckoned him toward her with one crimson-tipped index finger. He stood as if in a trance, not seeming to notice as he tripped over a chair. He just kept going.

Come to Mama. This was so not Tensley Tanner-Starbrook. But who had to know that? No one.

For a few minutes of her life, she could be someone else. Have a little fun. Ride on up to the orgasm bar and mix her own, instead of hoping someone like Bryan, who got points for congeniality, but couldn't rock her world if his cock was twice its size…would do it for her.

Head back, she thrust both arms in the air and her crotch toward the mesmerized man. Hell, yes. She *was* Delightful, thank you very much.

His hand snaked forward.

The voice of another man sliced through it all to jolt her brain, if not the body performing independent of her brain, to a screeching halt. "Back up, buddy," he said, loud enough to be heard over the music. "No touching her."

With a gulp, her arms still triumphantly in the air, she shifted an uncertain gaze to the chair, cloaked in shadows, where that voice had come from.

It couldn't be.

Razor-sharp memories pushed forward in her mind. The warm white bath of moonlight. A summer breeze washing over their damp, naked teenage bodies. The smell of newly mown fields. The lump in her throat before she worked up the courage to whisper, "I love you."

Nooooo. She had to stop dancing. Had to end the dizzying swirl of confusion that had caused her to think—

Shadow man got to his feet and her eyes shot straight to his tall, dark silhouette. His fingers flashed into the light as he lifted a drink to her. "Lookin' good."

Max.

With every bit of physical strength she could find, Tensley grabbed the finger still motioning the man in the striped shirt forward. She pulled both hands down and to her sides. Her tongue tried to poke forward to lick her lips again, so she sank her teeth into it, hard, and let out a screech. She tasted blood.

Her body wasn't giving up that easily, though. Before she knew it, she was back on her feet, gyrating and grinding, moving as though her two hands weren't engaged in a go–stop–go battle. Every time her hip shot to one side, she stomped her foot, in the vain hope that would stop it. Something halfway between a purr and a growl came out of her mouth as she concentrated on jamming both hands on her waist. And keeping them there.

Again with the hip thrusting. Again with the stomping.

The striped-shirt man backed up, his expression baffled. Possibly because he'd never seen a step-dance striptease before.

Her hips continued on and then her leg joined in, kicking high as the music hit a crescendo, undeterred by the fight she was having with herself. It wasn't until she ended up doing a vertical split of sorts, legs on the pole, fists still glued to her waist, that the music finally stopped and she regained control of her body.

Tensley eased her extended leg down and off the pole, inch by inch, and stood in the middle of the stage. After a minute or two of stunned silence, the crowd responded with polite applause and a few cat calls.

If he's here, really here, I don't want to know. I don't. The man in the striped shirt approached to drop a twenty on the stage. Tensley peered past him into the darkness, trying to get a better look at the man she didn't want to see.

The audience seemed to be waiting for her to do something. Tensley put one foot behind the other and bobbed a curtsy straight out of Miss Jodi's tap dance class. Miss Jodi had always said a lady should never leave a performance without a curtsy.

She wondered, though, if Miss Jodi had meant *every* kind of performance.

Footsteps again clattered across the stage and the woman who had threatened to evict her earlier grabbed the mike to demand, "Now, are y'all ready for Terrible Tawny, the Tahitian Temptress?"

The audience sounded its approval and the woman spread her arms wide, the sleeves of her sparkling costume nearly knocking Tensley off the stage. She stumbled backward, but caught herself. New music blared and Terrible Tawny began to move her hips from side to side in time to the beat. Then she backed up, one long-limbed step at a time, until she reached the spot where Tensley stood.

Another sharp gyration and Tawny pulled off part of her costume with a flourish. When it landed on Tensley's head, the crowd responded with hoots. Tensley reached up, yanked it to the floor and then tucked her hands under her arms, pulling them in tight as she shuffled backward out of the spotlight. *Get me out of this place.*

She hesitated at the top of the stairs, struggling to get her bearings. She had to call the police. Report this. And say—what? All she could remember was the flash above Madame Claire's head. And the words she'd said. A do-over. The psychic had said it was possible.

What if the idea for revenge that Tensley had tossed off had actually happened? If she'd punched Rhonda Reardon. What if—this strip joint was now her life?

A wave of nausea turned her knees to Jell-O. She grabbed the metal handrail for support as she half-teetered, half-fell down the few stairs, then sat at the bottom and closed her eyes.

It couldn't be true. She wouldn't let it be true. She'd click her heels together three times, like Dorothy, and…

Then she heard his voice, inches away, rocketing straight through the music. "Been a long time."

Her stomach did a double backflip. She remained perfectly still.

Warm breath ruffled the hair over her ear, caressing her skin. "I want a private dance."

Tensley opened her eyes and turned to the one man she'd never been able to get out of her system, even though he'd shattered her heart so badly, it had never properly healed. Virtual gymnasts began spinning, twirling, leaping, falling off a balance beam in her stomach, until she had to press a fist tight to her middle to make them stop.

"Max."

CHAPTER TWO

Max still had thick, dark hair that waved at the ends. But his lanky teen body had filled out considerably, given the muscles now straining at his T-shirt. His shirt was a dark ocean-blue. Like his eyes.

In that moment, everything else around her fell away, fading into a dull background of noise as though she and this man were the only two people in living, breathing color, while the rest of the world melted into black, white and shades of gray.

Max.

Over the years, she'd done everything she could to get him out of her mind. None of it had worked for long. Their sophomore year of college, her best friend had tried to help.

"Put him into a mental Tupperware container," Kate had advised, *"and store it on a shelf in your mind."*

As hard as Tensley tried, as soon as one of Max's legs went into the container, the other one climbed back out. "He won't stay."

"A plastic garbage bag, then."

"I think I have post-traumatic distressed-romance disorder."

"Put him in a metal safe."

What if she lost the combination? "A file folder."

"Just put him in something, already."

"He's in. The file folder." Tensley had felt bad about squashing him flat, though.

"Now shove that folder into the Tupperware container."

"But—"

"Put the container in the metal safe and lock it."

"I don't think—"

"Do. It."

So Tensley had tucked the folder inside the plastic container, placed it in a safe, turned the key and imagined Max's blue gaze disappearing from her life forever. His eyes had been her downfall, with their lethal combination of danger and vulnerability. Those eyes had made her forget he held their high school's record for the highest number of detentions.

Now those eyes had her locked in once again. As she sat on a stair offstage in a strip club, wearing almost nothing.

Of all the seeing-him-again fantasies she'd indulged in over the years…because of course the lock on the safe had broken, she hadn't sealed the Tupperware container right, and the folder had torn…this one had never entered the picture.

Tensley hugged herself tight, staring at the floor.

Maybe he would go away. Maybe everyone would go away.

Another male voice, from beside Max. "Hey, buddy. D'ya mind?"

Tensley looked up. The man in the striped shirt, the one she'd been playing with while on stage, grinned down at her, but his words were meant for Max. "I wanna buy this girl a drink."

"Later," Max replied, his eyes never leaving Tensley.

Striped-shirt man pulled out another twenty, rubbing it between his thumb and forefinger. "But Lila and I had a, you know, connection. Isn't that right, sugar?" He wiggled an eyebrow, beads of sweat dotting his forehead. He held up the money. "How about I help you stash this away?"

Tensley stared up at him and then turned to Max, struggling to keep the desperation she felt from reaching her eyes. There had to be some scrap of dignity she could hold on to in this situation.

Or not.

Max extended his hand. Waiting. As though he was Johnny in *Dirty Dancing*. And she was Baby. She'd always wanted to be Baby.

Tensley raised a trembling hand, laying her fingers in his. They were as strong, and as warm, as she remembered.

"Hey," striped-shirt man protested, running a nervous hand through his hair. "She was dancing for me."

Max ignored him, drawing Tensley up and away from the stairs as the other man's protests wilted away.

They wove through a blur of customers and writhing women, lights and music pulsating around them. Max held her hand tight, sending tingles through her body. Tingles she hadn't felt for a long time.

Tensley pressed her other hand to her chest, trying to slow her escalating heartbeat. He led her to a corner, behind a blue, see-through curtain that hung from the ceiling, lit from behind by a row of lights along the floor. Everything had a bluish tinge, including the lone chair.

Max. It was really him. He would get her clothes; take her out of this place.

He dropped her hand and sat down. "Dance," he said.

Tensley's heart thudded to her toes. "What?"

He sprawled on the wooden chair, legs spread, one arm resting on his thigh. "Private dance. Remember?"

After all this time, *that's* what he had to say? He strode up like Johnny Castle and was going to treat her like some—some—stripper?

If that's how he wanted to play it, Baby was coming out of the corner with her fists up. "You want a private dance." She jammed her hands onto her bare blue-tinged hips, as if that would force the wobble from her voice. "It's been, what, fifteen years—"

"And four months."

"Fifteen years and four months and you don't say 'how are you, what have you been doing, it's great to see you, you look amazing,' *anything.*" She stopped to catch her breath.

"Don't need to ask what you've been doing."

"You have got to be kidding. I don't work here."

One eyebrow rose as his gaze traveled the length of her body.

She should have been embarrassed. Furious. Terrified. She was, but she was also...*damn.* Turned on. Just what she needed right now, when she couldn't think straight as it was. "Okay, so it might look that way, but trust me, I do not," she snapped. "You think I'd leave my family's business for this?"

His lips parted, but she didn't give him a chance to speak. She was fighting too hard to keep herself from moving closer to him, from pressing her body against his to feel his heart beating. *Not going to do it. Not going to—*

"How about we talk about you. And how you cheated on me with Rhonda the big-boobed wonder." She'd promised herself that when she saw him again, if she ever did, he would only see all she had now, all she'd made of herself. She wasn't the same naïve girl he'd known. She had experience now. She'd grown into a successful woman. Without him.

Ow. Tensley pushed her fingers harder into her hips to make the pain in her heart stop.

It didn't work.

His jaw worked as if he was trying to decide what to say, but kept changing his mind. Finally, he gestured toward her chest. "So this is about Rhonda?"

As if. At least—she hoped not. "I don't know what you're talking about." She folded her arms.

His eyes held hers. "I remember."

Her breath caught. God help her, she also remembered. That was the whole problem. The scrap of fabric that passed for a thong was becoming damper by the second as she thought back to her arms, legs and heart wrapped around Max. With difficulty, she managed to say, "Don't change the subject." But she had to look over his head to get the words out.

He turned toward the main stage area. "You might want to start dancing."

Tensley followed the direction of his gaze, where she saw a short, barrel-chested man pushing his way toward them. "Why? Who's that?"

"Your boss." This time, Max was the one to look away. "If you don't dance, he'll bring me another girl."

Another girl. Over her dead, thinner-than-ever body. "Fine," she said between clenched teeth, "but only until that creep goes away and since I don't even know *how* to dance, it's not going to be anything great."

"That's where you're wrong."

He had one hell of a nerve, telling her she was wrong about anything. "I can't dance and never could, which means you must be thinking of someone else. That's no surprise, since—"

His words, rough and low, cut through hers. "You never did believe you were special. Guess you still don't."

The second flashback was so vivid, it bent Tensley forward. Max sharing with her, and only her, his secret affinity for the works of Hemingway and Fitzgerald, the sidelong looks he'd given her in class, the fiery sweet touch of his fingers beneath the desks in the back of the room that practically had her climaxing during Senior English.

And he'd only been touching her hand.

She had given Max everything, including her virginity, and it had nearly destroyed her. And now he had the balls to say she'd never believed she was special.

She wasn't going to dance for him. Wasn't even going to keep talking to him. She'd find her clothes on her own and run, not walk, out of this place and leave him sitting in that chair, looking like a fool—

Oh hell, no. Her body had started dancing again, moving easily and provocatively, as though she had done it for years. Which she hadn't. She *hadn't*.

Max held up a fifty-dollar bill.

Tensley's alleged boss turned around, though he continued to watch her over one shoulder.

Her hands reached for the ceiling, one by one, breasts moving in time to the music. She felt a lazy smile cross her face as she thrust her crotch toward Max, teasing her bottom lip with her teeth. A mating dance.

One he was responding to, though he appeared to be doing his best to look nonchalant. He raised the back of his hand to his mouth and cleared his throat, while shifting in his seat. That fold of denim appeared to have become pretty well…filled up.

Good.

No. *Not* good. Tensley's rational thoughts were being shoved out of the way by an overwhelming urge to grab the waistband of Max's jeans, rip that zipper open and take hold of him. Now.

Remember the Tupperware. Slam him back in there, legs and everything else.

It took a full minute of picturing plastic containers, in all colors and sizes, before she could clear a path through the haze of desire flooding her senses. Finally, she shoved him into a purple one and found her voice, scratchy as it was. "Bet you're a regular here." She should have known things would turn out like this for him. He probably had a wife and kids he'd left sitting at home so he could hang out in a strip club.

"Didn't say that." His voice sounded scratchy, too.

"Talk to me," she commanded as her abdomen rippled, crimson nails dragging themselves along her skin.

"You charge extra for that?"

"If I had to charge by the number of words coming from you, I'd be broke."

A short laugh. "So Tensley found an attitude."

"Oh, for God's sake, Max, I am not a stripper," she hissed. Her hands cupped her breasts, offering them up.

Again, his eyebrow lifted. "You're giving it one hell of a try."

One of her hands traveled to her thong, pulling the string playfully away from her skin.

Max straightened, suddenly alert. "Stop."

What was she doing? Tensley forced her free hand to grab the one that had hooked itself into the string, wrestling with herself until she'd managed to pull her wayward fingers back. With a concentrated effort, she made her body stop moving, which left her standing awkwardly, legs spread and her breath coming fast, while the music continued to play.

He glanced at the crowd, then back at her. "You okay?"

She shook her head, willing her eyes not to fill. "Told you I couldn't dance."

"You know that's not the issue."

The only thing she knew was that mortification could spread as fast as molten lava. She felt her cheeks flame. "You seemed to be enjoying yourself a minute ago."

He pulled his mouth tight, averting his eyes.

So he thought she'd sunk so low, she didn't deserve an explanation. That she was a stripper no longer worth his time. And he had the nerve to criticize her for not thinking she was special. *Welcome to the world of me.* She closed the distance between them to grab his face between her hands, the stubble of his whiskers raking the sensitive skin of her palms. He'd talk to her if she had to force him into it.

This time his voice sliced straight through her. "Damn it, Tensley. Don't touch me. Back up."

"Don't touch you?" She choked on her laugh. "Why, afraid you'll catch something?" All of the Tupperware containers opened at once, spilling their contents until her lungs squeezed the breath from her. The hard stares of Max's friends, her friends, the popular girls. The things they whispered, just loud enough for her to hear.

Rhonda's lips on Max's.

There had been only one other time when she'd felt so naked, so vulnerable. Max had been there that time, too. But he'd taken her into his arms and held her close, as if he'd never let her go.

He shot to his feet, causing her to stumble backward. The lighting cast shadows across his face.

She squeezed her eyes shut, folding her arms over her breasts and drawing her chest inward, sinking into herself. "Get me out of here. *Please.*"

"Tensley." He was close enough that his breath caressed her cheeks. She felt him tuck something into her hand, his touch shooting sparklers of anticipation up her spine.

"I'm sorry," he said, low in her ear. She felt every footstep as he strode away. If he'd said those words in her ear fifteen years, four months and three days ago, things might be different now.

She opened her eyes and looked down to see another fifty-dollar bill. Tears trickled from the corners of her eyes.

"Hey!"

Tensley turned to see the barrel-chested man bearing down on her. "Whaddya doin' standing here? Got someplace better to be?"

She drew her shoulders up and back, swiping at the tears with the back of her hand. Her body shook so hard, it jarred her voice. "As a mat—matter of fact—"

"Matter of fact, my ass. You're done with that customer. Go find another one."

Another swipe of tears. "You can't talk to me like that."

"The hell I can't." He shook a stubby finger at her. "Think you're going to get special treatment? As long as you work for me—"

She sniffed. "I don't. Work for you."

"Fine." He shrugged. "Then get your shit and get out."

Asshole. "Fine. I will." Her voice had climbed so high, though, she was pretty sure only a dog could hear it.

"I'll take that." He plucked the fifty from her hand. "See ya." He turned on his heel and disappeared into the crowd.

And she'd thought things couldn't get any worse.

She lifted her head and began retracing her steps through the place. Slowly. Deliberately. One foot in front of the other. As she moved, she made a mental checklist, forming perfect little boxes next to each item. *Find my clothes. Find my purse. Get home. Call Kate.*

Murmurs of "hey, baby," and "lemme buy you a drink, sweetheart," reached her ears, but she ignored them, keeping her eyes straight ahead, focused only on that first item on her list. Clothes.

She saw a black curtain behind the stage, partially pulled back to reveal a hallway painted a nauseating color of green. From out of nowhere, the bouncer showed up to block her way. She stopped, her heart pounding.

"Where you headed, Tensley?" His words carried a warning, more gentle than menacing, that pierced the layer of cotton around her brain.

He knew her.

A red-headed woman wearing scraps of black leather held together by silver chain grabbed the man's arm as she passed by from behind. "Hey Milo, who's lookin' good tonight?"

"Table six. Lots of cash."

"Thanks, honey." She gave his arm a pat and disappeared.

His features squashed into a good-natured smile until seconds later, his attention was caught by someone approaching from Tensley's right. He held up a hand and said, "Dancers only." Tensley felt the person slink away.

His next words were for Tensley. "Gary'll be pissed if he sees you tryin' to take a break this early."

Gary had to be the short guy who'd made her skin crawl. "That man is not my boss."

"You quit again?"

Again? "I don't belong here."

"Come on, Tensley." He shook his head. "You know Gary's just harder on the ones with a record."

She stared up at him. "A record?"

His brows lifted in the age-old "duh" expression. "At least you were still mostly a kid. You should tell him that instead of letting him give you all this crap. You're a good enough dancer and besides…"

The man's words faded into the roar of the background until she could only see his lips moving. *At least you were still mostly a kid.*

The do-over. Punching Rhonda when she'd had the chance.

She'd never hit anyone; never even had so much as a parking ticket. Then she looked down to see her hand form a fist. As it slowly rose, she flashed on the feeling of her fingers connecting with the cartilage and small bones of Rhonda's surgically perfected nose. Nothing in her life had ever hurt so good.

Oh, no. No, no, no. In her one chance for a do-over, Tensley had chosen punching Rhonda.

Milo grabbed her under the arms before she hit the floor. She struggled to regain her footing, but couldn't make her legs work.

From above her, she heard him say something unintelligible. Next thing she knew, he had picked her up and was moving her down the hall, her toes skimming the floor, as though she weighed nothing at all.

Milo shoved a door open. Tensley's brain registered a paper gold star taped to the wood, its edges crumpled. The bouncer somehow maneuvered her into an upright position in a chair. "Breathe," he commanded.

She did her best, choking back the aroma of cigarettes, burned coffee and perfume. After a few minutes, the adrenaline surge subsided, leaving her seasick.

Milo stood. "Better sit it out for a while," he said over his shoulder.

She raised her head, no longer sure what was real and what wasn't. "If I don't shake my scrawny ass, I won't have a place to live." She wanted him to tell her that was a mistake, at least.

Instead he sighed and said, "You're in worse shape than I thought." He sounded sorry for her. Tensley's self-esteem, fragile at the best of times, slunk off to a corner to sit things out.

"Go on, get dressed and get outta here," Milo said. "I'll cover for you." He closed the door behind him.

She stared at it for a few minutes, waiting for her brain to kick in with instructions. When it did, the directive was urgent.

Clothes. Now.

She pushed herself off the chair, legs trembling. It didn't take a lot of looking for her to find her station, a mirror above a table littered with makeup. Beneath the bright bulbs, a flyer had been affixed to the glass. It was a picture of Tensley, with hair longer than she normally wore it, pointing full, perky boobs at the camera while one finger pulled her bottom lip into a pout.

"Lila Delightful," the poster screamed. "Now appearing exclusively at Gary's Gorgeous Grecians."

Ohhhh hell no.

Her lungs stopped working. All of the items on her mental list blurred together, tumbling around her brain, their virtual boxes filled with questions instead of tidy check marks. Shoving them aside, she forced herself to gulp air, waving her fingers in front of her nose.

First things first.

She wrenched a metal locker next to the station open, chest heaving, and began digging around inside until she found something to put on—worn, tight jeans with a threadbare knee, an oversized Seattle Seahawks T-shirt, socks and white tennis shoes. Hand shaking, she dragged a comb through her hair and used a tissue to wipe away the layers of makeup.

She pulled a leather purse from a hook in the locker and opened a wallet inside. A wad of crumpled bills, mostly tens and twenties, fell to the floor. The wallet's plastic pockets held a blood donor card, a debit card used so many times that half the bank's name had worn off, a library card and a driver's license. She inspected each. *Tensley Tanner-Starbrook*, read the license, with an unfamiliar address and a weight she hadn't seen since high school. Birth date matched. *October 1*. Height matched. *Five foot eight*. Eyes matched. *Green*.

Then her hand closed on a piece of crisp white paper tucked inside. A checklist, in her handwriting. "Pay rent" was the first item. "Touch up roots" was the next. Tensley lifted a hand to her hair. "Ask Gary for more hours. Repair costume."

The boxes were small, perfectly drawn squares—evidence as damning as a fingerprint. She'd always said there wasn't much in life that couldn't be handled with a checklist.

Until now.

Tensley tried to fold the list, but her fingers were shaking so badly, she had to give up after only a few seconds and shove it back inside the purse, along with the money she grabbed from the dusty floor. Purse clutched to her chest, she walked to the door and opened it, blinking at the green cast of the lights.

Not going to think anymore. Just going to get out of here.

She followed a long hallway, her shoes squeaking, to a door that led outside. It opened to cool night air that washed over her, awakening her senses. In the distance, a siren wailed through night air spiced with the flavors of someone's cooking.

Her eyes drifted closed. Was stripping a trade she'd learned in prison? Because she sure as hell didn't know how to do it before. If she had, there would have been a lot more guys hanging out in the high school library.

She needed a plan. A hotel room, a night's sleep, a call to Kate. In that order. Not perfect, but it was all she had. For now.

She heard a sound to her right and opened her eyes to see a tall figure, in the shape of a man, emerge from around the brick corner of the building. Masked by the shadows, he was bearing down on her. She tried to shout a warning, a demand to leave her alone, but nothing came out of her mouth. And she still couldn't move her legs.

So this was how it would end. Her body, broken and bruised, found lying in the back of a strip club. Milo would lean over her, shaking his head. "I always said Gary should've cut her a break," he would say, before going back inside to finish his shift. "She was barely eighteen when she did her crime."

The shadowy figure continued coming toward her. She hoped she'd been able to pick up other skills in prison. Boxing. Or combat yoga. She tried a scream. This time it worked.

"Tensley." The voice was hushed, urgent. A hand reached out to grab her arm. She started to pull away, but stopped when she realized she knew the voice. "Ssshhh," he hissed, coming into the light long enough for her to catch a glimpse of his face. "Come with me."

Max.

She'd thought he was gone forever. Again. Her knees gave way at the same time she shot back at him with, "Get the hell away from me."

CHAPTER THREE

Max grabbed Tensley's arm before she hit the ground, but she shook him off, steadying herself against the back of the building.

Get away from her. *Right.* He'd tried that before. And it hadn't worked out so well.

She was thinner than he remembered, with a hard, shiny body instead of the softly voluptuous one that had cost him so many sleepless nights as a teenager.

But it was still her body. And he still wanted it like he'd wanted no other before or since.

She turned her face upward and his chest squeezed tight. Her eyes had always given her away, always said exactly what she was thinking and feeling, no matter how hard she tried to hide it. What he'd seen in her eyes all those years ago had nearly made him forget about the stupid bet that sent him to the high school library in the first place.

Fifteen years later, her eyes said, *I hate you. I don't hate you. Don't go. I hate you. I want you, right here, right now.*

Okay, maybe the last part was his dick talking. But this was all he fucking needed. Why couldn't she have acquired a jagged edge of distrust like any other self-respecting stripper?

He stepped back into the protection of the darkness. "You asked me to get you out of here." He wasn't sure what he'd expected from her, but it hadn't been this.

"And then you left." Her chin, held high, began to tremble.

"I couldn't—" He raked a hand through his hair. "Couldn't do anything inside."

"Except watch." She looked away. "And pay."

"What the hell, Tensley." As if that wasn't her job. He'd felt like shit giving her money, but it was pretty much the way it worked. Couldn't tell her why he was really there. At least not yet. "You said you wanted to go. Let's go."

"Can't stay out too late? Have to get back to the wife and kids?"

The thread of hysteria pulling through her voice heightened his alert system, drawing him to her. She'd somehow managed to come out of a strip bar smelling like summer and clean sheets. Or maybe his memory was just working overtime. Didn't matter. He took her elbow and softened his tone. "C'mon. My truck is close by."

"Don't. You. Tell me what to do." Her index finger, inches from his nose, shook.

That was it. Max shut his eyes, fighting the urge to pick her up and throw her over his shoulder, caveman-style. The thought of her body on his, though, killed that idea. He'd be lucky to make it the two blocks to the car. Finally, he managed to say, "Suit yourself."

He strode away, ear tuned to even the slightest movement coming from her. *Follow me.* All alone in this part of town at night, she'd be an easy target for creeps, which would add to everything else about her already weighing on his conscience. *Follow me, dammit.* He wouldn't, couldn't actually leave her. She only had to think he might.

He'd gone several yards, taking in every empty doorway and shadowed corner, before she started coming after him, sneakers padding across the pavement. When he heard her trip, his breath caught, but she recovered and kept going. He slowed his steps enough to let her overtake him if she tried.

It took another half a block for her to try.

At last, he heard, "Wait."

He stopped. When she reached his side, he started walking again without looking at her. "Truck's over there." He pointed his remote toward a brand-new charcoal gray F-150, gleaming quietly in the light from a nearby streetlamp. It lit up at his command.

If only everything would behave that well.

He opened the passenger side door and helped her up and onto the leather seats. Then he walked around to the driver's side and climbed in to start the powerful engine, doing his best not to focus on the fact that it was Tensley...*Tensley* beside him. Her thighs had been softer than the buttery leather of these seats.

He spent more time than necessary concentrating on the workings of the truck as they pulled out of the spot on the street.

"Where are you taking me?"

"Depends. Where are you going?"

With a sideways glance, he saw her look down, staring at her hands. He wondered why the question was so hard. Then his traitorous memory diverted him to wondering if her breasts, bigger though they were, would still fit perfectly in the palms of his hands. If she still made that soft, high-pitched sound when her nipple was nibbled into a pink mound of erect perfection. If she was still genuinely surprised by the power of an orgasm. *Shit.* Max shifted in his seat, trying to find a more comfortable position.

The girl he'd known was gone. In her place was a woman who made a living out of taking off her clothes. The two were not the same.

"I don't know."

He couldn't remember the question. "Don't know what?"

"I don't know where I'm going." Her words were flat. She stared straight ahead, into the darkness.

He did the same, while using his peripheral vision to process the too-few clues she was giving him. Injured? Drugs? His gut didn't think so, but she had a tight hold on that purse and just as tight a hold on herself. Her shoulders were drawn in, her chin defiant.

He flicked on his turn signal and made a left onto a side street. One where he knew people shuttered themselves inside their houses at night. No one would try and peer through his tinted windows or wonder why he was parked here. Even the bad guys lurked in corners, unwilling to venture into the open.

A darkened house with no streetlight offered a parking spot. He eased the truck to a stop and switched off the ignition, watching as a cat surfaced from the unkempt lawn to streak across the street.

He turned toward Tensley, resting his arm across the top of the bench seat while making sure his gun remained out of sight, safely tucked into the waistband of his jeans. He tried to sort through the questions thundering through his mind, at last landing on, "How long have you been back in town?"

She looked surprised. "I've been gone?"

No matter how much he wanted to think otherwise, she could be dealing with a mental issue. He fought the anguish that rushed through him, pushing it to the pit of his stomach. "For several years."

A nod. Slow, but deliberate. "Not long. I think."

"Back in touch with your family?"

A tip of her head as she appeared to consider this. "I would hope so." Her mouth pulled tight.

Several seconds, or maybe hours, passed before Max spoke again. This time, his voice scraped across the edges of his throat. "I tried, you know. The whole thing with Rhonda. I tried to tell them it was my fault."

Even in the darkness, he felt himself being pulled into the heart-stopping stillness of her gaze, just like the mesmerized punk kid he'd once been.

She searched his face, questioning. "You tried to tell them?"

That fast, he felt eighteen again, a mess of pent-up anger, frustration and insecurity on the inside, while maintaining a cool, arrogant façade on the outside. The only times the mask had slipped had been with Tensley. "Hell yes, I did. And when the cops wouldn't listen I went to your arraignment, figuring I'd get it cleared up then. But you screwed everything up by taking off."

She leaned closer. "Let me get this straight. *I* screwed everything up."

"That's what I said." But it hadn't come out right.

"It *was* you all over Rhonda, right? Practically swallowing her face with your mouth, grabbing her ass, grinding up against her. The day after you told me—" He watched her gulp air as naked pain stood out in her eyes. She hated him. "Told me—"

That I loved you. "Yeah."

"Perfect. I just wanted us to be clear on how it was that *I* screwed everything up."

"You did not have to hit her."

"Apparently I did."

"You could have hit me instead."

She appeared to consider that. "True."

He turned away. "Or better yet, hit no one and gone off to college like you were supposed to." A sideways glance told him that one took her aback for a minute. Oh hell, why couldn't he just shut up?

Enough talking. Max turned the key in the ignition and jammed the truck into drive, peeling out of the spot on the quiet street. "Tell me where you live."

No answer, but when he glanced over, he saw her open her purse and pull out a wallet. She bent her head and her hair fell forward, obscuring his view of what she was looking at.

She stashed her wallet back in her purse and gave him an address. Then she turned away to stare out the window.

Clearly, this wasn't the time to tell her what was really on his mind. That would have to wait. But not for long. He didn't have a lot of time.

***

Tensley breathed a sigh of relief when Max's truck pulled up before a fairly new apartment building in a decent part of town. Before she thought about it, she blurted what had been terrifying her into silence on the ride. "Thank God. That Tawny woman said I was behind on my house rent." She bit her lip. He'd think she was even crazier than he already did.

"Your house rent."

She ventured a look at him. "I thought, you know, maybe I shared a crappy house with her." *Don't laugh.*

Max rested one forearm on the steering wheel and the other on his thigh. He drew his brows together and lifted his chin, evaluating her. She felt like a bug, under his microscope. A weird bug.

"House rent is what you pay to the club," he said. "For every night you dance there."

She felt her jaw drop. Slowly, she closed her mouth and tried her best to look as though she knew that. "Oh. Right." *Brilliant, Ten.*

"But why would you think that meant you live somewhere else? Is this somewhere you're staying?"

"No. I um…live here." Possibly. "What can I say?" She touched her forehead. "Forgot for a minute." She reached for the door handle. "Thanks for the ride."

"I'll walk you to your door."

"That's okay," she was quick to say. "You don't need to do—" His door slammed behind him. "—that." She had no idea which key, if any of them, on the ring she'd found in her purse would open the apartment listed on her driver's license. She could be someone who moved a lot.

But he was already opening her door and extending his hand to help her down. Electricity shot through her at the touch of his warm skin. The teenager she'd loved had grown into a man. His voice the smallest bit deeper, his shoulders broader, the stubble of whiskers across his chin filled in, his clean-jeans-and-leather scent now blending with a woodsy cologne.

The set of his chin was just as firm, yet his face was different, as though becoming a man had filled in his edges somehow. She thought she could see a small scar close to the line of his jaw. It hadn't been there before.

She flexed the fingers of her other hand nervously, hoping she wasn't responsible for the scar.

When he let go of her, she slung her purse over one shoulder and gripped it tight with both hands.

Max looked like he was waiting for something. "Ready?" he asked finally, angling his head toward the building entrance.

Oh. He was waiting for her. "Sure."

She walked up to the entrance, as confident as a person who had no idea where she was or what she was doing could possibly be. "Okay. Thanks." She lifted her hand in a shaky wave, not sure she trusted herself enough to look at him. If she did, she might not be able to let him go.

He stood right behind her, not moving.

"See ya," she called, giving the door handle a yank.

It didn't open.

"Oh. Sorry. Not thinking." She pulled out the ring of keys, jangling them to stall for time. "You can go ahead and leave," she suggested over her shoulder.

"Want to make sure you get in all right."

So did she. But without him watching to wonder why she didn't know what she was doing. She wished she could just tell him what had happened to her, but the warning from the psychic was ringing in her head, the strangely accented words bouncing off all sides of her brain until she could barely hear herself think. *If you speak of this, events would unravel most unpredictably.*

As if it could get any worse. Still.

Tensley fumbled with the key ring, pulling out one that looked halfway likely. No luck. She tried another one. It didn't fit either.

She heard his voice in her ear. "How about a keycard?"

"A…what—?"

He pointed at a keypad to her left. Damn. She hadn't even noticed. She plunged her hand back into her purse, rummaging around on the bottom until her fingers found a thin, flat piece of plastic. Trying her best to look as though she'd known it was there all along, she pulled it out and swiped it across the pad.

A beep and a click. The door had unlocked. She grabbed the handle before it could change its mind.

"What's your apartment number?"

"4182." She wasn't sure if the rapid answer came from what she'd seen on her license or because she remembered it somewhere in the recesses of her mind.

"I'll take you there."

Noooo. Suddenly her throat felt tight, as though her emotions had supersized and blocked off every functioning part of her. *Max.* She'd never see him again. The last time, it had taken her years to get over him.

Except that she hadn't.

"Thanks again for the ride." She couldn't look at him. "But you need to leave now."

His hand closed on her shoulder, turning her around. She dragged her gaze upward to meet his, hoping that every thought and feeling wasn't on full display. When it came to him, she'd never been able to hold anything back.

"I didn't think I'd ever see you again."

"You didn't." She made a strangled sound. "Not the real me."

His hands cupped her face and his head bent, but right before the "Hallelujah Chorus" erupted in song, his lips abruptly veered away to brush against her forehead, their still-familiar touch sending throbbing beads of desire and disappointment through her.

"If you need anything," he said, "call me."

Then he began walking away. She couldn't let him. She *couldn't*. If he knew how long she'd literally ached for his touch, his kiss... How she'd punched holes in the damn Tupperware and dragged out his memory to invent fantasy after fantasy of seeing him again. "Max!"

He hesitated.

"I—" What could she say? "I—"

Something she couldn't read crossed his face. "You don't have to say it. I know."

The hell he did. How could he know what she was going to say when she didn't know herself? "For the record, you're the one who screwed up, and screwed up bad, by cheating on me. Hope it was worth it."

Here's where he was supposed to beg for understanding, tell her what a huge mistake he'd made. She'd see the pain in his eyes, know that he'd spent years beating himself up for what he'd done and how he'd sullied something truly beautiful, something neither one of them would see again. She'd forgive him. Maybe. Then allow that maybe she shouldn't have punched the Skank.

Instead Max simply said, "It was." Then he turned to leave.

And Tensley, once the words hit her with full force, retreated inside the door to the apartment building so that Max wouldn't see her crumble to the floor, the Tupperware container melting into a virtual pool of burning, melting plastic.

CHAPTER FOUR

Tensley had a cat. She knew she had a cat because the minute she turned the key in the lock of the apartment door, she heard an annoyed meow.

After a small hesitation, because it felt so weird to be letting herself into a place she thought she might live in only because of what her driver's license said, she'd ducked inside and closed the door behind her, flattening herself against it.

Then she'd felt brave enough to flick on the light switch. She didn't want to think about how she knew exactly where it would be in the darkness.

The cat sat directly in front of her, a few feet away, swishing its tail in a wide swath across the wooden floor. Its face was half gray, half white, right down the middle.

Tensley felt like a teenager caught sneaking in after curfew.

"Hello?" she ventured.

She'd never had a cat because 1) A cat required attention. Regular feedings. Litter box cleanup. Her schedule had always been too crazy for that kind of commitment. And, 2) She was allergic to cats. Not in the "I-can't-breathe" kind of way, but in the sneezing, watery eyes kind of way.

A long, slow blink of gray eyes. *Swish* went the tail.

"If you could just— Let me through."

No response.

Tensley scooted around the animal with a small get-away flick of her fingers. Big mistake. The cat stomped away, shaking each paw with disdain one by one, as if it had stepped in something disgusting.

Judgment. From a cat. "The attitude," she called after the animal. "It's not working for you."

Except that it was.

Tensley cautiously stepped ahead. Any minute now, there would be lights and sirens, handcuffs. Someone shouting that she was a burglar, with a key. The cat pointing a paw straight at her, identifying her to the police.

But she heard nothing.

She turned on a lamp and when soft light flooded the room, saw that she was in a cozy, small living room. The walls were painted a sunny yellow, accentuated by a sofa in a bright floral print. A large, plump chair sat across from the sofa, a pile of books on its seat cushion. A cheerful rug held an intricately carved chest that apparently served as a coffee table, with magazines scattered across its top, as well as candles in different colors and sizes.

The overall effect was comfortable, rumpled and inviting. Before she even thought about it, Tensley crossed the room to scoop up the pile of books from the chair and drop onto its seat cushion. She moved the books to the chest and leaned back against the chair with a sigh, closing her eyes.

Interesting. The seat cushion fit her exactly, the stuffing settling in against her thighs as though it had been expecting her. Must be her chair of choice. Was it possible to have two completely different lives?

Tensley opened her eyes and reached over to pick up the top book in the pile. Its title surprised her. *The Scarlet Letter.* One of her books from high school. She ran a finger down the cover, reveling in its familiarity, the connection to her past. She hadn't seen this book in years. For a moment, she clutched it to her chest and then set it down in her lap. It opened to a page that had obviously been read many times.

Something soft brushed up against her leg. "Not now, Gemini," she whispered, eyes still on the book.

Her head jerked up. Tensley looked down at the cat rubbing against her leg. *Gemini.* Of course. The cat's markings divided its face into two halves. She started to lower her fingers, but pulled them back. She wasn't sneezing. Strange. A cat had never been this close to her before without her eyes tearing and her nose seizing up.

Maybe her allergy had fled her body, along with her clothes.

This time, she let her fingers make it the full distance to stroke the soft fur. "I get it. You're like your name, aren't you? Wanted to kill me a few minutes ago and now you want to be my best friend."

An assenting meow.

And still no sneezing. She let her fingers remain in the cat's fur, where they moved to rubbing behind the ears in a motion so familiar, she felt as though she'd done it a hundred times. Gemini accepted the attention, eyes closed and chin lifted.

Tensley had redeemed herself. For what, she wasn't sure. But it felt good. Calming. She had a cat.

As soon as her eyes returned to the book's pages, one passage leaped out at her. Possibly because it had been circled in red in what had to be her own scrawl. A circle with ends that crossed over each other, instead of closing. She'd never been able to draw one that closed properly. Taking a deep breath, she read Nathaniel Hawthorne's prose:

The scarlet letter was her passport into regions where other women dared not to tread. Shame, Despair, Solitude! These had been her teachers—stern and wild ones—and they had made her strong, but taught her much amiss.

Much amiss.

Well, that was one way to put it.

***

The knocking sound became louder, stirring Tensley's brain into a series of question marks. *What—? Was that—? Why?*

When the knocking turned into a full-fledged pounding, she opened her eyes, wincing at the sunlight flooding through the windows. A dizzying disorientation overtook her when she saw a sofa, candles and lamps she didn't recognize. Then came the pounding again. On the door. Of the apartment. She shoved herself to her feet, a book...*The Scarlet Letter*...falling to the floor with a thud.

Ow. Her legs were stiff. She'd fallen asleep. Not curled up and tucked in, but with her feet flat, her arms on the chair. Her arms were protesting, too. *Ouch.* Who was making all that noise?

Eyes still heavy with sleep, Tensley stumbled toward the door, every other step a trip-walk, at best. Gemini the cat ran in front of her and the toe of Tensley's sneaker missed landing on the long tail by less than an inch. Gemini voiced high-pitched disapproval.

"Yeah, get in line," Tensley muttered to the cat, ready to lay into whoever was on the other side of the door. As much as she could lay into someone, anyway, with her brain foggy, her stomach rumbling, her eyes half-closed and her cat ready to take her out.

She threw open the door.

Max lowered his hand from the knocking position, flexing his fingers. "Good morning."

She leaned against the doorjamb and stared at him, trying to decide if he was in her dream, she was in his dream, or it was something in between. She hadn't seen Max in fifteen years and four months and now she'd seen him twice in less than twenty-four hours.

What did she even say? Something brilliant and witty.

"How did you get into a secured building?" So much for brilliant and witty.

He lifted one shoulder. "I have my ways." Then he extended the other hand forward.

In it he held—God help her—a Tupperware container. With its lid firmly on.

"Can I come in?" he asked.

"I don't think that's a good idea…" Her voice trailed off as soon as she realized her head was nodding, instead of shaking from side to side.

He smiled. An easy Max smile. The one that tucked in at the corners of his upturned mouth and made hummingbirds fly in her stomach, their wings beating a hundred times a second. Courtship speed.

"My neighbor made me muffins." He pointed at the container. "Thought you might want to have breakfast with me."

She couldn't think exactly why, with her impaired brain and all, but Tensley was pretty sure that would be the stupidest idea in the world right now.

So she stepped aside to let him in. It made as much sense as everything else.

He walked past her, down the short entryway and into the living room. She followed him, watching as he looked around. "Nice place."

"It is," she acknowledged. Then just as quickly, she added, "I mean thanks."

"Kitchen this way?"

She didn't answer, instead letting him take the lead past the sofa and into a combined kitchen/dining area, where he set the container of muffins on a square table of rich dark wood. Tensley herself hadn't made it this far last night. Suddenly, she wondered why and where the bathroom was, hoping she had a toothbrush in there.

Max was taking the lid off the plastic container, releasing the smell of freshly baked muffins. Yummm. Blueberry. Her favorite. Her stomach rumbled again, right on cue.

He grinned. "I know. I have great timing."

"Why does your neighbor make you muffins?"

"She just likes to look out for me. You know, me being a single guy and all. My idea of a fancy breakfast is a McMuffin."

Her heart leaped unreasonably at the news he was single at the same time she conjured up a mental picture of the neighbor. Probably blonde, model-perfect, dead sexy. Hoping she could feed her way into Max's heart. Tensley still hadn't learned to cook. It had been a repeat item on her checklist forever, even though she had yet to check it off.

She fixed her gaze on the muffins, cursing the obvious talent of the baker. "Nice to have someone so concerned about you."

Max leaned down, intercepting her fix on the perfectly rounded muffin tops. "She's a widow in her eighties. All of her family's gone, so she's sort of adopted me." Again with that smile. God help her, the man was gorgeous. He wore a crisp, striped shirt today over jeans that fit him perfectly. The top few buttons of his shirt were undone, just enough for her to see the tanned skin of his neck and upper chest.

She could feel each one of her internal defenses look at each other and shrug, ready to lay down their weapons. "Oh." She felt heat rise in her cheeks. "Would you...uh...excuse me for a moment?" *While I either crawl out of a window or transform myself into a woman who will make you forget all about stupid muffins in favor of ravishing me in my bed, wherever that might be.*

"Sure. Where are your plates?"

She blinked, mentally dressing him again. "Over there. Somewhere." She gestured vaguely in the direction of the cupboards, doing everything she could not to press her hands to her now-even-hotter cheeks.

"I'll find them. Want me to make some coffee?"

"Oh, yes. Please." It seemed like forever ago that she'd been to the mother ship, Starbucks. For all she knew, it might have been forever ago. *Please, please, please let him find a coffeemaker in there somewhere.* Just her luck, she'd discover that she didn't indulge in caffeine in this new life.

Some things didn't even bear thinking about.

She glanced behind her, spotting what looked like it might be a bathroom door, on the other side of the living room. "I'll be, you know, right back."

"Take your time."

"Don't start without me." The casual chuckle she'd intended sounded a little hysterical and the index finger she pointed at him shook. The sexy wink never happened because her eye flat out refused to operate independently. She ended up scrunching her face and shutting both eyes. Twice. "Ha, ha." She backed out of the room, hands gripped tight in front of her, only to let out a yelp as she stepped on the tail of Gemini, who screeched at the injustice.

Through it all, Max watched her, his head tipped, his expression quizzical. Actually, he looked as though he was trying not to laugh.

"Drama queen," Tensley shot under her breath to the cat. Then she turned and bolted for the bathroom, where she closed the door behind her and sank against it to the floor.

After a minute, she opened her eyes, only to meet the scrutinizing gaze of the cat. "You followed me in. Really. We're that close."

A blink of gray eyes. Apparently she and the cat *were* that close and Tensley was the only one who didn't know it.

Through the door, she could hear the muffled sounds of cupboards opening and shutting in the kitchen. Then a rattle of dishes.

"Found 'em," she heard Max call.

"What am I going to do?" she whispered to Gemini. "This can't be good to have him here. Can it?"

The cat responded by nuzzling against her and burying its head in her stomach. A second later, Gemini's head had moved to behind her back and Tensley found herself nudged upward. Hard.

"Okay, okay." Tensley grabbed hold of the edge of the sink and pulled herself to her feet. "You don't have to be so bossy."

Oh no. One look in the mirror told her that, even if she'd been imagining an extended sexual feast with a muscled Max, he could have only been thinking about the possibility of her being mistaken for a homeless person.

Her hair fell around her shoulders in a tangled mess, while the crumpled Seahawks T-shirt she wore was big enough to hide a couple of linemen in. Bare of makeup, her green eyes looked naked. And startled.

"Didn't realize it was this bad," she said to Gemini, who responded with a simpering gaze that said the level of badness was precisely the reason the cat had made Tensley stand up and look in a mirror.

"Oh, be quiet. If you know so much, you wouldn't have let me answer the door in the first place, looking like this."

From across the apartment, she heard the unmistakable whirring of a grinder. "Thank God," she breathed. "At least there will be coffee."

No time to linger on a full transformation. She'd have to work some sort of miracle in the space of a few minutes. Never let it be said that Tensley Tanner-Starbrook wasn't up for a challenge.

She opened the opposite door in the small bathroom, hoping it led to her bedroom and breathing a sigh of relief when she was right.

A few seconds later, she'd located the master bathroom and peeled her clothes off to step into the shower, not waiting long enough for the water to get warm. *Get in. And out.* She was only temporarily derailed when the bar of soap skittered off the bigger boobs she forgot she had and landed on the shower floor.

She refused to give herself even one second to think about the fact that she was naked and wet, while Max was...just a couple of rooms away. Well, maybe one second. Or ten. But no longer.

Lightning fast, she dried off, putting on a thong and bra she'd found in a drawer and identified immediately as being from the newest Victoria's Secret collection. At least she still had good taste in underwear.

She rummaged around in bathroom drawers until she located mascara and blush and then brushed her hair until it shone. She had new highlights. Red ones that brought out the auburn in her hair. Nice. She wondered why she hadn't thought of doing that before.

"Coffee's ready," she heard Max call.

"Coming!" Not in the way she would have liked, but first things first. She brushed her teeth, wiped off her mouth and headed for the closet.

It was neatly organized, as she would have expected. To the left, costumes and slips of fabric corralled on hangers. To the right, normal clothes. Jeans, T-shirts, sweaters, pretty dresses. Even a long, beautifully beaded dress. She wondered where she'd worn it.

The aroma of fresh coffee, with its sweet siren call, drifted into the bedroom.

Tensley grabbed a pair of skinny jeans and pulled them on. Then she selected a sleeveless print top, in a flowy fabric that both hugged her body and shimmered away from it. A pair of long earrings and a swipe of pearly pink lip gloss and she was ready.

For what, she wasn't sure exactly, but whatever it was, it would be on her terms.

"Do I look okay?" she asked Gemini, losing the battle to not let her anxiety show.

The cat stared at her for a second and then padded to the door.

"I'll take that as a maybe," Tensley said as she followed.

She walked through the apartment, in bare feet this time, until she reached the kitchen. The cat had better not be steering her wrong. Maybe she shouldn't have rushed through her cleanup. Or maybe she should have found something else to wear. Something less clingy.

"One blueberry muffin, coming up—" Max spun around, extending a plate. Then his mouth opened and his jaw dropped. So did the plate, crashing to the floor in a frenzy of china and crumbs.

Great. She'd either really screwed this up.

Or she hadn't.

CHAPTER FIVE

Max's best-laid plans shattered like the plate as it hit the floor. This was going to be a whole hell of a lot harder than he'd thought.

He'd told himself he could deal with Stripper Tensley. And that he could shove aside the memories of Teenage Tensley.

But this woman, the one who stood before him now, was someone different. Someone who brought to life every "Playmate-meets-wholesome-beauty-queen-next-door" fantasy he'd ever had. She'd caught him so off guard, he'd lost control of the fingers that had earned him a coveted sharpshooter trophy five years running.

"Sorry," he said to the plate, because he couldn't let the woman see the confusion raging through his brain. The last thing he needed was for her to see she could mess with him even more than she had years ago.

The cat sauntered over to lick up the crumbs.

"Max, are you okay?"

The concern in her voice pissed him off. "I'm fine," he shot back at her. "Where's your broom?"

When she didn't answer, he started moving through the kitchen until he found a broom and dustpan stashed in a corner. Never let it be said he didn't clean up his messes. Except—*shit*. When it came to Tensley. Must be some kind of karmic payback that she had to be working at one of the clubs he'd been assigned to investigate.

He swept the broken plate and muffin into the dustpan with a vengeance, the pieces of china clanking together. The cat leaped onto a chair outside the danger zone.

"Hey!" Tensley was in front of him, her hand on his wrist. "Stop. Put it down."

Even the way she moved through a room had changed. In high school hallways, she'd done her best to blend in with the background. Now she'd covered the distance between them in a few long strides that said she was here to be seen.

He put the dustpan down. Slowly. *Get a grip, Hunter. You can do this.*

She released her hold on him, but didn't move away. The damn cat jumped off the chair to pad between the two of them, choosing Max's calf to rub up against.

"She...or I mean, he..." Tensley cleared her throat. "This cat likes to be in the middle of things."

So she felt it, too. This electricity between them. It wasn't just him. She was so close. The scent of just-washed cotton and flowers drifted to his nostrils and wrapped itself around him. He felt the warmth radiating from her body; watched the faintest jump of her pulse. The breasts he'd ached to touch in the strip club were only a couple of inches from his chest.

Centerfold Slash Miss Apple Pie, meet your willing victim.

Before he knew it, his hands were on her waist, his fingers sending jubilant distress signals to a brain that couldn't think clearly. He pulled her closer. When her breasts met his chest, his dick made its presence known, rock hard and ready.

Years melted away and he was back in high school. Holding the girl he could never get enough of. A girl who had grown into one hell of a fantasy-inducing woman.

Somewhere in his scrambled thoughts, he registered her hands closing on him, curving around his belt to his back. Each one of her fingers pressed in on him with an urgency that matched his.

He'd thought about this moment a hundred times over the last fifteen years, but a thousand times more about what came after it. When they were skin to skin, sin to sin.

He tipped his head and bent to kiss her as everything around them slowed and he succumbed to a tsunami of raw lust. He didn't want to think anymore. Didn't want to come up for air. They had a lot to make up for—

Right before his mouth met hers, he felt her fingers still, her body stiffen.

"What the hell is that?" She dropped her hands.

He swam through the tidal wave that had flooded his senses, clawing his way to the surface. "I—what—?"

"You have a gun." She stepped away from him, face tight, and fired off questions that made his head spin. "Why, Max? Why a gun? Normal people don't carry guns." Her voice climbed several octaves. "What have you gotten yourself into?"

"Hold on." Max put a hand to his forehead, trying to block out the sound of his dick screaming for mercy. "What's the big deal?" He hadn't intended for her to find out this way.

"The big deal," she said, emphasizing each word, "is that you show up here after letting yourself into a building that's supposed to be secure, with muffins in your hand and a gun hidden under your shirt. The surprise visit and the muffins I can live with, but I want to know about the gun."

"It's not what you think."

"I think it means you're in trouble."

Nothing about this woman made sense. Most strippers would correctly think "cop" and go into survival mode. "I'm not. Trust me." *Can we get back to where we were?*

"Trust. You." She dragged the two words out until they took on several syllables and left them to swirl in the air between them.

His temper rose. "I came back for you as soon as I could last night."

"You cheated on me with Rhonda the Skank."

Max exhaled. Somehow he'd managed to forget Tensley's nickname for Rhonda. "That's a little harsh."

"So you weren't cheating on me with her."

"No. I meant—" He'd been kidding himself to think there weren't buried explosives in this reunion. "I told you. Things weren't supposed to go down the way they did."

"Because I wasn't supposed to find out about you and Rhonda."

"You were supposed to find out about me and Rhonda." *Hold on. That didn't come out right.* "There wasn't anything going on." He raked his hand through his hair and stared up at the ceiling. No help there. He didn't like being on this side of an interrogation. "You were just supposed to think there was."

This time, she shook her head. "I know what I saw." All of a sudden, though, she didn't sound so sure.

"Think about it, Tensley." Max was a lot of things, but he wasn't a cheater. It still cut to the bone that she'd been so willing to believe he was. Even though, at the time, he'd hoped she would.

"You think I *haven't* thought about it?" She moved into the living room, pacing across the wooden floor in her bare feet. "Tupperware didn't work, file folders, a damn metal safe. Nothing."

What the hell was she talking about?

She turned to pace in the other direction. "Other men didn't help. Gorgeous men. One of them, Bryan-with-a-y-not-an-i—"

At what point had he lost control of this conversation?

"—could talk dirty in French. Which is a whole lot sexier than it is in English. And believe me, it was a huge turn-on."

So he'd learn fucking French.

Another turn. Still pacing. Her red painted toenails caught his attention. Fiery, but delicate. She'd always had the sexiest toes.

She was still talking. "Great job, things going good. Beautiful condo. My mother and I getting along for once. Even working together—"

Hell, no. She did not just say her mother was working as a stripper. With a shudder, he recalled the uptight, wealthy bitch who'd warned him to keep away from her daughter. If that woman was stripping, total darkness and a whip had to be involved. Or— hold on. Working together could mean something else entirely. Something this cop would be interested in knowing about.

"And still, I can't forget about you."

Things were taking a turn for the better. Max opened his mouth, but she wasn't letting him get a word in.

"Why Rhonda? Why cheat with her when you and I were so good together? When we had something everybody wants but hardly ever gets?"

The first stab to his heart came from remembering how much he'd loved the girl who had seen in him things other people hadn't bothered to look for. The second was the realization that after all this time, she still hadn't figured out why he'd done it.

For every A she'd made in high school, she'd earned a D in street sense.

She stopped pacing back and forth and stared at him, hands on her hips. Even the cat was glaring at him, switching its tail in accusation. "You were kissing her." Her voice wobbled. "Like you kissed me."

Not even close. He closed the distance between them. "What would you have done if you hadn't found me with her?"

She pulled her mouth in tight and refused to meet his eyes.

"Tell me."

"I wouldn't have left."

"Exactly. You wouldn't have left."

The words echoed off each wall, making the silence that followed that much more deafening.

"You were supposed to go to college," he said at last. "But you said you were going to stay with me."

She dropped her hands from her hips, looking to the window, and back to him. He saw a tremble in her mouth. "I could have gone to college later."

"I wasn't even going to graduate from high school. What do you think we would have lived on?"

Her chin lifted. "Money isn't everything."

"It is when you can't afford a place to live."

Just as he'd expected, she didn't have an answer for that. He'd only had one answer himself, at the time.

"So it was a setup."

He jerked his chin in assent, watching her. For some reason, she kept flexing her hand, making a fist and then releasing it.

The punch replayed in his mind in slow motion. Tensley's fury. Rhonda's scream. His disbelief. If he'd had the training then that he had now, he could have blocked the blow. Things would have been different.

But "could-a, would-a" didn't matter for shit. Max had screwed things up but good.

Her eyes met his. "A pretty lame-ass plan."

He lifted a shoulder. "All I had at the time."

"Sounds like your intentions weren't...bad." She swiped at one eye with the back of her hand and shook her head, staring out the window again. "Better than mine, I guess."

He would let her blame him, but not herself. And he'd never been able to handle seeing her cry, so that wasn't going to work out well. "I'm a cop. That's why I have the gun."

She turned back. Her eyes widened and she made a little snort. The sound sent a tingle of memory through him. "A cop. If that's your idea of a joke, it's not funny, Max."

"It's not a joke."

"The police in this town would never have allowed that. You were number one on their most-hated list."

"I left after you did. Went to California. Finished high school, joined a police force and got a degree in criminal justice. Came back here. They offered me a job. I took it."

She considered that, her eyes narrowing. "You're kidding. You?"

He put a hand to his heart. "Thanks for the vote of confidence."

"I didn't mean—" She shifted her weight from one foot to the other, staring at the floor. "It's just that, of all the things I thought you would become, a cop never entered my mind."

"Right." He smiled, for the first time in what felt like years. "You thought maybe a car thief." He had shown her how to start a car without a key.

"Gambler." She also cracked a smile.

He'd almost forgotten. He'd also shown her how to play poker. "Con artist."

"Writer."

"Are you kidding me?" He would have laughed if her words hadn't sent such an unexpected thrill through him. She didn't know about the half-written murder mystery buried in his desk. No one did. "I had enough trouble graduating from high school."

"This is me, remember? You loved books. Words. You wrote me poetry. And it was good."

They needed to get off this subject. Fast. "Come on. Gangbanger. That's what you thought."

She hesitated.

"Don't lie," he said. "It entered your mind."

Her eyes met his, clear and steady. "I knew you'd end up fine."

"Not just now when you found the gun."

"I couldn't—think of a good reason you'd have one."

He screwed up his mouth. "Guess that's fair. I wasn't headed for anything good when you knew me."

"I never thought of it that way." Tensley turned away. She dropped into the chair and the cat jumped up to take what looked like a familiar position on her lap. She began stroking his fur. "So much has happened. I wish I could tell you." Her voice trailed off. "Things you wouldn't believe."

Unfortunately, he was pretty sure he would. He took a seat opposite her, on the sofa. "Do you want to talk about it?"

She seemed to consider it for a moment and then made up her mind. "No. I want to know about you and this whole cop thing. Do you like it?"

"I do. And I'm good at it."

Tensley's smile was wistful. "I'll bet. They probably have you deal with the teenagers just like you."

They had in his first job. "Sometimes."

"So an old lady bakes you muffins because you're single. Have you ever been married?"

Careful, Max. "Once. For about a minute."

"Any kids?"

"No. You?"

An odd expression, as though she had to think about it. "Not that I know of."

At least she hadn't lost her sense of humor.

Then she raised her head, fixing her gaze on him. "Why were you there last night?"

He leaned forward, clasping his hands in front of him.

Tensley sat up straighter, dislodging the cat.

Max switched into his best no-bullshit cop voice. "We need to talk about that."

CHAPTER SIX

"I was working last night," Max said. "But I'm sure you figured that out."

Tensley ignored Gemini the cat, who had leaped from the chair after losing his spot and was now attempting to sear his disapproval into her brain. "No. I didn't." Here's where Max would say he knew she didn't belong in that place. That a real stripper would be able to spot a cop the minute she laid eyes on him.

She leaned forward. Waiting. Hoping.

"First time I'd been to that club. Just got assigned." He hesitated, staring down at his hands. "I knew you worked there, though. Saw the flyer."

Right. How could she have forgotten the flyer? Lila Friggin' Delightful. Her heart sank. So much for her not belonging there. She leaned into the back of the chair, shoulders slumping.

"You must have been surprised to see me."

"You could say that." Tensley clasped her hands together so tight, her fingertips went red and her knuckles white.

"Or maybe not. Given the fact that you remember me as number one on the cops' most-hated list."

Oh dear God, his smile made her knees go weak. She hoped she didn't have to use them any time soon because, if he kept smiling, she was pretty sure her knees would wobble. She loosened her fingers, as numbness began to set in, and shifted her gaze to the cat. "What?" she asked Gemini, who turned and left the room with an annoyed switch of his tail.

Tensley braved another look at Max. Her fingers, now that they had regained feeling, longed to touch the curl of dark hair below his ears. She remembered how it used to wrap perfectly around her index finger.

"You know, though, I have to say, Ten. When I saw you…" He leaned back against the sofa, drumming his fingers on one jeans-clad leg.

Her inner roller-coaster ride began another steep ascent of hope as a clock she hadn't noticed ticked off the seconds. Loud seconds. *Keep talking, Max.* What had happened when he saw her? He'd realized what he'd thrown away, that he'd never stopped loving her? Or maybe he'd thanked his lucky stars for a narrow escape when he saw what he thought she'd become. *Okay, don't talk.*

A sharp rap on the apartment door jolted Tensley from ticking off the possibilities. She jumped, looking at the door and then back at Max.

"Do you need to get that?" he asked, when she didn't move.

"No." Nothing good could be on the other side of that door.

Another knock, more insistent this time.

"Ignore it," she said. She drew a steadying breath as the roller coaster crept upward. "You were saying?"

He looked puzzled for a second, but then leaned forward, deep blue eyes focused on her. "When I saw you last night, I couldn't believe—"

The apartment door screeched open and a heavy footstep sounded in the hall.

Tensley turned, picturing herself in a slow motion suicide leap toward the intruder, the word *n-o-o-o-o-o* roaring from somewhere deep inside. No more surprises. No more terrifying revelations into a life that wasn't hers. No more.

"Babe! What's the deal? Why didn't you answer the door?" A man moved into view. A short, muscular man with huge, tattooed arms. He was wearing a sleeveless tank top. In October. Jeans with a hole in one knee. And a grin that showed even, white teeth.

The man's expression changed to a frown that settled into deep creases between his dark brows. He looked to be in his thirties. He looked to be someone who lifted weights full-time. And he looked to be...not very happy. "Who's this joker?" He jabbed a stubby finger in Max's direction.

Max stood. "Just an old friend."

"Old friend." Thunderclouds formed in the man's eyes.

Tensley also stood. *Combat yoga, anyone?*

"From years ago." Max's tone was smooth, unruffled. "We ran into each other and were catching up. My wife and I went to high school with Tensley."

That stopped her. His wife? *Is he lying to muscle man...or me?*

"We were talking about getting together for dinner sometime soon," Max went on. "Tensley told me she had someone special she wanted to bring." He aimed a questioning look at her. "I'm thinking this must be him."

Her mouth opened, but all she could do was stare at muscle man, at Max, and back again.

Uncertainty flickered across the other man's face, but then, after appearing to make a decision, he stepped toward Max. "Name's Razor," he said. "Razor Burns."

Seriously? Razor Burns? This wasn't happening.

"Yep, I would be her someone special." Razor dipped his chin toward Tensley. "That's my girl."

And the roller coaster, having reached the top, plunged straight downward, Tensley screaming silently until her lungs ached. She did not have a boyfriend named Razor. Razor Burns.

"Nice to meet you." Max extended his hand, barely flinching when Razor did his best to crush it. "I'd better get home. It was great to run into you, Tensley." He flashed a smile at her. "Rhonda will be excited. I'll have her call you to set up dinner."

Rhonda? As in Rhonda the Skank? What the fuck. Of all the names he had to pull up for a fake wife, he picked *Rhonda?*

"Yeah. Great," she choked out. "Tell Rhonda the Ska—"

She knew that look on Max's face. It meant "play along." He'd signaled her with it many times in high school.

"Ska—*git* Valley Homecoming Queen," she managed to finish, "to call me." As if Rhonda could have ever gotten off her knees long enough to walk across a stage. She tried a smile, but it disappeared before it even got started.

"I'll do that," Max said.

"Homecoming queen, huh?" Razor gave a hoarse way-to-go chuckle. "Yeah, I nailed the homecoming queen at my high school, too. She kept her crown on the whole time. Damn thing almost poked my eyes out." He shook his head, then brightened. "Huge tits, though."

Again. Seriously?

Max gave an easy answering chuckle.

She might have to kill both of them. From the deadly lotus position.

"They were nothing like yours, though, babe." Razor snaked a possessive arm around her waist and nuzzled her neck, causing every one of her nerve endings to shout its protest. He dropped his voice. "Don't worry. I don't even remember her name. And you don't wear a crown so your Razor-man is safe to keep on going a-l-l night long."

Give her a minute and she'd get a crown. A huge one that would stab her Razor-man in all kinds of sensitive places.

Max lifted his hand. "So Rhonda will be in touch. Good seeing you, Tensley. Nice meeting you, Razor." He strode to the door.

Tensley would have run after him, but Razor Burns held on to her as what felt like every hope she'd had of regaining her normal life disappeared with Max Hunter. She hadn't always had the greatest life, but it was hers and from this vantage point, it looked pretty damned near perfect. She wanted it back.

The door shut, leaving Tensley standing with a man named after a facial injury.

He landed a drive-by kiss on her cheek and took off toward the kitchen. "What's to eat? I'm starved."

She put a hand to her cheek, where his rough whiskers and wet lips had brushed her skin, and scrubbed at it with her fingers. As he walked away, he flexed his arms and pulled his hands into fists, swinging them from side to side like a boxer. Wine glasses hanging from an iron rack near the kitchen clinked together in alarm.

His walk reminded her of someone, but she couldn't think who. She couldn't think much of anything.

"Babe?" Razor called from the kitchen. "Some of the guys are gettin' a game going over at Rod's house. You care if I go, after the gym?"

She was one-hundred-percent sure she did not care what Razor did. Now or ever.

He appeared again, a stalk of broccoli in one hand, a bottle of vitamin water in the other, and an expectant look on his face. He tipped his head. "You okay? You look kinda funny." He took a big bite of broccoli, watching her as he crunched. Bits of green clung to the corners of his mouth.

"Uh, no. No, I'm not." She shook her head, hugging her waist. "I don't feel well." True enough.

"Oh, man. Really?" Another bite. More crunching. More pieces of broccoli refusing to enter his mouth. "Can I get you anything?"

"Nothing. Except…" She gestured toward the broccoli. "I don't think I can watch you eat."

"Sorry." Another large bite and a swig of water and he was done. He disappeared into the kitchen. When he returned a minute later, he was drawing one large hand across his mouth. "You gonna be able to work?"

If he meant work at Gary's, she was never setting foot in that strip club again. Not if they dragged her by her tiny thong. She shook her head. And then shook it even harder.

"Pops told me you were acting weird last night. Bet it was because you were feeling sick, huh?"

Pops. As in…father. That walk. She knew she'd seen it before.

"You don't have to keep telling him you're quitting, you know. You can just ignore him if he's making you mad. Hell, that's what I do."

Gary. The owner of the strip club. Was this man's father.

Razor started making his way toward her, but came to an abrupt stop when Gemini planted himself squarely in the man's path. "I swear," Razor muttered as he went around him, "that cat hates me."

Gemini was beginning to grow on Tensley. Something began to bubble in the back of her throat. Hysteria. Nausea. Maybe both.

It deflated as soon as Razor leaned in to kiss her. "Stay away!" She put her hands in front of her face.

He pulled up, looking hurt.

She felt bad. For all she knew, or didn't know, he was an okay guy. "Sorry. I just—don't want you to get sick, too."

His expression softened. "Aw thanks, babe. You don't want me to miss the game." He stepped back, rubbing his hands together. "'Cause I'm feelin' lucky tonight."

"So go be lucky." *And leave me the hell alone.*

"You *bet* I will." He chortled at his own joke. "Okay. I'm leavin' now." He aimed a finger at Gemini. "Stay," he ordered.

The cat ignored him, zipping by Razor's feet and causing him to stumble. "Shit. You'd better get over this, dude. I'll be movin' in here before long and she's not gonna let you get away with that crap anymore." He turned and winked at Tensley. "Right, babe?"

Tensley couldn't even begin to muster a response.

Razor didn't seem to mind. "Hey, I'm gonna call you from Rod's. Make sure you're okay. Can't have my girl being sick." He flashed his white-toothed grin at her. "Unless you want me to play doctor."

Her stomach turned over. "I'm good," she managed.

"Call if you need your Razor-man."

Not in a million years. "Uh-huh."

"Don't want you passin' out on stage and hurtin' yourself now. Pops will get all pissed off and—" He continued to talk, even as the door banged shut behind him.

There was apparently no sick leave for Gary's Gorgeous Grecians.

Tensley stood, riveted to her spot, for several minutes and then turned. She fell onto the sofa, face down, inhaling the smell of cloth and cat.

Max. Maybe with a wife. Who might or might not be Rhonda. And she still didn't know why he had come to see her or what he had been about to say.

A job at a strip club. Where she owed money. A flyer circulating who knew where. Her entire life, upside down and spinning.

Two days ago, even two hours ago, she never would have believed it, but right now it appeared as though a heavy-footed, broccoli-chewing alleged boyfriend named Razor Burns might be the least of her problems.

As Alice in Wonderland, the queen of upside down, had said, "It would be so nice if something made sense for a change."

***

Tensley sat cross-legged in the middle of the apartment's bedroom, surveying the damage. She'd gone a little crazy after her face plant in the sofa, making her way into the bedroom to overturn drawers and pile the entire contents of the closet into one corner. She'd even crawled under the bed to see if anything had escaped her tornado of scrutiny, though she'd only found dust bunnies. All that proved was that her housekeeping skills hadn't improved any in her new life.

She hadn't known what she was looking for. But it had seemed reasonable that somehow, somewhere, she'd find a clue. A clue that would lead her home.

But most of what she found only left her more confused than she'd been before she started looking.

She had two distinctly separate wardrobes. One belonged, quite obviously, to a stripper. Sheer fabrics, from bright colors to virginal white. Decorated with feathers, fishnet, leather, and even chains. Shiny tiny skirts with matching sheer bras.

As Tensley fingered the light, barely-there outfits, she couldn't help but wonder how she looked in them. How the spotlight caught her svelte body as she moved. If the lace-up shoes with the six-inch heels made her legs look miles long. If men...*wanted* her so badly, their brains turned to mush.

Now that would be a change.

The other part of her wardrobe was remarkably similar to the clothes she owned in her old life, minus the business suits. A size smaller, but in the same jewel tones she loved. She even favored the same designers, though in this life she'd substituted knockoffs for the real thing. Pretty decent knockoffs, at that.

She'd also found a few familiar things in a box tucked in the back of the closet, which had caused her heart to speed up with simultaneous relief and foreboding. An old picture of her and Max. Ripped in half and taped back together, more than once. Just as it always had been. A photo album from her childhood. The teddy bear she'd slept with every night until her first day of junior high, despite her mother's disapproval.

And on the dresser, she'd found her iPod, loaded with all the songs she loved, from country to hip-hop. She'd leaned against the wall and hugged all four treasured items to her chest until she felt brave enough to begin searching again.

In the nightstand, she'd found several novels, including one she'd been reading in her old life. A chill had run through her when she'd found a bookmark tucked into the same page of the same book she'd left off reading a few nights ago, before the visit to Madame Claire.

In a dresser drawer, there were several crumpled to-do lists, in various stages of completion, but the notes were so cryptic, they didn't give her much insight into the tasks. Carefully, she'd smoothed the papers and stacked them in a pile.

Another drawer had yielded a more disturbing discovery—a small gun, with her initials engraved on the side. She'd stared at it for several minutes, relieved that this had been the one drawer she hadn't dumped upside down before going through the contents. She didn't know how to use a gun and wouldn't have been able to tell if it was loaded. She'd never *had* to know before.

Worst of all, beneath several pairs of jeans, she'd found an envelope in her own handwriting that had been addressed and sent to her mother, but stamped "return to sender." The postmark was two years old. Had to have been important for Tensley to write a letter, instead of an e-mail.

She couldn't bring herself to open the envelope. Not yet. At this point, some things were better left unread. If she could figure out how to get back to her normal life, she'd never even have to know.

Please. She didn't want to know.

Piles surrounded her. A leather whip poked out from beneath a heap of underwear and mittens. A box of condoms rested on top of flannel pajamas, with a pair of black leather spiked-heel boots standing guard.

The whole room looked like the victim of a maniacal, unfocused burglar. Tensley couldn't bring herself to clean it up. Instead, she uncrossed her legs, pushed herself up off the floor and left, closing the bedroom door behind her.

In the midst of her investigative tornado, she'd realized that one person was missing in all of this. The person who had started it all and now had a hell of a lot to answer for.

This kind of thing was *so* not in the best friend handbook.

Tensley found a crisp white sheet of paper and a pencil. At the top she wrote, "To Do" in careful, precise letters. Then she drew a box and next to it wrote, "Find Kate."

After a minute, she drew a line through "Find" and wrote "Kill," pushing the pencil so hard, it broke through the paper. But then she reconsidered, putting a line through "Kill" and erasing the one through "Find."

She would give her best friend a chance to explain. Two minutes, max.

After that, all bets were off.

CHAPTER SEVEN

It was a pretty bad sign, Tensley decided, when you didn't recognize the ICE number stored in your own cell phone. Her emergency contact should be someone she at least knew.

She'd scrolled through the list once, twice, and then three times. None of the names, and there weren't a lot of them, were familiar.

But most importantly for right now, Kate's name wasn't there.

She, of course, had the number memorized. She called it, but someone named Joe answered and had the balls to insist he didn't know Kate. After the third time she'd said she couldn't believe him, he'd gone from marginally polite to pissed off, telling her she'd better not call again. He sounded like he meant it.

How could Kate not be a part of her life? They'd been best friends since the fifth grade sleepover at Megan Asmussen's house, when a custom-made glass door had slammed on the cast on Tensley's arm and shattered all over the hardwood floor. Megan's parents had been so upset, they'd cancelled the sleepover and sent the girls home.

Kate, the new girl at St. Alban's Academy, had been the only one to defend Tensley, who had not-so-wisely used her plaster cast to block Megan from slamming the door on her. Yes, Tensley *had* been trying to overhear what Megan and her two right-hand witches had been saying about Turner Wells III, who every girl in the class had a crush on, but that didn't matter as much as the fact that Megan had lied to her parents and everyone else by saying Tensley had put her cast through the door on purpose.

Kate had come to Tensley's defense, even tossing in a speculation that Turner Wells III despised curly-headed girls. Megan had begun straightening her hair the next day and never forgiven Tensley or Kate, who had become inseparable friends from that day forward.

A person did not just misplace her best friend. It wasn't possible.

Tensley called directory assistance, relieved when she was given the office number for Kate O'Brien, DVM. At least that hadn't changed. Kate was still a veterinarian.

"I would like to speak with Dr. O'Brien, please," she said when the phone was answered.

"She's with a patient right now. Can I take a message?"

Tensley knew that voice, with its slight southern drawl. Mary Sue, the woman Kate had felt sorry for and hired as her receptionist. Mary Sue was notorious for saying, "Now I could have sworn I put that right here…" Animals loved her. People loved her. And she was as disorganized as they came.

If she left a message, it might get to Kate in a few days, or a few weeks, whenever Mary Sue uncovered it and said, "Well, there you are."

Tensley had to see Kate *now*. "Um, actually, I'll make an appointment to see Dr. O'Brien."

"Well, sure, honey. Now what kind of a critter do you have?"

Tensley slanted a look across the room, where a sleeping Gemini lay curled up in the sun. "A cat."

"And what's your cat's name?"

"Gemini."

The cat in question lifted his head, on alert.

"How about this Thursday?"

"No!"

"No?"

"I have to see the vet today." From the corner of her eye, Tensley saw fur go by in a blur as Gemini made his escape from the room.

"What's going on with Gemini?"

"He's..." She wracked her brain for an answer. "I don't know, but it's something bad. He's lethargic. Won't play with cat things."

"Hmmm..."

This wasn't going to get her in sooner than Thursday. "And he won't eat," she rushed to add. "I think he has a headache."

"A headache—?"

Right. How would she be able to tell? "His head flops to the side. It's as though he can't hold it up. And his voice—I mean, his meow. It's high-pitched. Like he's crying."

"Oh, my." Mary Sue sounded distressed. "That does sound bad. We'd better get him in right away."

Tensley's body sagged in relief. "Please."

"Give me just a minute to check the schedule." A brief pause. "It's going to have to be her last appointment of the day, I'm afraid. Can you be here by five p.m.?"

"Yes. And I'll bring the cat with me." Although how she was going to wrangle him into going, she wasn't sure.

"It is important, honey," the receptionist replied carefully, "to bring him with you."

***

By 3:30 p.m., Tensley was outside, aiming the Ford remote she'd found in her purse down one direction of the street and then the other. When a Taurus obediently lit up, she sighed. It was a color somewhere between green and brown, several years old, and covered with a layer of dirt. A long, very long, way from her sleek silver BMW.

She'd gone back inside to find the cat. At least she didn't have to worry about him scratching the leather seats of her BMW.

Gemini, it turned out, not only knew the word "vet," but also apparently hated everything associated with it.

It took Tensley twenty minutes to find him, even though the apartment wasn't very big. When she finally spotted him curled into a ball on the top of a kitchen cabinet, she crossed her arms and directed her voice upward. "I see you."

One eye opened.

"Sorry I said the V-word." The eye closed. Gemini was doing his best to ignore her. Or wait her out.

"Don't worry. She won't do anything to you. She won't even look at you. But *I* have to see her. And to do that, I have to take you with me. So. Come down, please."

Fat chance, apparently. Not one hair on the cat's body moved.

Time for a change in tactics. Tensley took a deep breath and then called, "Here kitty, kitty," in the sweetest voice she could manage.

Still the cat did not move. She tried again. Nothing.

"Okay. This can go one of two ways. You cooperate and everything's fine. You don't and I can't promise what will happen. Either way, you're leaving with me." She tapped a toe on the floor. "If you won't come down, I'll come up."

No response.

She tried whistling. Gemini opened one eye a slit, just enough to convey his disdain. But he didn't move a muscle.

So begging didn't work. Neither did threats. And time was slipping away. If Kate's last appointment of the day was a no-show, she might leave early, and Mary Sue wouldn't buy the cat with the floppy head story twice.

She glanced at the clock. "Time's up. I didn't want to do this, but you're not leaving me any choice." She climbed onto the kitchen counter and began scooting her hands along the cabinet, trying to maintain her balance as she prepped for a grab.

Gemini stood, his back arched, tail switching.

It crossed Tensley's mind that she should have found oven mitts and put them on. Too late now. "One...two..." she breathed. Then..."Three!" Her hands shot up at the same second Gemini hissed and leaped out of her reach. "Whoaa-ahhh-eeek!" Tensley lost her balance, falling backward as the cat ran the length of the cabinet and jumped onto the refrigerator.

By some miracle, she managed to get her feet under her. They hit the floor hard as her hands splayed across the counter. Ouch. That hurt.

From his perch on the refrigerator, Gemini glared at Tensley.

From her spot on the floor, Tensley glared at Gemini.

"Fine," she said. "I'll find another cat. One who will cooperate. There has to be some starving stray out there who would love to have a new home."

He didn't even blink. She'd never had a cat call her bluff. It wasn't a great feeling. And exactly where was she going to find a willing stray in the next two minutes?

It wasn't until she'd closed the apartment door behind her and was fumbling for her keys that another idea occurred to her. Her chin shot up. It might just work.

She turned the key in the lock a few more times than she needed to. Then, instead of taking it out, she threw open the door and grabbed for the cat who had taken up his position in front of it.

He screeched, legs clawing at the air, but she had him. And she wasn't letting him go until she had answers from the vet he dreaded and the best friend she needed.

***

By the time they arrived at Kate's office, Tensley was convinced Gemini had used the filthiest cat language possible to curse her up one side of the car and down the other. He'd probably even made up new words. Just for her.

He'd clawed his way across her body, managing to get one paw stuck in her hair, and they'd driven that way for several minutes—Tensley struggling to keep the car in the middle of the lane while Gemini dug sharp, painful needles into her shoulders and hissed his fury into her ears.

She pressed harder on the gas pedal and muttered a quote from the old Blues Brothers movie, a favorite at the elite Catholic schools she'd attended. "Our Lady of Blessed Acceleration, don't fail me now."

When she pulled up to the vet clinic ten minutes late for the appointment, she jammed the car into park and reached up to grab his sorry cat ass and tuck it under her arm. She slammed the door behind them and strode toward the entrance, ignoring Gemini's yowls. They were on a mission.

The woman at the desk started as they stumbled through the automatic door, her eyes wide. Tensley recognized her. It was Marla, one of Kate's techs. "Can I—help you?" Marla skirted the counter to reach them. "Have you been in an accident?"

You could call it that. Tensley leveled a black look at Gemini, who quit squirming long enough to return it. Then she lifted her chin and calmly said, "Hello, Marla. We have an appointment. This is Gemini."

Marla wasted no time on greetings, paperwork or anything else. Less than a minute later, Tensley and Gemini were installed in a room decorated with a kitten calendar and a large poster detailing the anatomy of a cat. Gemini made straight for the corner while Tensley used the reflection in the poster's glass to assess the damage. From what she could tell, one entire side of her hair looked as though it had been styled by a KitchenAid mixer. No wonder the tech had made a quick escape.

Kate was going to have a fit. Sure, she'd laugh when she saw what Tensley looked like, but then she'd get serious when she heard what had happened at the psychic appointment she'd forced her best friend to go to.

Tensley rummaged inside the leather purse until her fingers found a comb. She was trying to decide how best to approach a massive detangle when the door opened. Tensley turned to see her best friend standing before her in a white coat with red letters that spelled out "Dr. Kate O'Brien," followed by a tiny paw.

"Kate. I am so glad to see you." Tensley's voice broke under the weight of her relief. Her knees gave way and she had to grab the edge of the exam table to keep from falling.

"Tensley." Concern lined Kate's forehead. She closed the door without a sound and moved to the exam table. "Are you all right?"

"So far." Then she thought about the picture her hair, furious cat and Jell-O legs must present and began to laugh. A desperate, near-wail of a laugh. "I have so much to tell you. You're not even going to believe it."

Kate opened and closed her mouth a couple of times, before seeming to settle for, "It's been a long time."

"What do you mean?" Tensley shook her head. "No, it hasn't." She was starting to get a very bad feeling. She'd seen Kate two days ago. And since when did she decide to get a shorter, more severe haircut without even mentioning it?

The other woman set her clipboard on the table and turned her attention to Gemini, who was still in the corner. "I hear you're worried about your cat." She knelt before the animal, softly clicking her tongue and extending her hand.

What the hell was going on? Her best friend in the whole world was acting as though they barely knew each other and that traitor of a cat was lifting a paw toward Kate, pleading his nonexistent pathetic case.

"Don't worry about the cat. There's nothing wrong with him," Tensley said, more sharply than she'd intended.

Cat and vet turned to her at the same time. "I don't understand."

"Kate, what's the matter with you?" This was not going well. "Have you ever known me to have a cat? I can barely take care of myself, let alone a cat."

Her friend rose slowly. "I wouldn't know. It's been years since we've seen each other. I didn't realize you were back in town."

Years. *Shit. Double-shit.* "Kate—"

"I'm really glad you're okay. I tried to find you after you disappeared." Despite her even tone, Tensley could hear the hurt ringing the edges of her friend's voice; see it in the pinched corners of her mouth. Kate reached down to pick up Gemini, who promptly buried his head in her white coat, purring his innocence. "Guess I can understand you not wanting to see anyone, even me."

Tensley's stomach squeezed tight. This was wrong. All wrong. First Max, now Kate.

"I would never not want to see you, Kate. You're my best friend."

"Couldn't believe they were so hard on you. Rhonda deserved it. I don't know what I could have done to help, but I tried." A rueful smile. "Your mother threw me out of her house when I said I wasn't leaving until she told me where you'd gone. The ice queen is stronger than she looks."

"Listen to me, Kate." Tensley laid her fingers on her friend's arm as her words tumbled over each other in her haste to get them out, to make Kate understand. "Whatever you think happened—didn't."

"It was a long time ago. Don't worry about it."

"Don't worry about it," Tensley repeated as she began pacing back and forth in the narrow space between the table and wall, each step pounding the tile harder than the last. "I'm not worried. Hell, no. I'm way past worried. I'm in some kind of a fucking nightmare. Ever since I found myself on a stage last night with no clothes, dancing for men with saliva and whatever the hell else dripping from them, getting sweaty money shoved at me and then having it taken away by a club owner who treats me like I actually work there and am lower than dirt, and then Max, *Max* is there and it's like high school all over again—"

She ran out of breath long enough for Gemini to voice his impatience and Kate to interrupt with, "You saw Max?"

Tensley stopped pacing. "I saw Max."

"I didn't know *he* was back in town, either. Was this the first time you'd seen him since—everything happened?"

"Yes." She hugged herself tight.

"Are you okay?" Kate's voice softened. "That had to be tough."

"I can't even begin to describe it." Tough, amazing, infuriating, incredible. The biggest turn-on she'd felt in forever.

"If it was anything like high school, I get it. I think I was electrocuted once when I accidentally walked between the two of you." Kate looked at Gemini and then at Tensley. "Speaking of which, I hope your hair didn't look like…you know…that when you saw him." She pointed.

"My hair is that cat's fault."

The cat in question yowled, right on cue.

"I'll translate. He says that's bullshit."

"Really." Tensley jammed her hands on her hips and leaned down, searing her gaze into Gemini's. "You tell *him* that—" She broke off when she saw Kate's expression. "I cannot believe I'm arguing with a cat. Now I know I'm losing my mind."

"In this place, it just means you're normal."

The laughter bubbled up in the back of Tensley's throat until it came careening out of her mouth, picking up steam as it rolled over Kate and she joined in. Once Tensley started, she couldn't quit. It felt as though she hadn't laughed for months, maybe years.

A few minutes later, her eyes were damp and her stomach hurt, but she felt better than she had all day. "It was so hard to get that demon cat here." She sucked in a breath. "And out of all that I just told you, the being on stage with no clothes on, all of that, the only thing you heard was that I saw Max. Really."

"I sort of knew about the other."

"You have *got* to be kidding me."

"People talk." Kate managed to look both chastened and miserable at the same time. "It was hard to believe at first, but then—" She lifted a shoulder. "Considering everything that happened to you…"

Tensley jammed her hands on her hips. "You know what? None of it would have happened if you hadn't made me go see that woman."

Kate froze. "What woman?"

"The psychic. Madame Claire."

Tensley watched as her best friend's face turned several shades of white. Now Kate was the one to grab and hold on to the exam table. Gemini leaped out of her arms. "You went to—Madame—why?"

"Because you made the appointment and told me I had to. Two days ago."

"Two days ago. That's impossible. I haven't even seen you since…hold on." Kate wobbled toward the sink, grabbed a paper cup and took a drink of water. She kept her back turned. "Why in the hell would I do that?"

The question was whispered so quietly, Tensley wasn't sure if her friend meant it to be heard. She decided to answer, anyway. "Bryan-with-a-y-not-an-i?"

No response. She tried again. "You said I had to stop trying to find happily-ever-afters with losers. Like Bryan. Remember? I quit my job and flew to Canada to be with him. It was supposed to be a big, romantic surprise. The one spontaneous moment in my life." Tensley paused and then kept going, desperate to spark her friend's memory. "Except I was the one who got the big surprise. He forgot to tell me he's already married. With a kid."

Something like a whimper came from Kate. Alarmed, Tensley crossed the small room. "Are you okay?"

Kate turned an agonized expression on her. "While you were there," she croaked, "at Madame Claire's. Did she ask if you wanted to erase a mistake from your past?"

Tensley closed her eyes and shook her head. Saying it aloud would make it real and if a part of her couldn't cling to the hope that this whole thing was just one giant misinterpretation, she wasn't sure what she would do.

"Thank God." Kate grabbed her wrist. Her breath came in short gasps. "Are you sure?"

Again Tensley shook her head.

Kate straightened, looking less relieved. "You're not sure?"

"Even if she *did*..." Uh-oh. Kate might have stopped breathing entirely. "That would just be crazy."

"Tell me." Her fingers closed tighter on Tensley's wrist. "You have to."

"Ow. Fine. She said I could have a do-over."

"And?" Kate pressed. "What was the do-over?"

"I told you. Crazy. It's not as though I believed her."

"The do-over. What was it?"

Tensley winced. "I said, if I had it to do over, I would have punched Rhonda when I had the chance."

She had never heard anything like the sound that came out of her best friend. It was a combination of a moan and a screech so high that every dog in the back kennels began barking. Gemini sailed from the table to the floor right as Marla threw open the door to yell, "Dr. O'Brien!"

Kate let go of Tensley's wrist to sink into the chair, head in her hands. Gemini shot past Marla's legs as the barking chorus rose and swelled.

"What happened?" the tech shouted.

Given the events of the last forty-eight hours, Tensley decided, the better question was what the hell *hadn't* happened?

Yet.

CHAPTER EIGHT

"I'll bet if there was a national poll, most women would say they made their biggest mistakes when they were teenagers."

Tensley took a bite from the apple she'd found in the clinic's break room and considered Kate's words as she crunched. "I think you're right."

"So why is that?"

"It's the one time we're sure we know everything." Tensley tipped her head, thinking. The apple gleamed up at her, red, crunchy, satisfying. "Well that, and the temptation of hot teenage boys." One in particular.

Kate stood, brushing dog hair from her white coat. Tensley was relieved to see color begin returning to her friend's face.

The clinic was finally quiet. Marla and Kate had soothed each of the wound-up, barking dogs while Tensley climbed atop a stack of kennels to apologize to Gemini, who had been so enraged by the whole incident, he shook from ear to paw. He'd refused to even look at her, but after she'd groveled enough for ten sorry humans, he'd agreed to come down. Or maybe it was the bribe of a plate of Kate's most expensive cat food.

If she came back in another life, Tensley decided, she would like to be a cat. No one questioned a cat's demands for a world that made sense.

But on to the larger crisis. She had just opened her mouth to ask why Kate had gone to Madame Claire in the first place when her best friend spoke again, gazing at a calendar advertising the seven unique and savory flavors of a particular dog food. As if a dog cared whether there was more than one. "Mitch Sexton," Kate mused. "He was my mistake."

Tensley aimed a skeptical look at her. "Mitch Sexton. The guy who read the *Wall Street Journal* every day. He was cute and I'm sure he's made tons of money by now, but your babies would have been born carrying a briefcase." Tensley shook her head. "Think how much *that* would have hurt. I know he liked you, but you were right not to go out with him."

Her best friend turned slowly, her clear gray-eyed gaze meeting Tensley's. "Actually, I did go out with him."

"That's—crazy. You would have told me."

"I did."

Alice down the rabbit hole again. "No. I would have remembered—"

"Senior prom."

Tensley rifled through the file drawers in her brain. She remembered helping Kate pick out a dress, couldn't remember who her friend's date had been. And why couldn't she think what she herself had worn...oh. Tensley hadn't gone. That had been the night she and Max first made love. And it had been so much better than any prom ever could have been....

She had to shove the memory aside before everything began to hurt again. "Okay. So you went to the senior prom with Mitch."

Kate dropped her chin, drumming her fingers lightly on the counter. Her voice softened and a sad smile teased at the corners of her mouth. "For a guy who read the *Wall Street Journal* for fun, he knew how to rock a kiss."

"Really." Her mental picture of Mitch was changing by the second. "And how well he kissed didn't depend on whether his stocks were up or down?"

Kate's smile became bigger, and sadder, at the same time. "I don't know what his stocks were doing that night, but *he* was definitely up."

"Mitch. Mitch *Sexton*. And you."

"He got us a gorgeous hotel suite. Paid for it with his own American Express card." Any humor in Kate's small near-laugh was canceled out by the pain in her eyes. "Remember how much trouble we had with the zipper of that dress when I tried it on?"

Tensley thought for a minute and shook her head. This was just weird.

"It practically melted off me as soon as I stepped inside that suite. And Mitch was either a teenage prodigy at mind-blowing sex or the *Wall Street Journal* gives tips on more than the stock market."

"You slept with Mitch."

Kate didn't seem to hear. "Maybe they printed a different edition for premium subscribers."

"And did he wear a tie while you were having this mind-blowing sex?"

This time, Kate almost laughed. "No. He didn't. And he didn't stop once to check his stocks."

The apple hit the counter with a thump. "How could I not have known about this?" Best friendship carried certain unwritten rules. This was clearly a breach.

Kate blinked and straightened, tugging her white coat into place. "Because it didn't happen."

She wanted to scream. Instead, Tensley kept her voice low and even. "You just told me it did."

"When I went to Madame Claire, she erased the biggest mistake of my life." Kate paused. "That night with Mitch Sexton."

Tensley tipped her head, looking at her friend. Kate was the level-headed one of the two of them. If anyone was given to flights of drama, it was Tensley. "So you had fun with a cute, geeky guy. That's not such a bad thing."

"As it turned out, it was."

Her friend's bottom lip quivered. "Why?" Tensley asked carefully.

"I shouldn't be talking about all this." Kate put her hand up, backing away. "It's crazy. We haven't even seen each other in years and all of a sudden, I'm telling you things I haven't told anyone—"

"Stop," Tensley ordered.

She did, letting her hand fall back down.

"Two days ago, you tried to fire Mary Sue for, I don't know, the tenth time in the last year? And you couldn't do it. Just like you couldn't do it the other nine times. Even though she misplaced the supply order and didn't submit it. Again."

Kate stared.

"Who did you call to beat yourself up for being weak? Me. Your best friend. And I reminded you what kind of a person you are. The kind that is a very good vet, but has a hard time firing people."

"Oh."

"You need an office manager. I told you that then, for…hmm…I guess the tenth time. And I'm telling you again now."

Kate crinkled her forehead. "I do need an office manager."

"And you need to remember, no matter what else you might think happened, that we have never stopped being best friends."

"If anybody should know things aren't what they seem, I guess it's me."

"Damn right. Now tell me what happened with you and who-knew-he-had-it-in-him Mitch."

Kate looked away. When she spoke again, her voice was small. "It was all so fast. We were dancing at the prom, then we were in the suite drinking champagne, then more champagne, then we were in bed…."

"Oh. My God." This time, Tensley was the one to drop into a chair. Her friend wouldn't look at her. "You mean—" She lowered her voice. "Did you get pregnant?"

In the several minutes it took for Kate to respond, Tensley flew through emotions at a dizzying speed—from concern for her friend to regret that Tensley must not have been there for her and then to anger that Kate hadn't shared something so monumental—before finally landing on empathy for the upheaval one night of teenage hormones must have caused.

"I got married," Kate said.

"You—what? When?"

"That night. We'd just graduated, the whole world was open to us and it felt exciting and grown up, but so scary. We didn't think anything would change. We'd still go to college, but we would have each other and somehow getting married felt like being adults. When we weren't sure we *could* be adults." She took a deep breath. "Plus, it felt so good to have someone love me. And to love him back."

"Wow," Tensley whispered in disbelief.

Kate's gaze took on a faraway look. "Remember when we were little, how we would plan our weddings? The dresses, the flowers. The gorgeous groom. The houses we would live in, the cars we would drive? We always started with 'once upon a time.'"

"And ended with 'they lived happily ever after,'" Tensley said gently. "I remember."

"Fairy tales should be banned."

"Maybe." Beads of worry began to form around her heart, ready to roll.

"Little girls turn into big girls who still believe in them."

Madame Claire's powers apparently didn't extend to erasing the remembered pain of a mistake. Tensley stood, putting her hand on her friend's arm. "Kate—"

From the back of the clinic, a dog began barking, diverting the vet's attention. She turned toward the door. "I have to go."

Tensley kept hold of her arm, not letting her leave just yet. "What happened? With Mitch. Before you went to Madame Claire."

"Early in the morning. Justice of the Peace. We had both just turned eighteen so we didn't need anyone's permission." If Kate's lip hadn't been trembling, she might have been able to pull off the playful lift of her brows. "And you were there, as my maid of honor. Wearing your best jeans. You looked great, if that helps. You brought Max with you."

It didn't. Tensley felt as though her brain, which had been sprinting to keep up with processing all of this, stopped with a wheeze and a go-on-without-me wave of the hand. "But I wasn't. There. Neither was he."

"Not after Madame Claire made it all go away."

Another dog joined in the barking.

"How long were you married?"

"Oh, let me think," Kate said. Her tone was casual, but laden with bitterness. "Right about nine days, three hours and thirty-one minutes. Mitch's father had the marriage annulled and Mitch didn't say a word. He just…" Kate turned her palms up, lifting a shoulder, "left early for Yale. And his father told everyone that I'd tricked his son into marrying me because he never would have ended up with someone like me otherwise. It was humiliating. I started wondering if his father was right."

"Like you would ever do something like that." Tensley pressed her lips together.

"That's what you said then." A small, sad smile. "But then everything happened with you and Max and I lost my best friend. Started drinking way too much and hanging out with people I shouldn't have. A few weeks later, I'd totaled a car and been arrested for drugs. The university couldn't pull my scholarship fast enough."

"I'm so sorry."

"Never graduated. Never became a vet. Never got over Mitch and his father making me feel like dirt."

"I had no idea."

"I shouldn't have had any idea, either." Anger surged through Kate's voice, building in intensity as she went on. "Madame Claire was supposed to be able to erase all of the memories, along with the mistake. That's what she told me. That's what I believed." Kate sucked in a breath. "But she got it wrong with me and now with you."

Kate's expression changed. "You have to believe me," she pleaded. "I don't remember sending you to Madame Claire. Until you came in today, I didn't even know we were still in touch, still friends. As far as I knew, you moved away after the whole thing with Rhonda and I'd never heard from you again."

"Which," Tensley felt compelled to point out, "didn't actually happen until I went to see Madame Claire."

"Right." Kate nodded her head and then shook it. "God, this is so complicated."

Understatement of the year.

"But obviously, we *were* friends and I *did* send you to Madame Claire."

"Best friends."

"Some best friend I am. I can only hope the reason I sent you to her was because she swore she'd figured out what she did wrong the first time. I'm sorry. I really am."

Tensley met the anguished gaze of her best friend. "Hey, you were trying to help. And you must have believed her when she said it wouldn't happen again." She tried her best and brightest smile, figuring she might at least be able to manage one that was semi-good and only slightly dim. "And you're a great best friend, by the way. Except for this one slip-up."

She watched as cautious relief crossed Kate's face. Then the barking dog chorus began hitting high notes.

"I have to see what's going on."

"No!" Tensley stepped in front of her, blocking the way. "I can guarantee it has to do with that cat I ended up with. Marla will take care of it."

"But it's my clinic. I have to—"

"No, you don't." Tensley shook a finger in her friend's face. "You, Kathleen Margaret O'Brien, have to figure out how we're going to get me out of this mess *you* got me into."

Kate's shoulders sagged. "If there is a way out of it."

"Of course there is." Tensley drew her own shoulders up and back.

"Okay." Kate was close to drawing blood from her lower lip, as hard as she was biting it.

"Remember the 'Problem Solvers Club' we cofounded in grade school?"

The ghost of a smile. "Yes."

"This is just a bigger problem." Tensley rolled her eyes. "All right, *much* bigger. Same principle, though."

"Bigger than the kid who kept farting in class and making us nauseous?"

"Yes. Bigger. But we did solve that one."

"You're right. We did. Except then we had another one to solve. He thought we had crushes on him because we brought him peanut butter sandwiches every day."

"He never figured out the crunchy part of the sandwich was Beano tablets." Tensley sighed. "I wonder what he ended up doing in life. Something alone. Has to be."

Kate's smile became a touch bigger. "I heard he's a dentist now."

"No." Tensley began to laugh. It felt good. "Can you imagine him asking patients if they want gas during their appointments?"

"And they think he means the other kind." Both women snickered.

"Some dental assistant has to be sneaking him Beano now. Otherwise, it would be hazardous working conditions." Tensley wiped the corners of her eyes. "So, fine. The 'Problem Solvers Club' is back in business."

"Guess so. Lead on, Tensley Theron Tanner-Starbrook."

"You had to go there." Tensley rolled her eyes toward the ceiling. "You don't remember we've been friends all these years, but you remember my middle name." She couldn't have a nice normal middle name, since she'd already been saddled with Tensley, which made people wrinkle their noses and ask how to spell it. No. It had to be Theron. Parents should be required to get a license before naming their children.

Kate's smile was genuine. "I did. I had to go there."

In spite of the head injury she must have suffered from landing at the bottom of the rabbit hole, Tensley smiled, too. "Apology accepted." Then she locked her fingers together, moving into urgent project mode. "We need a to-do list. Now."

"I'll get the paper and pen." Kate followed Tensley out of the door. "While you tell me what happened when you saw Max again."

Tensley pulled up short, nearly causing the two women to collide. "That's what I'd like to know."

***

The first item on the to-do list, of course, was to go see Madame Claire. But that would have to wait until the next morning. It was nearly eight p.m. by the time they'd caught up on Tensley's current bizarre life, settled the animals, and left the vet clinic.

Tensley had been tempted to leave Gemini there for the night, but his furious yowl was a clear protest and she was too tired to argue. Kate had offered to let them stay at her house, but Tensley had declined. Her brain felt so full, she wasn't sure how long she could continue to hold her head upright. On the other hand, if she tipped it to one side or the other, valuable information about her real life, like her address and phone number, might spill out. She couldn't afford to lose them by jamming in more information about a life where she was a stripper, with a boyfriend named Razor.

"Thank you. Really. Thank you," she said to Kate in the parking lot. "I'd love to stay with you, but I'd keep you up all night, asking questions." She paused. "And to be completely honest, I'm not sure I could handle the answers right now."

"Here's my address and phone number." Kate put a piece of paper into Tensley's hand. "If you change your mind, call me. Otherwise, I'll meet you at Madame Claire's first thing in the morning."

"Yes." The relief Tensley felt stretched the one syllable into several. Once everything had returned to normal, she wouldn't need to think about anything else. Including the squirming cat in her arms, who would become somebody else's problem. "See you tomorrow."

"Tomorrow." Kate hesitated. "I'm so, you know. I mean…"

Tensley threw her arms around her friend, folding her in a hug. "We'll figure it out."

"I know," came the answer in her ear. "But I'm still sorry."

"So you'll owe me. Big time." Releasing her friend, Tensley walked toward the Ford Taurus. The closer she came to it, the more the cool, crisp night air seemed to have a calming effect on her. Or maybe it was the chant she had assumed to block the thoughts that threatened to derail her. Step. *Breathe in.* Step. *Breathe out.*

Gemini shot her an exasperated look.

"Go with it," she told him.

She unlocked the car and slid into the driver's seat. Gemini scrambled over onto the passenger seat, tail thrashing against the vinyl, and glared at his faux owner. He'd apparently missed the soothing chant part of the agenda. "Relax," she commanded as she fit the key in the ignition.

He didn't. She could feel his eyes burning holes into the side of her head as she backed the car out of the parking place, gave Kate a wave, and began a less frenzied drive than the one she'd undertaken several hours before.

By the time she parked in front of the apartment and got out of the car, the events of the day had drained her so much, her legs wobbled and wiggled as she walked and it took a few minutes for her to locate her key and remember how to turn it in the lock. Gemini, for once, remained perfectly still.

When she opened the door, the cat shot from her arms and disappeared in a flash of fur. Tensley wouldn't have blamed him, she decided, if he'd gone back to his hiding spot on top of the kitchen cabinet. But then he wasn't the only one who had had a rough day. She wondered if that spot was big enough for her, too.

Speaking of rough... She turned to lock the apartment door from the inside and then grabbed a chair, dragging it across the hardwood floor to prop it beneath the knob. Razor Burns wouldn't be walking in here as he pleased tonight. She gave the chair one more push to make sure it was tight up against the door and walked down the hallway, her legs no more steady than they had been a few minutes earlier.

Tensley dropped onto the comfy couch, resting her head against its back. Now if she could just empty her mind. *No. Not empty. Just draw a curtain across it so that she didn't have to think, feel, or do anything until Madame Claire's shop opened in the morning. Once the psychic had put everything back, Tensley would be in her regular, blessedly normal life. With every problem she couldn't wait to have again. Because they wouldn't be *these* problems.

She closed her eyes, wondering if she would remember any of this once Madame Claire had undone the damage. Would she know that her dance moves could put men into full drool mode? Would she still clench her fist at the sound of Rhonda Reardon's name?

On second thought, she would do fine never remembering either one of those things. Instead, she'd gulp her pride and beg her mother for her job back. She'd consider herself lucky to have escaped a close call with someone like Bryan and she'd be more cautious next time. A woman did not need to have a man in her life to be happy.

Although, maybe, just maybe, she'd look up Max, now that she knew where to find him. She felt her mouth begin to curve in a smile as she thought of seeing Max again as herself, her real self. She'd wear her red silk dress. Or she'd first go to the gym for a month or two and then she'd buy a *new* dress. No more paying for a gym membership every month, while slapping the alarm off to go back to sleep every morning.

She'd be a new person. Or a new…old…person.

Her head ached. *Just get through tonight and it will be all over.* Her fingers fumbled for the to-do list she'd left on the table next to her. Her cell vibrated. Tensley opened her eyes and pulled the phone out of her purse, staring at the display. Private number, it said.

The phone stopped. Then started again. It could be anyone on the other end. She pushed the button and ventured a hello.

"Tensley."

Her stomach dropped five stories. *Oh God. It was him.* "Yes?" Her voice cracked.

"It's Max."

I know I know I know I know. "Hi."

"You know when I said we needed to talk?"

I haven't forgotten a single word you said. "I remember."

"Can you meet me tonight? Ten?" His voice was low, urgent.

She didn't hesitate. "Of course."

"Just you and me."

"S—Sure." The fact that her heart had leaped into her throat made it hard to breathe, let alone talk.

Max gave an address on the other side of town. Tensley grabbed the pen and paper and scribbled it down. His promise to see her in half an hour reached through the phone to caress her every nerve ending until her cheeks flushed with anticipation and she had to stand just to get her equilibrium back.

She was seeing Max again.

This was *so* not a good idea.

CHAPTER NINE

The Taurus groaned to a stop in a parking place right in front of the address Max had given Tensley. It was a restaurant, with the appetizing name of Sol's Good Eats.

The "n" was burned out of its neon "Open" sign. Sol's was, the sign announced in pink ringed by purple, "Ope."

Tensley turned off the ignition and sank against the headrest. Here she was, leaping straight back to high school at the sound of Max's voice over the phone, at the chance to see him again so soon. She'd thought she'd gotten over him years ago. But no. That would be something people who actually knew how to move on would do.

Now that she let herself think about it, she'd probably been comparing every man she'd dated since high school to Max. One hadn't ever read Hemingway and didn't even mind. One's smile was too perfect. Another one laughed at the right pitch, but too loud. Still another would brush the side of her face with his hand, but never make it up to her earlobe, even though she'd practically get her head in a horizontal position, hoping he would.

Damn it, Max. All your fault.

A man with scraggly hair and hands shoved deep into his jacket slowed his step long enough to peer inside her car. She glared a warning and he kept moving. What she really wanted to do was get out, toss him the keys and tell him to take off with the car.

People who drove a car like this were married, drove their kids to music lessons, knew what colors to paint the walls in their houses and what to cook for dinner.

People who drove a car like this didn't date good-looking men with the attention span of a flea, work in the family business because it was easier than not working in the family business, and keep hoping no one would find the huge, gaping hole inside her where a real person should be.

Next thing she knew, Dr. Drew would show up. Why not? What better reality show than Tensley, the only woman to screw up not just her life, but also her second chance.

Scraggly man was back. He ventured closer this time, bending down to look at her. Tensley flipped on the ignition and laid on the horn, hoping to frighten him away. He shook his head and kept walking.

She stared at her fingers, resting on the steering wheel. Minus her customary large, sparkling rings, they looked like someone else's hands. Bare. And vulnerable.

Then again, they *were* someone else's hands. A felon's.

To hell with it. Tensley got out of the car, slamming the door hard on her thoughts. So she'd see Max for a few minutes. Tomorrow, she'd be back at Madame Claire's and back to her life. And she'd get some new mental Tupperware to put him in. With a better seal.

She tried throwing open the door to Sol's Good Eats for dramatic effect, but the doorknob was greasy and it took her three tries to make it work. As soon as it did and she stepped inside, she grabbed a paper napkin from the table, her nostrils constricting at the smell of onions and coffee.

The welcome mat and the checked curtains were in need of a wash. Stuffing poked out of the red barstool seats at the counter, leaving vinyl edges that looked as though they could shred the butt of the toughest pair of jeans. A total of two customers, sitting a few stools apart, denim butts still intact, hunched over their plates of food. One glanced up at Tensley, but then went back to his French fries, drowning one in a puddle of ketchup before shoving it in his mouth.

No greeting. No wait staff. A sign by the door that said, "Please seat yourself."

She looked around the place. Also no sign of Max.

A twenty-something woman bounded out of the door to the kitchen, giggling at the man behind her, who was wiping his hands on a stained white apron.

The woman pulled up short at the sight of Tensley. "Hey. Sit anywhere you want. I'll be with you in a sec." She tossed a smile over her shoulder at the cook, who grunted and turned away.

"I was supposed to meet someone—" Before Tensley could finish, the woman had disappeared again.

If this was Max's idea of a joke, she was going to kill him. She told herself to leave, but the message didn't make it all the way to her feet, which stayed rooted to the mat. Then she saw a man lean out of a booth in a back corner. Max. He beckoned to her.

Go, she told herself. *Stay. No, go.*

This time, she managed to take a step back toward the door. He tipped his head, questioning.

Stay.

Her heart, traitor that it was, had sped up at the sight of him and heat flooded through her until she felt as though her crotch must be glowing its own neon "Ope" sign.

The waitress swung through the kitchen door, a glass carafe in her hand, following Tensley to the booth. "Coffee?" the woman asked as Tensley slid onto the dark-red leather seat opposite Max.

"Please." Vodka would be better, but she doubted it was on the menu at Sol's.

The waitress turned over a cup and splashed dark liquid into it. "Something to eat?"

Max lifted a forkful of scrambled eggs to his mouth. He'd sprinkled them liberally with pepper, Tensley noted, but there wouldn't be any salt on them. He didn't like salt. *Damn.* She didn't want to remember little things like that. Butterflies took off inside her, bumping against her rib cage. "I'm good with coffee," she managed to say.

The waitress refilled Max's cup of coffee. "How're your eggs?" she asked him, hip thrust in his direction. "They okay?"

"They're fine. Thanks," he said, never taking his eyes off Tensley.

The woman bounced away, sneakers screeching. She'd been gone less than a minute when the giggling began again.

Tensley took a sip of her coffee while her heart engaged in a full-out battle with her head. Her head won, but barely. "So what's up?" She averted her eyes, mentally talking the butterflies down, mid-flutter.

"How well do you know Gary?"

"I don't. Please tell me that's not what you wanted to talk about."

He didn't answer. After the silence had stretched over several seconds, she looked back at him. He was gazing through the window, his jaw working, as though trying to decide what to say next.

When he turned back and his deep blue eyes locked on her, the butterflies took off in a panic. She leaned forward, knocking the coffee cup with her hand and splashing hot liquid onto her skin.

"Here." He grabbed a napkin and her hand, blotting the coffee. "Did it burn you?"

Her skin tingled at his touch. She shook her head.

"It's red—"

"I am never going back to that place."

Max's chin lifted. "Fired?"

As if. She bristled. Tensley Tanner-Starbrook had never been fired from anything in her life. "No. I wasn't fired." Wait. Had she been?

"You can go back then."

She wasn't so sure she liked Cop Max, who seemed to have a single-minded focus. "Why should I? So you can watch?" Narrowing her eyes, she folded her arms in front of her. If he ever saw her naked again, and he should be so lucky, it was going to be on her terms.

The butterflies, no longer needed, flew an escape route.

He dipped his head, staring at his coffee. When he raised his eyes, his half-lidded gaze washed over her. "Because I need your help."

A dish crashed to the floor somewhere in the vicinity of the kitchen, followed by the raised voices of the waitress and the cook, one accusing, the other defensive. A barstool squeaked as a customer left. The door banged shut.

And Max needed her help.

Her cup had a hairline crack that had turned brown. She ran a finger along it, thinking. "I don't understand." She wanted to, though.

"Gary's a bad dude."

She looked up. "Tell me something I don't know."

"I can't tell you much until you agree to help."

"And you're saying that to help you, I would have to go back to Gary's Gorgeous Grecians." Just saying the name made her want to vomit.

He nodded, his eyes never leaving hers.

"I can't."

"That's hard to believe."

He had no idea what she'd just been through. Anger flashed through her. "I haven't even seen you for years, Max. All of a sudden, you show up at that—place. And then at my apartment and now you have me come here, just so you can ask for a favor. How exactly does that give you the right to not believe me? You don't even know me anymore." *Ow.* Really. *Ow.* This conversation wasn't going well.

"You're right."

Of course she was. But she didn't know what to do about it, maybe because it occurred so rarely. A half-snort escaped before she could catch it.

Neither of them spoke for a few minutes.

Then Max's fingers covered hers. He dropped his voice to barely above a rumble. "I've been working on building a case against Gary, and whoever he's working with, for months. But I've hit a wall. I need someone on the inside who can help me put the pieces together so I can nail this guy."

The butterflies were back, their wings banging against her ribs at the touch of Max's warm, strong fingers on her skin. "So let me be sure I understand." She paused to clear her throat. "Are you trying to say you want me to be that person on the inside?"

"You work there."

Not anymore. After tomorrow morning, she wouldn't have even heard of the place.

"And you're tight with Razor," Max went on. "You have access I don't."

Razor. Razor Burns. She shuddered.

Max's face hardened. "Has that asshole hurt you?"

"It's not that."

"Then what is it? Gary?"

"You wouldn't understand." Events would unravel most unpredictably, Madame Claire had warned, if she told anyone what had happened. "Just leave it alone."

He drew his mouth in tight. "Guess I can see why you wouldn't trust the police, after what you've been through."

Tensley rolled her eyes. "I'm still trying to figure out how you talked them into letting you be a cop."

"Want to see my badge?"

"Bet you say that to all the girls."

He ducked his head, having the sense to look embarrassed.

"I knew it." She took a long sip of coffee, looking at him over the rim of her cup. "Does it work even better than showing a girl how to outrun the police?"

"You remember that night." He was trying not to smile, but he couldn't manage it.

"Of course I remember. Now that you're 'the law' do you kick people out of that spot?" A dark little alley. Just big enough to hide a car and the two teenagers inside it, victorious after a slightly illegal street race. Max had said it was private enough to make love. No one would find them. No one had.

A twitch at the corner of his mouth. "Not even when I was a patrol officer. I had too many good memories. I didn't want to ruin them by finding someone else there."

"Oh." It came out as a squeak. She took a hasty sip of coffee.

The waitress came swinging back by, a carafe of coffee in her hand. Both Tensley and Max put up their hands and she left.

"Is it the house rent? Is that why you don't want to go back to Gary's?"

She searched his eyes. "Why me? There are other girls who work there."

A smile teased at his mouth. "You and I have a history."

"A history."

His coffee cup seemed to suddenly fascinate him. "Maybe I wasn't exactly disappointed at the idea of spending time with you."

My God. This was not happening the night before she would return to her real life. She slapped back the hope that surged inside her before it could take hold. Max the teenage boy had been amazing. Max the man was far more dangerous. Now his confidence was backed up by something real, something fascinating, something pulling her toward him faster than she could paddle backward.

This had to stop. Before things went any further. "So it's got to be me, you're thinking."

He nodded.

"Gary's a bad guy."

"Yes."

"Underhanded?"

More nodding. His gaze rose to meet hers, nearly undoing her resolve. But she kept going.

"Criminal? Violent?"

"Yes. And probably."

"And you want to put me, not someone else, just me, back in that place. Working for him."

Max stopped mid-nod.

Maybe he'd even made up that whole story about why she'd found him with Rhonda, to try and get on her good side. The skeptical side of her, the one that chimed in with an unhelpful I-told-you-so every time Tensley got hurt, urged her on, giving her words a clipped edge. "In fact, you want me to be the one responsible for getting the goods on him. Not that he'll be pissed off about that or anything. But it doesn't bother you at all. You're ready to send me in."

"Tensley—"

Back on solid ground, instead of emotional quicksand. "This is great, Max. Just great." Tensley snatched her purse from the seat and pulled out a couple of dollar bills, throwing them on the table. "After all we meant to each other, you would put me in danger and not even think twice about it." She stood, her knees knocking together. "Good to know what you really think about me. If I get shot up, you'll just move on to the next girl."

"It's not like that. I'll protect you."

"Like you protected me from seeing you with Rhonda?"

His mouth opened. And closed. He didn't answer.

She arched her brow. Damn. It was trembling like the rest of her. Just once she'd like to be able to make a dramatic exit. "Goodbye, Max. Hope you find someone to help you catch your bad guy. It isn't going to be me."

Another dish crashed as she walked toward the door. More yelling followed. She hoped Max was watching her newly thin ass, but she wasn't about to give him the satisfaction of turning back to see. He could actually kiss it, as far as she was concerned. She was never falling for him again, no matter how gorgeous those blue eyes, that dark hair, that hidden poet's soul was.

Never.

After tomorrow morning, if everything worked out the way it should, she wouldn't remember this brief, insane part of her life.

***

Kate was late. It took everything Tensley had not to charge through Madame Claire's door on her own. But she didn't. Her toe tapped on the pavement until she had a severe toe-ache, but she waited.

Finally, Kate came around the corner, head down. She glanced up. "Hi."

"Hi." Tensley scanned the worry lines on her best friend's face. "It's okay. Nothing bad is going to happen. We'll go in, tell her to make this right and then we'll leave once she does."

"It's just—" Kate shoved her hands in her jacket pockets. "I'm worried about what will happen if we have her try this again."

Dread began to ripple through Tensley. Kate couldn't back out now. "She has to. Nothing could be any worse than it is now. Trust me."

Kate looked over one shoulder and then the other. "I wasn't supposed to remember anything, once the mistake was erased." She focused her anxious gaze back on Tensley. "Then she *inserts* a mistake into your life *and* you still remember your old life. The woman screws something up every time. Can we trust her?"

"We can't afford not to." Tensley put her hands on Kate's shoulders. "Listen to me. I'm a college graduate, with a great condo, a closet of Jimmy Choos, plenty of successful men to date, and a good job. Once I get it back, anyway. But would anyone know that? No. Because they think I'm a stripper with a record." Her grip on her friend tightened. "And a boyfriend named Razor."

"Razor?" Kate's lips pursed like she'd tasted pickle juice. "You can't be serious."

"Dead serious." Tensley grabbed her friend's arm, pulling her toward the door. "And that's why we're going in." She opened the door, the tinkling of the bell and the smell of incense sending chills up her spine. The last time she'd been here… She loosened her hold on Kate and drew her shoulders back, focusing on breathing through her mouth.

The door at the back of the shop opened and Madame Claire appeared. Today she was dressed in black, with a heavy gold necklace around her neck and on her feet, leopard-print heels.

"So you have come," she said gravely. Once her gaze swept upward to take in the two women, she blanched and her eyes widened. "Oh."

"You weren't expecting us? Thought you were psychic."

"Tensley," Kate said under her breath. Her hand closed on Tensley's arm, radiating a warning. "Don't piss her off."

Tensley steeled herself to be polite. "We need your help."

"I see." The woman drew a breath and walked toward a small desk. "Unfortunately, it is fully booked today." She leafed through the pages of a scheduling book. "My appointment will arrive at any time. I do not know what has detained her—but yes, at any moment, she will be here." More ruffling of the pages, backward this time. She crooked an eyebrow. "Next week you may come. Or the week after."

Tensley and Kate didn't move.

Madame Claire walked toward the back of the shop, leopard heels clicking on the hardwood. She hesitated and then gave a dismissive flick of her fingers. "You will take your leave now."

"No."

The psychic turned.

Kate took a step forward. "I asked you to help my friend but instead, you turned her life upside down." Her voice shook. "You need to put things back the way they were."

"I do not understand this…" Madame Claire's hand lifted as though she were a stage actress burdened with an unappreciative audience. "…upside down."

Tensley surged forward. She'd never had an abundance of patience, but today it was nonexistent. "Cut the crap. You know exactly what we're talking about."

Madame Claire's gaze could have neatly sliced her in two. "It is a rare opportunity you were given. What you did with it was of your own choice."

"I didn't know what would happen."

"And that is where the opportunity lies, does it not?"

Tensley jerked a hand through her hair, tears frustratingly near. "I wasn't thinking. You asked me about a mistake and I just threw something out there. I didn't know you were serious."

"Did I not explain?"

"I—I didn't believe you." Tensley turned to Kate for help. Her friend's mouth was open, her eyes wide with alarm.

The psychic lifted one shoulder. "Perhaps it is that you should have." She turned again.

"Stop!" Tensley's voice screeched upward. "You have to undo this!"

"Please," Kate implored.

"It cannot be so." The woman kept walking.

Fear surged through Tensley's veins. "You made me a stripper. Do I look like a stripper? That's because I'm not!" She shook off Kate's restraining hand and charged toward the woman. "Get the hell back here and fix this or I—I'm going to the police!"

Madame Claire's shoulders lifted. She spun on one heel to face Tensley, who pulled up short before reaching her. "The police, what is it you will tell them? It is you who have caused these events to occur." She sniffed. "And you did not, as you say, 'throw something out there.' When it is this chance you were offered, the answer, it came only from your heart."

"Bullshit."

"How long did it take you to answer when I asked this question of you?"

"I—It—"

"Exactly. The regret is always with you. One question I ask and out it comes."

Tensley's heart beat so fast, it thudded in her ears. She could barely hear, barely move. "But I'm not me anymore," she whispered.

Kate was at her side in a flash, arm around her shoulders, hugging her hard.

Madame Claire looked from one woman to the other. "My mother, she said this would happen."

Kate spoke for both of them. "What?"

Madame Claire put her hands on her hips, looking everywhere but at them. "Never does she let me forget that...what can I say, errors, they can be made. Not that *she* ever made an error." She snorted. "Or so she does say. She has, it must be said, a convenient memory."

Tensley struggled to keep her voice even. "Let's go back to how you're going to undo this."

"My mother, she taught me things before she died, but not too much." She made a sound of disgust. "She said it would be too dangerous, that I was perhaps inclined to accidents."

"Great," Tensley breathed. "An accident-prone psychic."

Madame Claire directed herself to Kate. "It was sorry I felt for you, so I took a chance. And it worked, did it not? Except that you remembered what you were not to remember. Your life before."

Kate's hold on Tensley tightened. "You could have mentioned you didn't know what you were doing."

"It is complaints you have about your life now?"

"No." Kate screwed up her face, as if she had to think about it. "Not really."

Tensley folded her fingers into a white-knuckled plea. "Please tell us that your momma at least taught you how to undo this."

The psychic hesitated. "It is not so simple. There is a lesson that first must be learned before there can be, as you say, an undoing. Or the spell, it will not take."

Tensley and Kate looked at each other, baffled. "A lesson?" they asked in unison.

"My mother, I heard her tell that to a client who begged to have a spell undone. The reverse spell, it was...three hundred sixty-four. Possibly." Madame Claire tapped her chin with a bright red fingernail. "Part A...or was it B."

"You don't even know which spell it is?" Kate sounded horrified.

"The spells, they are on my iPhone," she sniffed. "That is not the difficult part."

"Of course it isn't." Tensley was pretty sure she might pass out at any minute. Her head felt so light, her arms and legs had to be acting like a giant balloon weight, holding it down.

Madame Claire pulled her mouth in tight. "The lesson, it must be learned from the journey. Yes." She paused. "Or no. It may be something else."

"I don't understand how you could not know this." Kate's voice was barely audible.

"I was but twelve years old. And not to be listening. My mother, she did not want me to go into the family business."

"But you did, anyway," Tensley blurted.

The psychic didn't seem to hear her. "It is, I believe, a lesson tied to the regret that has been undone." Madame Claire bit down on her bottom lip, transferring red lipstick to her teeth. "And now I have told you all that I know."

Kate squeezed her eyes shut. "I'm sorry," she whispered to Tensley. "So sorry."

"My next client will arrive at any moment," Madame Claire said. "You must now leave."

"Uh-huh. Bad for business." Once again, Tensley's knees were banging together, threatening to give up on keeping her upright. What exactly was she supposed to have learned from the last day and a half? How to pole dance?

"It is my best I will do." Madame Claire sounded aggrieved. "That is all one can ask." She sucked in a breath. "Please to stand there. Quietly. I will make a try with something."

"Like I'm going to trust you now." Tensley's voice rose to a shriek.

"And it is many choices you have?" the psychic snapped.

Tensley shut her eyes.

"Wait a minute," Kate said. "What are you going to do to her?"

"The reverse spell. Once the lesson, it is learned, all should go back as before."

"*Should*," Tensley repeated. "Nice."

"You said you weren't sure which spell it was." Kate sounded panicked.

Suspicious, Tensley opened one eye.

"Three hundred sixty-four…uh, Part A. That is what I believe."

"And what if you're wrong? I turn into a giraffe or something?"

"A giraffe, it has long legs." Madame Claire scanned Tensley from head to toe. "Could not hurt, I would say."

"Hey!"

"Your eyes, you will close them," the psychic ordered.

Tensley did as she was told. Maybe she'd find out she'd already learned her lesson, without even knowing it, and the spell would take right away. She wasn't half-bad at pole dancing, so if that was it, she was golden.

Please let that be it. Please, please, please. She closed her eyes as tight as she possibly could. And she held her breath.

CHAPTER TEN

Tensley snuck one eye open. And then the other.

Kate had turned several shades of pale. A vein jumped in her neck as she watched Tensley. "Well?" she breathed. The word barely left her mouth

"I don't know." Tensley looked down and up. She didn't feel any different and she had the same clothes on, but…

Madame Claire nodded. "You are to leave now. And you are welcome. No charge."

That would mean—what, exactly? "Did I get my life back?" Afraid to meet the psychic's eyes, Tensley instead stared at the woman's shoes. There was a small tear in the leopard print of one, near the toe.

The answer was sharp, impatient. "No. It is obvious to see."

"What do you mean it's obvious?" Her voice shook. Tensley imagined an actual leopard leaping from the shoe to swallow Madame Claire whole.

A faint mewing sound came from Kate, causing Tensley to glance up. Kate, who looked as though she might pass out, had grabbed the edge of a table.

"The light. We would have seen it," the psychic replied calmly. "And yet we did not."

"So you didn't do it right." Fingers of desperation crawled up her spine.

"It is correctly I did it." Madame Claire jammed her hands on her hips. "But nothing will happen until this lesson you learn." She shook her head. "I believe this has already been explained."

Tensley was ready to deck the woman. She raised a shaky fist, stopping mid-air when Kate recovered enough to talk.

"What the hell are you doing? That's what got you into trouble in the first place," her friend said under her breath. She released her hold on the table and stood up straight, directing her attention to the psychic. "Once she does learn her lesson, whatever that might be," Kate cleared her throat, "everything will go back to the way it was?"

"That is what I have said," Madame Claire replied, though she sounded none too sure. "Now please, you must leave."

"Let's get out of here," Kate said, putting her hand on Tensley's arm.

"But I—we can't—just leave."

"We have to."

The door shut behind Madame Claire right before the bells over the front entrance tinkled and a nervous-looking woman walked in, teetering on heels too high for her small frame.

A few seconds passed and Madame Claire appeared once again. "Ah," she said to the woman. "So you have come."

"Let's go," Kate whispered, tugging at Tensley's arm.

"But what about…"

The words died on her lips as Madame Claire speared her with a single look.

"*Fine.*" Tensley allowed herself to be led toward the front door. "We'll be back."

"This I know," the psychic replied gravely. She beckoned toward the nervous woman. "You will come now."

Kate half-pushed, half-shoved Tensley through the door, the bells overhead clanging in alarm.

"What the hell?" Tensley choked as they spilled onto the sidewalk.

Her best friend took her arm, propelling her down the street. All around them, Tensley realized with a jolt, it appeared to be a perfectly normal day. Seattle-gray skies overhead, bicycles going by, people emerging from beneath the green awning of a Starbucks, lattes clutched in their hands.

A traffic light turned yellow and then red. Cars stopped obediently, not knowing anything was wrong. That in a flash of light, Tensley Tanner-Starbrook had gone from a nearly-happy, financially secure businessperson to a stripper who owed rent to the "house." Even worse, no one cared. Except her best friend, who hadn't known until yesterday that they were still best friends.

"Think," Kate ordered. "What would you have to learn from that whole thing with Rhonda?"

"I don't know. I can't think. I can't even walk." As if to prove it, she stumbled.

Kate dragged her back up by the arm. "Well, you have to."

"You're the one who started this whole thing."

"I know. And I said I'm sorry. That's all you're getting until we figure this out."

They walked in silence for two blocks, until they reached a small city park, with weathered wood benches and a set of swings with black rubber seats. They stopped at the same time and then, without a word, Kate made for the swings.

Tensley followed. She fell into a swing next to Kate and grabbed the thick chains, holding on tight. There was comfort in the feeling of the cold metal against her palms, in the knowledge that it had safely carried too many children over the years to count. Digging the heel of her shoe into the sawdust, she pushed off, setting the swing in motion.

They swung back and forth as the chains creaked and moaned. The sound took Tensley back years, to the feeling of flying through the air at recess, hair streaming behind her as she stretched her legs forward and back. No worries but who she would sit with at lunch and how she would make herself pay attention in math.

"I heard Rhonda's opened up a boutique," Kate said at last. "Sounds like it's doing well."

"Specializing in what? Hard-to-fit sizes for women with bad boob jobs?"

"Okay, Bitter Betty." Kate flew by, toes pointed up.

"What do you want me to say," Tensley grumbled. "I'm happy her life's turned out great, while mine sucks?"

No answer.

Tensley hung her head, staring at bits of sawdust as she swung by. It had become such a habit over the years to hate Rhonda, it was disconcerting to find herself feeling a little bad about it. "Max told me yesterday that it was all a setup. That I was *supposed* to find him with Rhonda so I would leave him to go to college."

"Huh." Kate slowed down. "I suppose that might make sense, though I wouldn't have seen it then."

"Yeah, well. Neither did I." She borrowed a term from Madame Claire. "Ob-vi-ous-ly. But I'm not so sure I believe him. He might be saying that now because he wants something from me."

"What something?"

"Just—nothing. Never mind." She couldn't bring herself to think about going back to that place.

After a few minutes, Kate said, "You know, you might not be that far off about Rhonda."

"I was being mean. So she has her own boutique. Good for her." She tried as hard as she could to sound like she meant it.

"It's called 'Rags to Bitches.'"

"Are you kidding me?" Tensley started laughing.

Kate joined in. "I'm not."

"I'll bet she sells spandex evening gowns."

"With matching hubcap earrings."

"And gloves with detachable brass knuckles. For those *special* occasions."

The heavy load pressing on Tensley's chest lightened for a few minutes as the two friends giggled and swung. Then, after a few leftover snickers, they quieted.

"I wonder what would have happened if you had left him and gone off to college," Kate mused.

Tensley came to an abrupt stop, sawdust flying, and shot her friend an exasperated look.

"Sorry," Kate was quick to say. "I forgot. You already know."

A raindrop landed on Tensley's nose. She pushed off again, sending it sailing through the air. A minute later, there was more moisture on her face, but it wasn't rain. She swiped at her eyes. "That's my real life. This isn't."

"So quit whimpering and concentrate on figuring out what you have to learn."

"I do not whimper. I am not one of your patients." Tensley made a face. "You know, you're much nicer in my real life."

"I doubt that." Kate grinned. She backed up and took off again, stretching her legs high.

Tensley's answering smile disappeared seconds later. "What could I possibly have to learn from punching Rhonda? Or...not punching Rhonda." She aimed a quizzical look at her friend as she flew by. "Which is it?"

"Got me."

Tensley stood and moved to one of the poles that anchored the swing set to the ground. She leaned against it and folded her arms across her chest, watching children go down a slide on the other side of the small park. Each kid landed on the ground with a shriek of joy. "So if it's true it's a regret that has always been with me, I guess the question is, why? Out of all the things I've done in my life, why is that one my biggest regret?"

"She took your man. You wanted revenge."

"Which would definitely work if my life was a country song." Tensley thought for a minute, then shook her head. "I don't think that's it."

"You always wanted to be a pro boxer, but you didn't follow your dream." Kate was barely moving in the swing now. She leaned back all the way, her arms extended, face to the sky. "Wait. I think that one's a movie."

Tensley tipped her head, exasperated. "Are you going to help, or not?"

"I am helping." Kate sounded miffed. "So far, I'm the only one who's come up with anything."

Tensley began to pace, making a trail in the sawdust. "Maybe I'm supposed to learn to be more accepting."

"Of what? The girl you found kissing your guy?" Kate shook her head. "That can't be it."

"Yeah, I don't think so, either."

Kate sat up. "What about jealousy? Isn't that one of the seven deadly sins?"

"Let me think." Tensley wracked her brain, pulling open the mental file drawer that contained her childhood catechism. "Envy."

"Same thing."

"What exactly did I envy?"

Kate made a dismissive motion with her hand. "Rhonda. She had the skanky arrogance to talk herself out of every single clothing detention, had practically every guy in school panting after her—"

"Not *every* guy."

Kate ignored her. "At the time, she had *your* guy's tongue down her throat."

Tensley leveled a look at her friend. "Fine." She raised her arms, palms up. "I'll never be envious again," she called. The kids on the slide stopped shrieking and turned to look.

"You can't just say it," Kate reminded her. "You have to demonstrate it."

"A little hard to do since high school was a while ago. The only thing I really envy now is anyone with a Chanel reissue 2.55 bag. Don't think I'm going to find that here." She stopped. "Unless you have one?"

Kate shook her head. "I'd just get dog pee on it."

"That's okay. Not sure I could manage a lack of envy on that one." Tensley tapped her chin, thinking. "Maybe it's that I'm supposed to be more diplomatic. See a problem, solve it. Instead of making it worse."

Kate scuffed the toe of her sneaker, slowing the swing. "I don't know."

"I should have asked questions. Expressed my feelings and asked for feedback. Brokered a solution." She stopped pacing.

"Not sure if that's a journey."

"It definitely could be." Tensley paused, imagining herself calm, cool and in control. Taking the emotion out of a problem and solving it, to the gratitude and maybe even applause, of those around her. "I know I haven't been doing enough of it at my job." Hastily, she added a clarification. "My real job. I tend to get too caught up in the people involved and not focus enough on the problem and how to solve it."

"If that's your lesson, how are you going to prove you've learned it?"

Tensley's shoulders sagged. "I have no idea."

Kate rose and came to stand by Tensley's side. When she spoke again, her voice was gentle. "We'll figure it out."

"Right." Tensley pumped her chin up and down. If only Madame Claire's mamma had written a damn mamma manual. She took a deep breath and then said, "Max is investigating the strip club. He asked me to help him get information."

"What did you say?"

"I said no."

"Why?"

"It's dangerous, that's why. And he wasn't even thinking about that part of it, about putting me in danger. He only wanted to use me, to help make his case—" She stopped, turning to Kate. "Wait a minute. He has a problem."

"A problem."

"He doesn't have enough information to nail the guy. I can help him get it."

"A problem that needs solving." Though she sounded doubtful, Kate nodded her support.

Tensley sighed. "But I'd have to go back to that place. If I ever knew anything that would have helped him, it was gone as soon as Madame Claire did her thing and I could only remember my old life."

"Max can't put you into danger without a way to protect you."

A lone butterfly began flapping its wings against Tensley's ribs.

"I used to date a cop," Kate said. "They have procedures miles long."

"I can't go back." Tensley shuddered.

"He needs your help. You need to learn a lesson. This could be your ticket back to your old life."

"Maybe."

"Or he figures if he scares you enough, you'll jump into his bed for protection. Could be worse things to do while you're waiting for a flash of light." This time, Kate was the one who sighed. "There was something pretty sexy about sleeping with a man who put his gun on the nightstand."

"Great. Thanks for that." Half of her wanted to leap straight ahead to that fantasy and linger awhile, while the other half shouted a warning that, if she let herself fall for Max again, she'd be so much worse off than she was now. Pressing her fingers against her temples, Tensley decided to ignore both and concentrate on the right here, right now—doing what she had to do to get her life back. "So if I help solve his problem, I might end up with a lesson learned."

"Possibly."

"I don't know." Tensley shook her head. "This might not have anything to do with Max at all."

"You won't know until you try."

"There has to be something else."

"You're just scared."

For someone who couldn't remember being her best friend, Kate could still call her bluff. "Wouldn't you be?"

"Is he still as gorgeous as he was in high school?"

Tensley didn't hesitate. "Oh hell, yes."

"You two were so great together. You had something special."

The butterfly in her stomach found friends. Yes, she and Max had had something special together.

Something she had yet to recover from.

CHAPTER ELEVEN

Max didn't bother to look at the caller ID on his cell before he answered it. The way this fucked-up day was going, it didn't matter. "Hunter," he said, his voice a rough bark.

"What's wrong?"

Tensley. That fast, his heart started the weird happy dance thing it hadn't done since high school. "Nothing's wrong," he lied. "I'm glad you called." No lie about that. He sat up straight and then decided he was better off trying to relax, so he leaned back in his chair, staring up. The ugly, brown water stain on the ceiling tile above his head had become bigger overnight. Nice. "About the other night—"

"If you're going to apologize," she broke in, "don't. I overreacted."

He was silent for a few seconds, taking that in. Overreacting had always been part of her appeal. Tensley had a passion he'd never seen in other people. "No, you didn't," he said. "You thought I was trying to throw you to the wolves. Or in this case, one wolf. Gary."

"True," she admitted.

"So are we done apologizing to each other?"

"For now."

He could have sworn he actually heard her smile. "Good."

"The thing is…I'm calling to say I'll help you."

He sat back so fast, his wheeled chair nearly launched him into his desk. "You serious?"

"Hardly ever. But I am about this."

He heard something in her voice. Something that caused his detective instincts to kick in. "Why the change?"

"You're making this a lot harder than it needs to be."

Nothing had ever been easy when it came to this woman. "Right." He tapped a pencil against the desk. "I won't ask, then." Hell, yes, he would. But not now.

"Good idea." He heard her suck in a breath. "There's only one condition. You can't let me be gunned down in a hail of bullets. Much as I've always wanted to play the tragic, sympathetic heroine, I'm pretty sure I would suck at it."

The idea of a bullet coming anywhere close to her caused his stomach to clench with apprehension. He tried to hide it with an off-hand response. "Good to know. I'll take the gun battle off my to-do list. Damn. We usually get at least one a day in, but seeing as you don't want to do it..."

"The blood would mess up my hair." A nervous laugh.

"Not gonna happen. Trust me." As if he was trustworthy. Just the thought of his hands in her soft hair... He shoved away from his desk to try and startle his dick out of its ready position. Unfortunately, he forgot about the wheels again and his chair slammed into the desk of the surliest detective in their unit, who aimed a zero-tolerance frown at him. Max drew his brows together, pointed to the phone at his ear and shook his head at the guy— *nothing, man, ignore it*. His colleague turned away.

"What do we do now?" Tensley asked.

Good question. He went with his gut. "Meet me."

They made arrangements to meet at the diner again in half an hour. As Max put the phone down, though, the day became a little less fantastic. He'd be one hell of a stupid cop if he didn't ask himself why Tensley had suddenly changed her mind. And whether he would ever be able to keep his professional distance from the woman.

At least he knew one thing—he would do anything and everything to make sure he protected her. Especially since his reasons for asking her to do this for him probably weren't the best.

Now that he thought about it, really thought about it, getting her involved might have been the worst idea he'd had in a very long time. And that was saying something, given the number of bad ideas he'd come up with in his life.

***

Sol was behind the counter when Max arrived at the diner, but the flirty young waitress with the squeaky shoes and bobbing hips was nowhere in sight. Mid-afternoon, the place was deserted. "Hey."

"Hey." Sol acknowledged him with a nod.

"By yourself today?"

"More trouble than it's worth to keep help around." The owner of the diner rolled his eyes.

"So you pissed this one off, too." Sol fired waitresses as soon as they started catching on he had a soft spot the size of Texas for a hard-luck story. As a result, he went through a spin cycle of employees.

Instead of answering, the older man wiped his hands on his apron and turned away to grab the coffee pot. "You want something to eat?"

Max's stomach answered for him, with a rumble loud enough for Sol to hear.

"I'll take that as a yes. Cheeseburger, no onions. Fries, no salt."

With a thumbs-up, Max made his way to his favorite booth.

Sol arrived a couple of minutes later to splash coffee into a cup. "Meetin' somebody?"

"We'll see."

The older man grunted. "The last one sure left in a hurry. What'd you do, try and get too friendly?"

"I smell my cheeseburger burning."

Sol started, then said, "Shit. It's not even cookin' yet."

Max hid his grin. "Man, I hope it doesn't take long. I'm really hungry."

"Yeah, yeah." Sol left for the kitchen, calling over his shoulder. "Someone comes in, you tell them to sit down."

"Or put on an apron."

Most of what Sol muttered in response was unintelligible, which was probably a good thing. Max cradled his coffee cup as he looked through the window, telling himself he wasn't watching for that first glance of Tensley. The one where he would get to drink in everything about her before she saw him and her guard went up.

It didn't take long. A couple of minutes later, her car cruised to a stop. She got out, shut the door and then stood, arms hugging her body, looking at Sol's sign. A grown woman now, she still gave off that vibe of naïve fragility, but there was a thread of pure steel running through the middle of it. Not seeing it would be like mistaking Jennifer Aniston for the character Rachel she'd played on TV.

Come on, he urged. *I won't bite.* That fast, he added, *but you can.* His mind veered back to an open field, inhaling the scratchy sweet smell of grass as Tensley's hair brushed his naked body. Little nibbles from her perfect pink mouth, beginning at his shoulders and moving down, that had driven him half insane. His rock-hard dick standing so tall, he could have thrown a tarp over it and made a spacious shelter for them both.

He set his cup down, rattling the china. He closed his eyes, doing his best to bring his breathing back to normal. She would be a confidential informant. And he could not ignore the fact that she could even be involved in what was going on at the club. She'd changed her mind pretty fast about helping him. What was in it for her?

It did not matter, repeat, did not matter, what kind of memories she stirred in him. All of that was a long time ago. Done. Gone. He had a job to do.

"Let me guess. You've taken up meditation."

The sound of her voice brought him straight back to Sol's diner. "No." He pushed the word out of his throat so hard, it startled them both.

She took a step back.

"Sorry." He gestured. "Have a seat."

"Are you okay?" she asked as she slid onto the seat.

He cleared his throat. "I'm great."

Her nod was so small, he might have imagined it.

Sol appeared at the table. "Coffee?"

"Yes, please."

Once her cup had been filled, Sol jerked a thumb at Max. "Watch this one. He gives you any trouble, you let me know."

Tensley's eyes met Max's. "Thanks, but I can handle him."

"That's what all his women say." Sol shuffled off.

Tensley's forehead puckered. "How many women are we talking about exactly?" she asked Max.

He ignored the question. Damn Sol, anyway. "I need you to come with me to the station."

"Why?"

"Department policy. My captain has to sign off on you as an informant."

"Informant." She repeated the word carefully, as though she had to roll it around on her tongue.

Max swallowed hard. "You changed your mind pretty fast. Anything I need to know about?"

"Let's be clear." She leaned forward. "I do not want to do this. Be an informant."

Now he leaned forward. "That's not what you said when you called."

"All I said was that I would do it." Her breath tickled his nose.

"So back to my question. Why? Money?"

"No."

He hesitated for a beat. "Immunity from prosecution?"

"No." She also hesitated. "And that sounded very *Law and Order* of you."

"You'll need to sign an agreement."

"Terrific. Perfect. I think they do that on *Law and Order*, too."

"You haven't told me why the sudden change."

"For God's sake, let it go."

"They wouldn't let it go on *Law and Order*. And that's apparently our standard here."

She fought unsuccessfully to keep the corners of her mouth from turning up. "It should be."

"Then spill."

"Maybe it's because you and I have a history."

He ordered his own smile to a halt. Then he leaned in further, until his mouth was barely separated from hers. "So what are you saying?"

Her lips parted. "I'm saying—"

"Cheeseburger, no onions," Sol growled as he slid the plate between them. Max and Tensley jumped apart.

Guilt stabbed at Max, as though he was a high school kid again, caught with the girl he'd been ordered to stay away from.

"Fries, no salt." Sol looked from one to the other. He wiped his hands on his apron. "You decide yet what you're having, young lady?"

"Um...I..." She blinked.

"Grilled cheese," Max supplied.

Her cheeks turned pink. "You remember."

He shrugged, as if it wasn't any big deal, but a warm feeling spread through him. He reached over to finger the salt shaker.

Sol gave a good-natured snort. "One grilled cheese, comin' up."

Max watched as Tensley's gaze dropped to her hands, folded and resting on the table. "I never could figure out," he said, "why your mother would ban a whole sandwich."

"She said that much cheese would clog up a person's thought processes," Tensley said to her hands. She glanced up. "That could explain some things. Maybe I ate a grilled cheese before I slugged Rhonda."

"Your mother doesn't know shit. Never did." Max didn't try to keep the disgust from his voice. Esme Tanner-Starbrook had run Tensley's father out of the house and then tried to mold their toddler daughter into a mini version of herself, ruthless, rigid and as driven as they came. She hadn't counted, though, on her only child being born with a compassionate heart and a romantic soul. The mini-me process hadn't worked out so well and Tensley had been the one to suffer for it.

Tensley snorted, then covered her mouth, obviously embarrassed. "Sorry. I mean—try telling her that."

"I hear another cable company is making a serious run at this market. Wonder how your mother's handling that."

"By ignoring it." She tipped her head. "Just one annoying gnat flying around the giant picnic spread of Tanner Cable." Bitterness peppered her words.

Max left the salt shaker alone, turning his gaze back to the woman on the other side of the table. "I guess it's good to have that kind of optimism."

"Optimism isn't so much a part of the equation. It's more that this city wouldn't dare choose another cable provider when Tanner has been here for three generations." She opened and closed her mouth, finally settling for, "And that's all there is to it, according to my mother."

They were silent for a few minutes, cradling their coffee cups and listening to the muffled sounds of Sol banging pans in the kitchen. Oddly enough, it was a comfortable quiet, Max decided. As though they'd picked up where they once were, instead of having been apart for all these years.

He lifted the burger bun, inspecting the tomatoes. "So she figures if she doesn't acknowledge the competition, it isn't there."

"Pretty much. A shot of bug spray and any competition will give up and die or move on."

"Do you agree?"

"No. I don't think a business that keeps doing things the same way for three generations can survive. She's severely underestimating our customers and what they want and expect."

Our customers. Had he missed something?

"I've been trying to convince her to—" She broke off.

He waited. She didn't finish, so he prompted her. "To what?"

"Nothing. Not important."

He'd lay odds that wasn't the truth, but before he could respond, Tensley straightened, dropping her hands to her lap. "So tell me what's next. How soon do I meet your captain and get this whole informant thing going?"

He'd leave it. For the moment. "First thing in the morning."

"How about now."

His eyes met hers. God, she was beautiful. And he could not fathom how she'd managed this turn in her life without taking on that hard edge that kept people at a safe distance. Or kept them away, period. "Guess I might be able to make that happen."

Sol appeared again to slide a beautifully browned grilled cheese sandwich in front of Tensley. Her eyes lit up.

"But how about we finish eating first," Max said. He took a bite of his cheeseburger.

"I could do that," she agreed.

Max watched as Tensley took her first bite of Sol's gooey, crispy grilled cheese sandwich. Pure pleasure spread across her face as she closed her eyes, lifted her chin and chewed. "Mmmmm," she said.

He nearly choked on his burger. When he brought his hand up to cover the coughing, it ran straight into his water glass, spilling liquid over the table.

Her eyes flew open, startled.

"Damn." He grabbed a paper napkin to try and mop up the mess, but in the process, managed to knock over Tensley's water glass. More liquid on the table, now spilling over the side.

Tensley picked up her plate with both hands to protect it from the flood. She laughed, a small sound at first and then bigger. "Eat out much?"

"No." Water was dripping onto the floor. "I mean—yes." The napkin holder was empty. "Wait here."

"You think I'm leaving this grilled cheese?" She took another bite.

Max grabbed napkins from the neighboring booth and threw them onto the table, pressing hard, determined not to look at her.

Sol appeared with a large cloth. In less than a minute, he'd expertly wiped up the mess and restored order. "More water?" he asked Tensley. Before she could answer, he shot a warning finger at Max. "You, on the other hand, are cut off."

"Very funny," he grumbled.

Tensley looked at him, eyes dancing, after Sol left. She extended her glass. "You can have mine."

"No. Thanks." He waved her off, not even hungry anymore. Shit. He felt like a twelve-year-old.

Some cop he was. Despite awards, accolades and a reputation for being a coldhearted son-of-a-bitch when it came to nailing bad guys, he could still be rendered totally useless by one woman. When she did something as innocent as eat a damned grilled cheese sandwich.

This could not be good.

And the best part was—it was too fucking late to back out now.

CHAPTER TWELVE

Max's captain said less than three words to Tensley, but his glare pinned her to the wall for what felt like hours. When he finally glanced over at Max, she nearly choked on her relief. She'd bet the police captain had won every staring contest he'd ever been challenged to as a kid. She, on the other hand, had usually been the first to cave.

Max stared back at him.

Did these people ever actually talk?

The captain broke it off first, scrawling his name on the piece of paper and shoving it across the metal table.

She couldn't understand why she felt relieved. It wasn't as though she was interviewing for a job. She didn't even want to do this. Had to be other ways to "learn her lesson." Well, maybe.

Tensley focused on the paper, sorting through a blur of words until she found the place for her signature.

The police captain got up and left, closing the door hard behind him.

Max turned to her. "Don't worry about him."

Tensley folded her arms across her chest and sat back against the chair. Metal pushed against her shoulder blades. "Your captain doesn't talk much."

"He's had some bad experiences."

She narrowed her eyes. "Bad experiences. With talking."

Max choked back a laugh. "You might say that."

"Seriously. Why's he so angry? You would think he'd be happy to have someone agree to help."

"I'm sure he is." Max picked up the paper she'd signed. "Your signature's changed."

"Don't even try changing the subject." Tensley tipped her head. "You know better."

Max drummed his fingers on the table, the only sound in the room for a couple of minutes. Then his hand stilled. "I don't know everything about my captain, but if I had to guess, I'd say it's his bulletproof vest." He abruptly stood, shoving his chair back, her signed agreement in his hand. "Let's go."

He wasn't getting off that easy. "So get him a new one."

His dark-blue eyes met hers. "I meant the kind you can't see."

She didn't want him looking at her like that, with a heavy-lidded, intense gaze that saw right through every flippant remark she wanted to make right now, making her chest go tight and a party begin down below. As if things weren't already complicated enough. "The one that keeps him from having to feel much of anything." The sarcasm she'd intended disappeared in the breath she couldn't quite seem to catch.

"Pretty much. Job's a hell of a lot easier if you keep it on twenty-four seven."

"I'll just bet it is. If you don't get to know someone, if you barely even look at her, you don't have to care about what happens to her."

Instead of answering, he motioned toward the door. "Let's get out of here."

Ha. Cops weren't the only ones who could lay claim to wearing protection from emotional bullets. Not by a long shot. Pun...well, *intended*. Tensley went through the door, chin high. She may not be in her right life, but she was in her right mind and she knew what she had to do.

Since Max was behind her, she didn't think he could hear what she murmured, more to herself than anyone. "Should try taking yours off once in a while."

But his response was immediate and right in her ear. "Not on your life."

She flinched in surprise. *Fine, Detective Hunter,* she thought. You take care of your virtual vest and I'll take care of mine. Yours is probably made from some sort of camo fabric and riddled with holes, anyway.

While mine is pink. With Swarovski crystals. And an early warning system.

There's no way it's coming off for you.

Ever again.

***

Max climbed into the driver's seat and started the truck. It took everything Tensley had to keep her eyes and mind off his muscled legs and thighs. The teenager few adults had given a chance to succeed had become a strong, self-assured man others now looked up to. And his every movement radiated an effortless sexuality that quickened both her heartbeat and the fantasies that had begun to tumble through her imagination.

Help him. She would. So she could go back to her real life. "Give me my assignment."

"First, I want your word you'll be straight with me."

Tensley made a cross over her heart. "Whatever I know, you'll know." She didn't have to mention she knew hardly anything.

"Second, don't be stupid." He slid a glance across the seat to make sure she was listening.

That was going a little too far. "Are you calling me stupid?"

He exhaled. "I mean, don't try to do anything, like confront someone, on your own."

Had she called it, or what? This stuff was dangerous. Five quick I-told-you-sos ran through her head at once, each mentally pointed at Kate. At the very least, her best friend had better throw her one hell of a funeral. And cry. No, *sob* with guilt for trying to mess with Tensley's functionally dysfunctional love life in the first place. "Don't worry. I'm not big on confrontations."

It was only after Max shot her a skeptical glance that she remembered why she had ended up here in the first place. Rhonda. "Generally speaking, anyway," she clarified. She could have sworn she saw the corners of his mouth begin to turn up, but he was back to cop mode before she could be sure.

"Look, this isn't my first vice assignment," Max said. "Just about everybody's got a little something going on outside of the rules, but Gary's got more than a little something going." He eyed her.

"There are rules?"

Max's brows drew together.

"I mean, of course. The rules." Whatever those might be. She motioned for him to go ahead. "Sorry."

"Tell me I'm wrong."

Tensley sighed. "I don't know what to tell you. I believe it, because the guy makes my skin crawl, but I haven't seen anything."

Max looked at her long and hard. A horn honked and he had to brake fast.

Tensley clutched her armrest. "Maybe you should let me out here."

He ignored the suggestion and kept driving. This time he addressed his words to the windshield. "That's why I thought you could help. You haven't been there long enough to get drawn into much yet." He paused. "Right?"

Now she was the one to give the long, hard look. "Seriously. You need to ask me that?"

He shrugged, but the offhand gesture wasn't reflected in his tense expression.

"All I do is dance." She really, *really* hoped that was true. "So what is it you think Gary's doing?"

"For starters, I'm thinking there's a separate menu of services."

"Oh." She thought about that.

"It's that or drugs." He gave her a sidelong glance. "Or both."

"Wouldn't surprise me."

Silence for a few minutes. Tensley looked over at him, watched the hard set of his jaw. "There's something more. What is it?"

"I've seen a couple of people in the club who shouldn't be there."

In Tensley's opinion, no one should be there except maybe those with membership in the perv-of-the-month club, but she kept that thought to herself. "What kind of people?"

"Let's just say they're pretty highly placed."

"Even highly placed people could have a thing for watching naked women."

"They weren't there for long. And they didn't pay any attention to the dancing. They disappeared into the back with Gary."

"Drug buy?"

"Could be. But it isn't adding up. There's something I can't put my finger on."

"So they're silent partners in the club. Or running the drug operation. Or...?" She tapped a finger on her chin.

"Yeah. It's that last 'or' I'm working on figuring out."

"And you're thinking that's where I come in."

"My captain's not so sure. That's part of what you were picking up on from him."

She leaned closer, making sure he turned to look at her. "Thought it was his bulletproof vest."

"It is. He's been burned before." Max refocused on the windshield, his jaw muscles working. "Not so ready to take chances anymore."

Tensley settled back into her seat. "You must have convinced him it was worth looking into."

"For now." His chin lifted. "Let's start with you telling me anything you already know."

"I don't know anything." Truer words could not be spoken. "At least not yet."

"You and Razor. Tell me about that."

She'd like to know about that one herself. "Not much to tell," she said, staring straight ahead. "He thinks there's more to it than there is."

"Did he get you the job?"

How in the hell would she answer that one? "You don't think Gary took one look at me and hired me on the spot?" Her laugh stuck in her throat.

"Absolutely. Way back when, I took one look at you and—" He cleared his throat. "Never mind."

Tensley smiled, but felt it disappear slowly, bit by bit. "I don't know anything," she repeated.

He looked at her again and then back at the street. After a moment that seemed to stretch into an hour, he said, "I believe you."

Warmth rushed through her. For a second, she wondered if he would believe her about other things, like the fact that she was not, nor had she ever been, a stripper. She came within a breath of spilling the whole story, stopped only by the memory of Madame Claire's words. *Events would unravel most unpredictably.*

Which meant there was a possibility things could get even worse than they already were. Hard to believe, but she couldn't afford not to.

She shot up straight, the shoulder strap of the seatbelt tightening across her chest. Telling Max was *not* an option. "How can I help?"

"Get into Gary's office if you can. Look for files, paperwork, receipts. Don't take anything. Just let me know what's there. If he's stupid enough to have left his computer on, see what he's been looking at. Also, listen to what the other women are talking about. Some of them have to know what's going on."

"Okay." Sounded easy enough. She'd watched a ton of cop shows; she knew what to do. A mental picture flashed before her eyes—Tensley flattening herself against a wall, then making stealthy moves toward Gary's office, where she would slip the lock with her American Express card and be inside in one fluid motion. She'd never actually slipped a lock, but it couldn't be that hard.

As if he had read her mind, Max said, "This isn't TV, Ten. Make sure no one has a clue what you're doing."

That fast, she saw herself stumbling over a chair and hitting the floor with a crash, lights flooding the room as a furious Gary, brandishing a gun, threw open the door to see what was going on. She ducked her chin. "I know that."

"You can't trust anyone."

"What do you think I am, an idiot?"

He didn't answer for a minute, which irritated her enough that she began jerking on her seatbelt and opening her mouth to demand she be let out of the truck.

Before she could, he pulled to a stop and she realized they were in front of her apartment building. She unsnapped the belt and reached for the handle.

"Wait."

She turned to him.

"Look. What I'm trying to say is..." Max hesitated, looking down at his jeans to wrap his finger around a stray thread. "Be careful. These people aren't like you."

"You don't know that." The bitter words slipped out before she could stop them.

"I know you."

Her bottom lip trembled, making it hard to answer. She could not let this go further. There were only two things she needed to do. Learn her lesson. And then get the hell out of here and back to her life. He had no right to interfere.

"You only think you know me." She kept her eyes focused on her hand, which was gripping the door handle so hard, her knuckles had turned white.

"How did you end up in that place?"

Oh, let's see. Mix one well-intentioned best friend with one under-trained psychic. Fold in one massive regret...

And you have one Lila Delightful, baking under the spotlight at Gary's Gorgeous Grecians. Served up to a dozen drooling patrons.

She turned to look at the man who was the heart and soul of her massive regret, and said, "It doesn't really matter." Then she pulled on the handle and pushed the truck door open.

"Hold on," he said, leaning across the passenger seat to catch the door before it closed. With his other hand, he pulled a card out of his pocket. "Take this."

When she did, their fingers touched, sending a ripple of excited awareness through every part of her body.

"That's how we'll keep in touch."

Tensley focused on the card, which had a phone number written on it in black ink. She nodded. Then she turned and walked away as fast as she could without breaking into a full-fledged run.

If she'd stayed in close proximity to him one second longer, the only lesson she would have learned would have been how to rip the clothes off a cop in broad daylight without getting dragged off to jail.

Somehow, she suspected that particular lesson wouldn't meet the Madame Claire criteria.

***

It turned out Gary wasn't any more pleasant on the phone than he was in person. If she'd translated his obscenities accurately, he'd said he didn't have time for Gorgeous Grecians with attitude. All because she'd said she still wanted a job, but didn't want it to be on stage.

Jerk. She pulled the cell away from her ear. A few seconds later, she heard a knock at the door, accompanied by a rough-edged voice. "Hey, babe. Open up."

Her gaze traveled from the cell phone to the door.

Razor. Razor Burns.

Another knock. This time it sounded as though he used both hands. "C'mon. Why you gotta lock the door?"

Tensley stood up so fast, she knocked over the chair. It fell with a crash against the wooden floor. "You okay?" Razor asked, rattling the handle.

"Just a—a minute," Tensley called. She wondered if she could crawl out a window. Lock herself in the bathroom. Claim head trauma and total amnesia. Within the next sixty seconds.

From across the floor, Gemini watched her, his tail swishing, judgment in his eyes. No matter the situation, you could count on a cat to think he had a better idea. "Fine," she shot in his direction. "*You* answer the door then."

The cat looked down and raised a paw to lick it, as though Tensley's problems were too trivial to bother with.

"Babe!"

Tensley shot Gemini a "thanks-a-lot" look as she veered around him on her way to the door, without so much as a garlic clove or an onion for protection against a hello kiss. When she opened the door,

Razor, who was leaning against it with both hands, nearly toppled over.

He recovered his balance. "Whoa. That was close." He flashed a grin and then planted a wet kiss on her lips.

It took everything she had not to blurt "Eww!" and swipe her arm across her mouth.

He moved around her as she stood with her hand on the handle of the open door. She popped her head into the hall. It looked like a nice enough escape route, long and narrow, with stairs at the end. No neighbors in the vicinity to act as witnesses. She'd have a head start since Razor seemed to have disappeared into the kitchen.

A muffled "Yougomintowerktanight?" came from behind her. Tensley blinked and turned to see Razor, clutching a piece of bread folded over some kind of meat, his mouth stuffed with food.

"Um...what?" She blinked.

Razor made a show of swallowing, his Adam's apple bobbing. "You going to work tonight?" He took another bite of his sandwich.

"I was, but—" Hold on a minute. Razor might turn out to be useful. "I asked your father if I could do something different than be on stage and he hung up on me."

Razor looked genuinely puzzled. "Why don't you want to dance?"

He made it sound like it wasn't any big deal, which left her struggling for words. "I...you know..."

He shook his head. "Nope. You're the best one."

Oh. In spite of herself, she brightened. She was the best at something? Huh. Who would have thought—now she was the one to shake her head. This was insane, having to explain to her...boyfriend...why she didn't want to take her clothes off for strangers.

Think fast. "I hurt myself." She dropped a hand to her thigh. "That's it. I pulled a muscle or something." She grimaced. "It really—ouch."

Concern crossed Razor's face. "Oh man, that's tough. Did you tell Pop?"

Tensley shrugged. "I tried, but, well…" She let her voice trail off, hoping for the sympathy vote. "Maybe you could talk to him for me."

The stocky man looked doubtful. "I could try, but it didn't go so well last time."

Last time? She took some comfort in knowing this wasn't the first time she'd tried to get out of dancing onstage. "I can still work. He probably doesn't know it, but I'm a hell of a bartender." Not exactly true, but she had learned how to make two drinks from a cute bartender she'd flirted with at a friend's wedding reception last year. She unfortunately hadn't been paying that much attention to the instructions because she'd been caught up with how great the guy looked in his tux, but she could probably fake it. How hard could it be to tend bar?

Razor's features mushed together with the effort of deep thought, but then his expression suddenly cleared. "Becca," he said, snapping his fingers.

"Becca?"

"I just remembered. Her grandma's sick. She's leavin' today to go home and see her. I could ask Pop about letting you be the one to cover for her."

"Yes. You could." Tensley grabbed his arm. "Where's your phone? You could do that right now."

"You sure about this? You always said—"

"Whatever it was, I didn't mean it."

"So the thing about not wanting to have to look people in the eye—?"

Tensley shuddered. God, no, she didn't want to have to look them in the eye. Not the people who went to Gary's. But if she had to do it to get off the stage, she would. "Don't know what I was thinking," she assured Razor. "Will you call him?"

He pinched the skin between his brows. "But you said—"

"Please?"

Razor hesitated, then shook his head. "Women," he said, pulling his cell from his pocket. He took another large bite of his sandwich and wandered back toward the kitchen. Seconds later, she heard him mumble something into the phone.

She sank into a chair, closed her eyes, and waited.

Razor's voice rose, fell, and then went silent. He appeared in the doorway, sandwich-less. "Okay," he said. "You're in."

"I'm in?"

"You're fillin' in for Becca at the bar. Pop wasn't happy, but he finally said okay."

"He said okay."

Razor looked confused. "That's what I said."

She could help Max while keeping her clothes on. Tensley shot out of her chair toward Razor and threw her arms around him. "Thank you." He was round and solid, like a teddy bear with muscles, and smelled of soap.

"Sure, babe." His big arms swallowed her. "You know I'd do anything for you."

He was sort of sweet in a lumbering kind of way. Must be why she was with him.

"Wouldn't want you to be hurtin' yourself." Razor released her and took a step back, looking down. "Hold on. Did your leg get better?"

Uh-oh. Tensley bit down on her lip, staring at him. "No. I just— wanted to hug you, so I, you know, pushed through the pain." She put a hand to her leg. "Big mistake, though. It hurts even worse now." She was such a bad liar.

Razor apparently couldn't tell. His face relaxed. "Aw, you can't be doing that to yourself, just so you can hug your Razorman."

"I…uh…" Tensley could think of no response to that.

"Come on now. You can have a hug any time you want." The big man smiled, pulling her back to him. "Wanna show your Razor some lovin' before you go?"

Oh God. No. She did not. "I can't be late!" She pushed away and began speed-limping in the direction of her bedroom before realizing she was favoring the wrong leg. She came to an abrupt stop and turned to blow him a kiss. "I'm out of here in a few minutes, so see you later. You'll let yourself out?"

Without waiting for an answer, she took off toward her bedroom again, this time remembering to limp with the correct leg.

"Oh-kay," she heard him say, his voice uncertain, before she shut the bedroom door behind her. And locked it, for good measure. Then she pressed her back up against it, eyes locking on the annoyed cat sprawled across her bed.

Her apartment door opened and closed. Razor probably wasn't sure what had just happened. Thankfully, he didn't seem like the type to pursue finding out.

Gemini voiced his displeasure at the interruption.

"Really?" Tensley asked. "What else was I going to do?"

The cat blinked.

"That's what I thought." She left the door and went to her closet to push through hangers of clothing in search of something to wear. Didn't take her long to settle on dark skinny jeans, super-cute stilettos and a black tank top. She needed to blend in, especially if she was hanging out anywhere near Gary's office.

Speaking of blending…

"It can't be that hard to make drinks, right?" she asked Gemini, who turned away to lick a paw, apparently hoping she'd take her questions elsewhere.

A lot of help he was.

"People don't go to strip clubs for the drinks," she announced as she began changing clothes. "So no one's even going to notice what I give them. They'll probably all want beer, anyway."

Once ready, she ran a brush through her hair and stopped for a quick look in the mirror. She'd never looked so good in a pair of jeans. It was maybe the one perk of her new life.

She grabbed her purse and keys. "Wish me luck," she said to Gemini. "Drinks to pour; bad guys to catch; lessons to learn." A premise for a TV show, if she'd ever heard one.

Gemini responded by burying his face in the covers.

Damn cat.

He was right.

CHAPTER THIRTEEN

Twenty minutes into her shift, Tensley realized how wrong she'd been about bartending being an easy job. At first, she'd thought a smile and a clean counter could carry her through anything. Then a topless woman walked up and fired off drink orders so fast, all Tensley could do was look at her open-mouthed. "I, uh, what was that again?"

The woman focused in on her for the first time and the exasperated sound she made was loud enough to be heard over the pounding music. "Why are you here? Where's Becca?"

"Family emergency." Tensley tried out her bartender smile, which she'd decided should be a mix of hell-yes confidence and don't-come-near-me cheerfulness.

The woman's layers of dark eye makeup made it hard to tell for sure, but it looked as though her eyes narrowed. "Maybe you could think about writing this down."

The hell-yes confidence part of Tensley's smile froze as she scrambled to find a piece of paper and something to write with.

"Something wrong, Pepper?"

Tensley glanced up. It was Milo, the bouncer. The guy who had covered for her the other night.

"Got a dancer behind the bar and she doesn't know what the hell she's doing," Pepper responded. "That's what's wrong."

Tensley's fingers closed on a pad of paper and pen. She gave Milo a nod of recognition, trying her best not to look like a dancer-slash-bartender who didn't know what the hell she was doing.

Milo pointed at her. "Her leg's messed up so she can't dance. And Becca's gone."

"So what's the big deal? I danced with a broken ankle."

"Really?" Tensley asked, genuinely curious. "Didn't anyone notice?"

Pepper looked at her as though she'd asked if two plus two equaled four. "They weren't looking at my ankle."

"Oh. Right." Tensley wrapped her fingers around the pen as though her life depended on it. "What were those drinks again?" She could do this. She really could.

Milo left and Pepper propped an elbow on the counter and repeated each one, slowly and deliberately. A screwdriver, a vodka and tonic, whisky with a water back, a salty dog, three beers. When she'd finished, she asked, "You got that now? 'Cause you're costing me money."

"Got it." At Tensley's nod, the other woman walked away.

The music pounded and a male voice announced Terrible Tawny, the dancer from Tensley's first night at the club. Tawny took the stage to enthusiastic applause and cat calls, while Tensley, clutching the piece of paper with drink orders, paused to watch.

Razor had told her *she* was the best. Was that even possible or was he just speaking boyfriend-ese?

Tensley had never been the best at anything.

Tawny was pretty good, but those legs didn't look like they were straddling the pole at a perfect parallel to the floor, as Lila Delightful's had. Still, *that* was an interesting move; how had Tawny been able to transition so smoothly to a handstand with one foot wrapped around the pole, especially when that foot was tied up in a shoe that didn't bend—

"You doing okay?"

Milo.

"Yes! Perfect!" Tensley put the list on the counter in front of her and grabbed the two closest glasses she could find, doing her best to look busy.

It must have worked because he moved on.

Tensley stared at the drink orders. She herself preferred cosmos, martinis and chocolate cake shots. Vodka and tonic was easy enough, but what the hell was a salty dog?

She squared her shoulders. Easy stuff first.

Thanks to college parties, she could pour a beer with a beautiful head on it. As more than one gentleman of Delta Tau Delta had hopefully observed, though it hadn't gotten them anywhere, she gave good head.

Tensley poured three beers and set them carefully on a round tray, murmuring a silent thank you to the Delts who had taught her well.

Next, she moved on to the vodka and tonic, but turned up her nose at the bottle of no-name vodka she spotted on a shelf close by. She ran her eyes up and down the bottles until she found one of Absolut tucked in the back. Much better.

She grabbed it, threw a few ice cubes into a glass and then poured out a generous portion of vodka. Nearly too late, she remembered the tonic part. She found that bottle, added a thin layer of tonic water and then stood back to appraise her work. Something was missing. Color. She sliced a lime and threw it on top. Vodka and tonic. Done.

Next, a screwdriver. She'd heard of it, but had no idea what was in it. She made a stealthy grab for the purse she'd placed on one of the lower shelves, rummaging through it until she found her cell phone. It only took a minute to pull it out, open the Web and type "screwdriver" into search.

A photo of a drink had just come up, listing the ingredients as vodka and orange juice, when she heard a familiar growl at the other end of the bar. "Tell me you're not on the phone when you're supposed to be working."

Tensley jumped, the cell clattering to the floor. She reached down to pick it up as Gary's gaze burned through her. She threw the phone back into her purse and straightened. "Of course not," she said, despite all evidence to the contrary.

"Don't be thinking you're going to get any special treatment from me," he warned. "This is a one-time deal, only while Becca's gone."

"Yes, sir." The sarcasm in her voice fell into the swirl of applause for Terrible Tawny.

"And that's only because I was feeling like being a nice guy to my son. That doesn't happen much." He leaned forward. "I ain't a nice guy."

"Can't think why anyone would ever say that about you."

Gary grunted and then slapped the counter. "So get to work. I'm not telling you again."

She resisted the urge to slap him, focusing instead on the fact that her helping Max should put Gary out of business. That thought made her smile, a real one this time. Gary looked suspicious, but left.

Vodka and orange juice. Okay, then. She grabbed the bottle of Absolut, again pouring an ample amount into the glass, but this time remembering to leave enough room for the orange juice she'd found in an under-the-counter refrigerator behind her.

A few ice cubes tossed in for good measure. And another drink down.

Whisky with a water back. Whatever that meant. She searched for and found a bottle of Maker's Mark, hidden even better than the Absolut. Her absent father had imparted few words of wisdom, but one thing he had said was that there wasn't whisky, there was only Maker's Mark. She'd been ten years old when she'd overheard him saying it to some other man. It had sounded grave. And wise.

"Here's to you, Dad," she murmured, pulling the bottle out.

But the water back part... She glanced up to see Pepper making her way over to the bar, followed by another topless woman. Time was nearly up.

Tensley plopped ice cubes into a glass and filled it with Maker's Mark. The water part could happen when the ice melted.

A customer flagged down Pepper. She stopped to talk to him, giving Tensley another minute or so.

Next, a salty dog. Short of coaxing a canine into standing under a shaker and then on top of a tray... She smiled, picturing it, and then ducked her head so no one would see.

There was always the margarita approach. Tensley ground the top of a glass in salt and debated what alcohol to put in. Pepper was on the move again. Tensley grabbed the bottle of Absolut and poured it in the salted glass and then shot in something clear and fizzy from the flexible hose. Looked like soda.

There. About as dog-ish as things were going to get. "Your order," she said to Pepper, who had just reached the bar. Tensley pushed the tray toward her and turned to the next woman, who thankfully only wanted one whisky and soda and five beers. That she could do.

"Where's the water?" Pepper asked.

Oh. Who knew it was that simple? "Sorry." Tensley filled a glass and put it on Pepper's tray before turning to the next woman's order.

Pepper returned a few minutes later. Tensley's stomach turned over, fearing the short turnaround might be because of angry customers, but then she noticed the glasses on the woman's tray were empty.

"The guy said that wasn't exactly a Salty Dog, but whatever it was, he wants another one." She made it sound like a question.

"Great." She did her best to sound like it was no big deal, but she knew she'd packed a fifth of relief into the one word.

For the first time, Pepper looked as though she might smile, but she managed not to. "They all want another round, even the screwdriver guy."

"On it." What did Gemini the cat know? She wasn't doing so badly.

Pepper sauntered over to another table, boobs bobbing, while Tensley got busy making the drinks. Terrible Tawny left the stage and two other women took her place, each grabbing a pole to call her own.

A few hours later, Tensley had faked her way through most of the requested drinks, covering her lack of knowledge with generous amounts of alcohol. One customer ordered several rounds of rum and coke. Probably because she made it with two-thirds rum and one-third coke.

The only thing that mattered, though, was getting information for Max—wherever or however she had to do it. As busy as she was, she continued to look around the club, watching for anything that seemed unusual. One problem. She didn't know what *usual* was here.

"Hey." Tensley flagged Milo down. "I need a break."

He hesitated, casting his gaze around the darkness.

"Seriously. I do. Or it's not going to be pretty." She raised an eyebrow.

Milo jerked his head. "Go on. I'll watch the bar."

"Thanks." She grabbed her purse before he could change his mind and began weaving her way toward the back of the club, staying close to the walls to be as inconspicuous as possible. Probably didn't matter, she realized. Who would be looking at her when there were nude and semi-nude women all over the place?

About halfway across the club, she came to a private area lit in blue, with a sultry, slow-moving dancer and a man sitting in the shadows, watching. *Oh hell.* Her stomach knotted at the memory of her and Max, locked into that same horrible, thrilling dance.

She touched her fingers to the wall to steady herself, breathing in the potent scent of lust and sweat mingled with perfume, hating herself for almost, *almost* wishing she was back inside there with Max.

There was so much about this new life she was going to have to forget.

Keep moving, she told herself. Eyes straight ahead. At least she wasn't attracting attention. All eyes that weren't riveted on Pepper's bouncing boobs were focused on the dueling dancers on stage.

No one was guarding the black curtain that shielded the dancers' dressing room. Tensley reached up to pull it back and slip inside.

She saw that same long, green hallway, nicked and bruised by passing cigarettes and careless people. Not far down, the door with the paper gold star. As softly as she could in four-inch stilettos, she crept past the door, glancing behind her every few steps to make sure no one saw or followed her.

On the right, a women's restroom, where someone had endowed the stick figure on the sign with generous breasts. Next to it, a men's bathroom with a similar drawn-in enhancement, this time of a penis long enough to do serious damage.

Even the restroom signs in this place were X-rated.

Further down was the exit door she'd opened onto the street after that disastrous time on stage. She took a deep breath, fighting the temptation to slam through it a second time. If she was fast enough, she might be able to outrun this outrageous life and leap back into her new one.

Her brain was a millisecond away from giving the order to hit the door and run when she spotted something she hadn't seen that night. Another hallway, more dimly lit. She did a Scooby-Doo double-take. This could be important. This could lead to Gary's office.

Another glance over her shoulder told her no one else was around. Yet.

Tensley crossed quickly into the second hallway, where she spotted two closed doors. Pulse throbbing in her ears, she laid her fingers on the first door, pressing her ear against the wood. Nothing. She tried the knob, but it didn't turn. Locked.

Then she heard the sound of a male voice, echoing off the walls in the first hallway. With a shudder, she registered who belonged to that half-snarl, half-grunt. Gary. He'd probably been the one who'd drawn the penis on the restroom sign, as some sort of delusional personal marketing campaign.

The voice was coming closer. "I am not gonna tell you again," Gary said. "Don't fuck with the business."

Tensley squinted in the half-light. It was so dark, she couldn't see if the hallway was a dead end or led somewhere else. She darted away from the first door and on to the second.

She heard another familiar voice. "But Pop," Razor pleaded. "It was a good idea."

Relief washed through her when the knob turned in her hand. She opened the door and ducked inside a pitch-black room. Then she closed the door without a sound and leaned her back against it, hands splayed.

Seconds later, she heard the rattle of keys and the sound of someone entering the room next to her. Gary was talking again, but she couldn't quite make out what he was saying. Inch by inch, she scooted her back along the door, feeling with her right hand for the wall. If she could get closer, she should be able to hear.

No wall, yet. She sidled her body closer, leaving the relative safety of the door frame, and stretched her arm full length. Air...air...*there*. A solid surface. She scooted over and put her ear to it.

Gary spoke again, his voice higher, angrier. "That's what you call a good idea. Putting girls in bikinis in a fucking hardware store?"

Tensley drew her brows together. A guy who ran a strip club had a problem with girls in bikinis?

Razor's voice also rose. "Brought in more customers in one day than we had all last month."

"Let me take a guess here, Einstein. You're thinkin' those guys are actually coming back once their wives find out what they've been lookin' at in the hardware store."

That must have stopped Razor, because all she heard was something that sounded like Gary dropping hard into a chair.

It took a minute, but Razor rebounded. "Hell, yes, they'll be back. Not every guy has a wife and if they do, they're not gonna tell her. I'm only doin' this one day a week. Callin' it Wiggle Wednesdays."

Even through the wall, Tensley could hear the note of pride in Razor's voice.

Something slammed together hard. Gary's fist on the desk? Razor's head—she hoped not—against the door?

Then she heard Gary's voice again, lower, more menacing this time. "Listen to me. And listen good. I do not pay you to think of ideas. I do not pay you to put girls in bikinis in my hardware store. Hell, if you weren't my son, you wouldn't be there in the first place."

Sympathy rippled through Tensley. No one deserved to be talked to like that.

Gary went on. "I pay you to show up and make sure the place sells its fucking screws, hammers and nails."

She heard what sounded like a nervous laugh from Razor. "Speaking of screws, one of the girls had this funny idea for a sign—"

"What the hell is wrong with you?" Gary thundered, hurting even Tensley's ear. She backed away from the wall.

Razor mumbled something she couldn't make out, but it sounded apologetic. Tensley leaned in again.

"You want the cops sniffing around the place? Because I sure as hell don't."

"I made sure it was legal," Razor offered, but Tensley could practically see him cringing. "And I stopped the guy who was tryin' to put a tip in Tiffany's—"

"Oh, that's just perfect. You asked somebody if it was legal? Somebody else. But not me. The damn owner of the place."

Interesting. Gary owned a hardware store.

Razor mumbled something Tensley couldn't hear. She turned her whole body to the wall where her elbow knocked into something metal and sharp. She stifled a yelp of pain. As she reached out her other hand, to cup her injured elbow, it, too, hit the metal object, knocking something off what had to be a shelf. It fell to the floor with a soft thud.

Silence on the other side of the wall. *Ouch.* She could feel wetness on her skin. Great. Her elbow must be bleeding.

And she smelled soap.

She took a step back in the darkness and slipped on liquid, her feet going out from under her to crash into the metal shelf. Unable to suppress a cry this time, she landed hard on her backside, legs flailing. The shelf hit the floor next, with a screech of rickety metal and thuds of whatever objects it had held.

The soap smell was so strong now, it stung her nostrils.

She coughed and then held her breath, hoping with every part of her being that Gary hadn't heard the commotion in the room next to him.

The door flung open and an overhead light flipped on, nearly blinding her.

"What the fuck is going on?" Gary roared.

Tensley looked down to see the floor covered with liquid soap, her legs at awkward angles against the wall, her elbow bleeding, and a now-empty metal shelf on the floor beside her.

Razor's head appeared behind Gary's, his eyes widening.

Tensley gave him a weak smile and lifted her hand. A blob of soap dripped off her palm and onto the floor.

This was so not how things went on *Law and Order*.

CHAPTER FOURTEEN

Since no one was talking, Tensley thought she'd better. Gary's face was growing redder by the minute and he had his jaw clenched so hard, she expected his teeth to begin popping out of his mouth, one by one, like Chiclets gum.

Razor tipped his head, looking perplexed.

"I needed soap," Tensley said.

It took several seconds for Gary to loosen his jaw enough to answer. "And you didn't turn on the light because, what? Soap glows in the dark?"

"Good one, Pop," Razor chortled. Then he stopped, apparently realizing he might be lining up with the wrong team. "I mean, yeah, if you need soap, you're just gonna go where the soap is and get—"

Gary reached back to whack him. "Stop talking."

"Ow." Razor rubbed the spot on his arm.

Tensley lifted her chin, determined not to let Gary see the beads of sweat forming on her forehead. "I couldn't find the light switch."

"I hid it. Because you're not supposed to be back here." Gary's singsong tone of exaggerated patience crawled up Tensley's spine. "You need something, Milo gets it." His eyes narrowed. "You know the rules."

So no one but the bouncer was allowed back here. Why? She held his gaze. "Milo was busy. And I don't leave a restroom without washing my hands."

A little tough to pull off righteous indignation when she was sprawled on the floor, covered in liquid soap that wasn't even the kind that smelled of pomegranates or lemons. Where did Gary buy his soap, Cheap Goo, Inc.?

Gary looked her up and down. Slowly, and with malice laced with lust. "Ri-ii-ght. You wash your hands, your ass, your—"

"Pop!" Razor interrupted. "That's my girl." To his credit, he didn't shrink away when his father shot him a venomous look.

Tensley's fear turned to a pulsing anger. That slimeball Gary had no right to look at her like that, as if he—*owned* her. She clenched her slippery fists and forced her voice to remain even. "Speaking of rules, Gary, I saw one of the new dancers out there breaking at least three. You might want to pay some attention to that since you're not going to need any soap if the cops shut this place down."

She had no idea what the rules were, but there had to be at least three, just as there had to be at least one new dancer. She crossed her legs as if she had all the time and reason in the world to sit in liquid soap, breathing through her nose in short, sharp bursts.

Gary's color turned from red to nearly purple. "Which one?"

Oops. "You know damn well which one," she snapped.

She took satisfaction in the fact that he could barely choke out his next unintelligible words.

He jabbed a finger at her. "You're paying for this mess."

She opened her mouth to protest, but thought better of it. Things could have gone so much worse for her.

"Get it cleaned up and get outta here," Gary snarled, turning to leave. "Now." Next, he jabbed his finger at Razor. "How about you get in there and help her, since she's your girl."

Razor lifted his hands in the air. "No problem."

After his furious father had left the room, Razor closed the door. Then he turned toward her, running a hand through his hair. "What a..."

"Mess. I know." Tensley did her best to stand up, but lost the battle, her stilettos slipping and sliding across the floor. After landing hard on her butt again, she wrenched the shoes off one at a time and tossed them across the room to an area where the soap hadn't traveled yet. "I'm not even sure how to clean it up."

Razor walked to the edge of the soap lake and reached down with a beefy hand to help her up. He surveyed the situation. "Shelf first."

He took off his shoes and socks, set them by the door, and waded gingerly into the whitish liquid. "Damn. Who would have thought all of these bottles would bust at once?"

"Not me," Tensley said with a sigh.

Razor picked up the metal top of the shelf and walked it back upright. The soap began dripping down to each level in trails of cheap cleanliness.

Ever since Tensley could remember, housekeepers had taken care of anything having to do with household order. That included cleaning up messes. She ran a toe through the liquid, watching as it filled right back in again. "What do we use? A broom?"

Razor gave her a doubtful look. "Nah. That'll make it worse." He brightened. "Hey, I got an idea. Stay here."

"Sure thing." As if she could go anywhere. The stuff was already beginning to harden into a layer of film on her once super-cute jeans. She had a feeling it had gotten into her hair, though she didn't want to check, and she was pretty sure that, should she try to move, she'd only hammer her bruised backside yet again.

At least she didn't have to worry about her pride. It was long gone.

Razor returned in a flash, a grin on his face and a bag of kitty litter in his hands. "Your Razorman saves the day," he announced, dumping the contents of the bag onto the soap. "Tawny thinks nobody knows about that stray cat she takes care of."

"Tawny takes care of a stray cat. Seriously?" The woman looked like she ate nails for breakfast.

"Don't tell nobody. She keeps it behind the stage."

Tensley crossed her fingers over her heart. "I won't say anything." About the cat, anyway.

"So in a minute, we get the broom. And then, yeah, we have to mop it or something."

The kitty litter already appeared to be working, turning the liquid gunk into solid gunk. "How did you know to do that?"

"One of my guys did this when some stuff spilled at the store. It worked pretty good."

"I'm impressed."

"It's nothin'." Despite brushing off the compliment, his cheeks tinged pink.

Once again, Tensley felt a stab of sympathy for him. The guy must not receive many compliments.

She cleared her throat. "So, the store." She kept her tone casual, nudging the blobs of congealed soap with her toe while pulling out her virtual pencil and notepad. She had to remember anything and everything about Gary that might somehow be helpful to Max. "How's everything going there?"

Razor went to the corner to retrieve a broom and dustpan. "Same as always."

That would be helpful if she had any idea what the "same" was. "How did Wiggle Wednesday go?"

He turned and stopped, broom in one hand, dustpan in the other. He frowned, bringing his brows together in a deep V. "I told you 'bout that?"

She sure hoped so. Tensley held her breath.

Razor thought. "Guess I must have."

She exhaled slowly, quietly. "And I said I thought it was a great idea." The fibs were rolling off her tongue now. Then again, maybe she *had* said that.

"Yeah, well. Pop doesn't think so."

She took the dustpan from him and bent down to position it. "I would think he'd be fine with anything that brings in customers."

Instead of answering, he concentrated on sweeping.

The globs clunked their way into the metal pan. Tensley tried again. "Hardware's a tough business to be in right now." As if she knew anything about it. At all. She glanced up at him.

"No shit. Sometimes there's only one or two customers all day." He flashed a toothy grin. "But it's still the only place you can get a screw for under a buck." He chortled at his joke.

Her sympathy for him ran screaming from the building. Tensley rose and emptied the dustpan into a bin. She reached for the broom. "Give that to me. You go. I'll finish this."

Razor shook his head. "Can't. Pop said—"

"He says a lot of things," she interrupted. "Most of them bullshit."

There went that V in his forehead again. She'd never seen anyone who could make thinking look so painful.

"Go," she repeated, pushing him toward the door. Or trying to, anyway. The man was as solid as a brick wall. "Buy another bag of kitty litter before Tawny finds out hers is gone and dumps the used stuff over your head."

His eyes widened. "Oh, man. She would, too." This time, he let himself be pushed. "But what about your bum leg?"

Oh. Her leg. She couldn't even remember which one she was supposed to have hurt. She settled for an overall grimace. "Falling like that didn't help, but I can take care of this."

He hesitated. "I should help."

"No. You shouldn't. Because then both of us will be limping. Tawny will hurt you."

"She might not... Yeah, she will." His expression turned bleak. "You're gonna clean up fast and get out of here, though, right?"

"Right."

She opened the door and he lumbered through it. She had just shut it behind him and turned to debating her next move—because this confidential informant stuff was a lot harder than she'd thought—when it opened again and Razor stuck his head inside.

"I'm not kiddin'," he said. "If Pop finds you still here—"

She didn't have time for this. Before he could finish the sentence, Tensley had reached down and thrown a blob of litter at his head. He ducked and closed the door fast enough that it only hit the wood, spattering harmlessly to the floor. "Ma-a-n, babe," she heard him say from the other side.

Tensley's fingers ached for a piece of paper and a pen. At the very least, the police department should give every confidential informant a checklist to follow, so she didn't have to make her own.

Eavesdrop. *Check.*

Ask questions of unsuspecting party. *Check.*

Get damning documentation. *Um...not yet.*

Keep from getting killed. *Ch-e-ck.* So far, anyway.

Then again, maybe three out of four wasn't bad. She'd only been on the job for a day.

***

Once she'd cleaned the supply room, minus the shine she figured had to be lurking somewhere beneath the soap film, Tensley slipped back through the door, closing it behind her without a sound. Several minutes with her ear to the wall had convinced her Gary was not in his office, which meant she might have an opportunity to try and get into it.

She took one step toward the office and then another, the back of her jeans crackling with caked-on soap.

How hard could it be to break in? What were the odds she'd get caught? She'd been caught once today, so she might have used up her share of bad luck. On the other hand, she'd been caught once today. One more time and Gary would forget she was his son's girlfriend and make sure she never tried again.

Tensley pressed her lips together, narrowing her eyes at the closed door. She was on a mission.

She pictured Max's face, his voice, when she was able to find and give him what he'd asked for. He'd lift and twirl her, round and round, like the prince in a Disney movie, as her hair streamed behind her. They would laugh. The birds would sing. Small forest animals would peek out from behind the trees. Music would appear from out of nowhere, strings soaring, as Max pressed against her, his heart pounding, his skin warm beneath his princely clothing, his über-hard cock growing by the second, promising everything it had delivered in high school. And then some.

Eyes closing, she swayed on her feet and had to reach for the wall as the movie in her head continued to play. There went her clothes, sheer, floating...and carried off by happy little bluebirds. She was naked in Max's arms now, wrapping her legs around his waist and ripping the buttons from his shirt even as she moved against that bulging, hot, huge—

"Lila!"

Sucking in a breath, she opened her eyes, the instruments in her mind's orchestra all ending on a different sour note at once, cymbals crashing to the floor.

Milo stood at the end of the hall. He extended both hands in a plea. "What the fuck are you doing?"

"I...uh..." What was she doing, besides fantasizing about a man she had no business fantasizing about because not only did she not belong in his life, she didn't even belong in *her* life? She blinked. "There, uh, wasn't any soap in the bathroom...and I came to get some...and there was an accident...and I cleaned it up."

He clasped his hands together, shaking them at the ceiling as if to ask, *Why me?* "Gary went behind the bar, looking for his Maker's Mark."

She shook her head. "So? It's his place. If he wants his—" Midway into a shrug, she stopped. "Oh."

"Yeah," Milo said. "Oh. There isn't any."

Because she'd emptied out the bottles, making drinks.

"Pepper told me nobody's ordered or paid for the good stuff," he continued.

"Oh," she said again.

"Tell me you stashed it somewhere. Maybe so it wouldn't get mixed up with the cheap stuff."

He sounded as though he really did want her to say that.

"No," she said, crossing her arms and then uncrossing them. She couldn't meet his eyes. "I'm pretty sure I used it."

"Damn, Lila." Milo rubbed his face. "Gary's gonna kill you."

So much for checking "keep from getting killed" off the list. "The customers seemed to like it."

"I'll bet they did." He heaved a sigh and jabbed his finger in the air, pointing down the hallway toward the curtained entrance. "Get back out there. I'll call my buddy and get more here pronto. Gary asks anything, you tell him you put it away to keep it safe. Soon as I get it, I'll slip it to you without him seein'."

"I...um...thank you."

"Yeah, yeah. You're gonna pay me back."

"I will," she promised.

He pulled out his cell phone. "Get your butt back out there."

So she did, crackling denim and all. She would have to stay clear of those mixer hoses or there could be an unexpected bubble show behind the bar.

Come to think of it, though, it might distract Gary from killing her over a bottle of Maker's Mark.

Or, well, four bottles. No wonder the tips had been so good.

***

By the end of her shift, Tensley's feet were killing her and she never wanted to see, smell or use liquid soap again. Her jeans were in a not-wet, not-dry, not-gonna-bend state sure to draw puzzled looks if anyone could actually see her in this darkness.

Milo's buddy had delivered on the Maker's Mark, thank God. There had been a few tense moments when Gary approached the bar, thunderclouds on his face, but he'd turned away and disappeared into the crowd.

Once Milo had slipped her the paper bag, she'd stashed it in a safe place and waited to triumphantly pull it out and pour Gary's stupid drink. But he didn't show. Not then or later.

Before leaving the club, Tensley stopped in the dancers' dressing room. She pulled off her shoes, sinking into a worn leather chair to rub her feet.

And just as quickly slid off the chair and onto the floor, landing with a thump.

A giggle from not far away. Tensley looked up to see the red-headed woman she remembered from her first night, now in jeans and an oversized pink top, instead of the scraps of black she'd been wearing then. With her face scrubbed of all makeup and a sprinkling of freckles across her nose, she looked like a teenager on her way to a football game.

"What are you doing?" the woman asked as she closed the door to a locker. The name on it, scrawled in marker pen across masking tape, read, "Fiery Farrina."

Tensley did her best to rise from the floor with at least a small amount of grace, failing miserably as the heel of her foot slipped and she landed on her backside yet again. Even her feet, apparently, were coated in soap.

"Here." The redhead walked over and put out a hand.

"Thanks." With the help of the other woman, she was able to move back into the chair. This time she anchored herself by gripping the arms. "I had an accident. With soap."

The woman grinned. "Why does that not surprise me."

Good to know…or not…that some things carried from one life into another. Tensley was apparently as clumsy as a stripper as she had been as a corporate executive. She lifted a shoulder. "Shouldn't store that much soap on a cabinet that isn't anchored to the ground."

"Wait." The redhead frowned. "You were in the supply room?"

A raised voice from the other side of the door. "Sarah, your ride's here."

"I'll be right there," she called. Then she turned her attention back to Tensley. "Nobody but Milo goes in there."

"I—guess I forgot." Tensley looked away. "What's the big deal, anyway? There wasn't any soap in the restroom. I went to get some."

"You serious?"

Tensley felt herself slipping down the leather again. She gripped the chair's arms until her knuckles turned white. "Despite all appearances to the contrary, yes."

Sarah lifted one brow. "I gotta go." She pointed a finger at Tensley. "Don't go into Gary's hallway again unless you're invited." Sarah headed for the door.

Interesting. "So how do you get invited?"

The woman paused, her hand on the knob. She looked back at Tensley, her gaze clear and steady. "You show Gary you won't make trouble, you don't stick your nose where it doesn't belong, like in the supply room, and you don't ask questions like 'how do you get invited.'" She turned the doorknob.

Great. So far, she was zero for three. "Wait!"

Sarah hesitated.

"I like being a part of things. Could you put in a good word for me?"

"Tensley, I've got a kid to feed. You know that. I can't—" She pulled her mouth tight. "I can't risk making Gary mad. About anything."

No. She hadn't known.

Sarah looked back again. "You going to be okay? You're not going to trip over something and break your leg or knock over a candle and burn the place down?"

Well, there weren't any guarantees, but... "I'll be fine."

"Good. See you tomorrow." Sarah tossed her a smile and went out the door, closing it firmly behind her.

Tensley released her hold on the chair and allowed herself to slide back onto the floor, wincing as her now-tender backside hit the floor.

Again.

***

Max waited in the shadows near the door to Tensley's apartment building. It wasn't safe for the place to have this good a hiding spot, he noted with disgust. The building manager needed to get off his ass and cut down some of these trees, making it less likely that someone other than a cop could be hanging out here. Waiting.

The thought of someone going after Tensley made his blood boil. Job hazard, he told himself. Nothing personal, just because it was Tensley he was thinking of. He was trained to go after bad guys.

Still, he might have to get an axe and take these trees down himself.

His phone vibrated. He pulled it out and glanced at the caller ID. Rhonda. Ever since her most recent divorce, she called Max when she couldn't sleep in the middle of the night. Most of the time, she'd talk about what they'd been through together. And then she'd cry.

Max hated it when she cried. He felt so helpless, his first instinct was to crush the phone in his hand out of pure frustration and his second was to throw it as far away as possible.

Instead, he listened. When moisture pricked at the backs of his eyes, he squeezed them shut, put the phone on speaker, set it down, and began cleaning his service revolver. The methodical steps helped him distance, which kept the phone intact but didn't do much for Rhonda.

But this time, he pressed ignore on the phone, mouthing *sorry* as he slipped it back into his pocket. He'd call her after he'd had a chance to check in with Tensley to see if she'd learned anything.

Right on cue, he saw her. Moving toward the door to the building, her head bent as she searched in her purse. He shook his head, knowing he'd have to have a talk with her about being such an easy target. Any lame ass creep could be hanging around here at night.

He watched as she found her card key and passed it in front of the reader. A beep and the door opened. That fast, Max was out of the shadows and behind her as she went inside.

She whipped around, eyes wide with fright. She cut off the beginnings of a scream and pressed a hand to her heart. "Max," she choked out. "What are you doing?"

"I need to talk to you."

"And to do that, you had to sneak up and scare the life out of me? I thought you were somebody—bad."

"Yeah, speaking of that." Taking hold of her elbow, he steered her toward the elevator. "Ever heard of being aware of your surroundings? You're all alone at this hour and your head's in your purse, looking for something."

The elevator doors opened and they stepped inside. Tensley jabbed at the button for the fourth floor. She had no right, in Max's opinion, to have that pissed-off look on her face right now.

He leaned against the back wall. "Know how long it would take for someone to overtake you when you're that distracted?"

She turned, hands on her hips. "Let me guess. You timed yourself."

"Not me. Somebody else."

"You were the only one there."

He decided to ignore that. "Five point two seconds."

"You made that up."

He had, but that wasn't the point. "I'm concerned about your safety." The words came out sounding self-righteous, even to his ears. He looked away, giving the elevator a floor-to-ceiling professional scan while his peripheral vision did the same with her. She was a hell of a lot more enticing than the elevator. And most everything else.

The doors opened and she stepped out. "Then don't hide in the bushes."

"Trees," he said, as if it made any difference. She was already well ahead of him on her way to her apartment. When it occurred to him she might shut the door on him once she got inside, he picked up the pace. He couldn't figure out why she seemed so annoyed.

She turned the key in the lock.

"Can I come in?" he asked.

Her skeptical look compelled him to add, "It's business. I want to know what you've found out."

"I don't know." She narrowed her eyes, gazing at a spot over his shoulder. Then she shook her head. "It can't be a good idea to let someone in who crawled out of the bushes and tried to overtake me. In five point two seconds."

He moved forward and shut the door behind them. "Very funny."

She flipped on a lamp and set her purse down on a table. "Only thinking about my safety."

"I'm not just someone."

The teasing light left her eye. "No," she agreed, holding his gaze. "You're not."

Something inside his chest pulled tight. Damn, she was beautiful. And hard as he tried, he couldn't get the picture of her naked body out of his mind. He hadn't been that turned on since—high school. "So," he announced, his no-bullshit cop voice practically bouncing off the walls, "what did you find out?"

She looked away from him, rubbing a hand across the back of her neck. "I tried my best, but don't think I have a lot to report, yet."

She looked so disappointed, he wanted to reassure her it was okay, that she didn't have to have anything for him yet, but he wrenched himself back into police mode before that could go any further. "Then tell me what you do have to report."

A look of surprise flitted across her face, probably at the gruffness of his tone.

"Okay. Well." She took a deep breath and he had to fight like hell to keep his eyes off her chest.

"There's a hallway in back and I'm pretty sure that's where Gary's office is. He keeps it locked."

"Go on." *Eyes up, dammit.*

"One of the dancers told me tonight that you can't go back there without being invited. When I asked how you get invited, she said you have to be someone who doesn't ask questions."

That's not Tensley.

"That isn't me," she continued with a sigh. "But I did manage to get back there."

At that, his dick and the rational side of his brain paused in their ongoing battle, lowering the boxing gloves. "You did?"

"Into the hallway, anyway. The door to his office was locked, so I went into the supply closet next door when I heard Gary coming. He was arguing with Razor."

Max nodded. What did Tensley see in that guy, anyway? The only book he probably ever opened was a bathroom reader of fart jokes.

"Did you know Gary owns a hardware store?"

"A hardware—? No." Max shook his head.

"Razor apparently had the idea to attract more business by putting girls in bikinis in the store. It worked, but Gary was furious. Told him to stop doing it."

"Interesting, given Gary's line of work." Max scrunched his forehead, trying to think of laws that would prohibit bikini-clad girls from being in, or working in, a hardware store. He couldn't come up with any.

"That's what I thought, especially when it sounds like the hardware business isn't very good right now. I don't know why you'd go to all the trouble of having a store if you're not going to do whatever works to get customers in there." She paused. "Maybe Gary has some sort of moral code about little kids or something."

They answered that at exactly the same time.

"Nah."

"Nah."

"While they were arguing," Tensley went on, "Gary told Razor he didn't pay him to think, which I thought was a really terrible thing to say to the guy, especially when he's your son, and then he asked him, did he want the cops to come sniffing around the place?" She stopped mid-sentence, her gaze on Max. Questioning.

His eyes riveted on her. "Gary has a hardware business—"

"—that he doesn't want the police in," she finished. "Razor said that sometimes there's only one or two customers all day. That would make it pretty hard to turn a profit."

"Could be a tax write-off. But that wouldn't explain him not wanting the police to come around." Max rubbed his chin, thinking about the men he'd seen slinking along the walls of the strip club.

Men who didn't belong there and didn't want to be seen. *Shit. Would Gary be stupid enough to—?* His pulse sped up. "He could be using the store for something else."

Tensley's eyes lit up. "You think?"

"I think." His thoughts raced. If Gary had illegal activities going on, he could run the money through another business, like an innocent-looking hardware store. Or, the illegal activities were happening *at* the hardware store. Why else would he berate his son for doing anything that might attract the police?

Oh, fuck yes. He'd been right. This could be good. Before he'd even stopped to think about what he was doing, he'd grabbed Tensley and begun spinning her around the room. "Do you know what this means?"

"I—uh, something good?"

Why was she slipping out of his hands? He reached down lower and hoisted her up, holding on tight. "Hell, yes. Could definitely be."

She laughed. No one laughed like Tensley did, with that half-gulp that kicked off a giggle and ended up in a sound of pure joy that shot straight to his heart and made him want to join in.

Instead, he leaned down to kiss her. Hard. On those full, soft, parted lips.

Tensley's brain stopped functioning the second Max's mouth met hers. A gang of butterflies took over her stomach as her heart leaped somewhere into the back of her throat, and she had the overwhelming sensation of falling, falling… Over a cliff, a ledge…

Or onto the floor. She hit it with a plop. "Ow," she said faintly.

He made a deep, rumbling noise in the back of his throat that caused her heart to race and her knees to forget they were supposed to be holding her up.

"What have you got on, Crisco?" Without waiting for an answer, he picked her up.

She wrapped her arms around his neck, not caring where they were going or why. She wanted to entwine her fingers in his hair, breathe in the warm, musky scent of him, feel his heart thudding against hers, and have him bury that hot, moist, hard, thrusting cock in her—

Okay. So maybe she did care where they were going.

CHAPTER FIFTEEN

He kicked the door open with his foot. Actually kicked it. *So Scarlett and Rhett.* That much registered in Tensley's mind before he laid her on the bed, his warm, sweet, achingly familiar mouth covering her cheeks, her mouth, and then her neck with kisses that sent shivers through her.

He drew back long enough to mumble, his breath half gone and his eyes heavy-lidded, words that sounded like, "…bad idea."

A bad idea. On so many levels. She could barely manage to nod before he closed in with the urgency of a man with his foot on the pedal of a race car, ready to roar into the night, tires squealing, at the flick of a flag.

The butterfly gang in her stomach threw on leathers and furiously flapped their tattooed wings in a show of tough fear.

Tensley waved the green flag by grabbing Max's face between her hands and kissing him like she'd never kissed anyone before, including him. His whiskers scraped against her fingers as his tongue probed the depths of her mouth.

She tore off his jacket. Through the haze of lust wrapped around her brain, she heard a thump when the jacket hit the floor and sent up a vague hope it wasn't his gun.

Max grabbed hold of the bottom of her shirt and she raised her arms so it would come off fast. When their gaze locked in again, she caught her breath at the darkening blue of his eyes. He peeled off his own shirt and she rose toward him, reaching between her breasts to unsnap her bra. Her new, bigger breasts spilled free in an invitation to be held, cupped, massaged. His hands were a man's now, no longer a teenager's.

And...*ohhhh-my-gawwwd* if they didn't fit her boobs perfectly.

A ripple of pleasure went through her at the feel of his fingers, his mouth on her. "Max," she whispered, right before his lips closed on hers again, and his bare chest, muscles rippling beneath, pressed against her skin.

It felt so good, so right, so...she was falling again, tumbling over a cliff there was no turning back from. He was going to find out she was no longer a girl. That she was one hot hell of a lay...even if...she had to figure out how to be.

She wrapped her legs around him, holding on tight as he enfolded her in his arms. And then they were sliding, falling, into another universe.

Right off the bed and onto the floor. She landed on top of him. He grunted in surprise.

They pulled back to look at each other, the only sound their joint ragged breathing.

"We shouldn't—" He sat up, struggling to get the words out. "We can't—do this."

"I know." Why was that again? She couldn't think. She raked her hair back with her hand, arching her back. "Bad idea."

"Really bad," he murmured, shaking his head. He pulled her close, his breath caressing her face and his lips nearly touching hers. Her nipples brushed his and the thrill that shot through her set off tiny explosions powerful enough to bring down a substation.

His hands traveled down her back to grab her bottom. "Damn, Ten," he said, his voice rough and laced with heat, "What *is* that all over you?"

Bad idea or not, sometimes you just had to go for it. She stood, peeling off her jeans and panties one leg at a time, her eyes never leaving his. "You. I want you all over me." As simple as the words were, as much as they sounded like a line from a bad porn film, they came straight from a place inside her that had never been able to loosen Max Hunter's grasp on her heart.

She'd always known it. And now he was going to know it, too.

She had a second of terror that he might turn away, that he might leave her standing over him. Naked and alone. Her heartbeat pounded in her ears.

He put a hand to the floor and slowly rose until he stood before her, so close she could feel the warmth of his skin radiating to hers. His index finger brushed the underside of her chin. In his eyes, she glimpsed the sliver of vulnerability, wrapped tight in a tough guy wrapper, that had first drawn her to him, all those years ago. It was the side of him he had refused to let anyone else see.

"This isn't high school," he said.

"Damn right it isn't," she whispered, rising to her tiptoes to kiss him, softly at first and then harder.

Max groaned and pulled her tight. She put both hands on his chest and pushed away, breathing hard. Waiting for her brain to send words, any words, to her mouth.

He waited, his eyes continuing to darken.

"Strip, Hunter."

"So you're giving orders now."

"You're…" She jammed her hands on her hips and looked up, at the ceiling. "…wasting time. I might change my mind." Like there was *any* chance of that now.

"Wouldn't want that."

At the sound of his low, gravelly chuckle, her gaze shot back to him. He tugged at the waistband of his jeans and began unsnapping them, but he was moving agonizingly slow. At this rate, *he* might change his mind. She tried to help, but ran into trouble right away, given the strain on the denim.

One of his hands caught her by the wrist, while the other moved his jeans and underwear over and around his rock-hard penis to free it. He released her, stepped out of his clothing, and pulled her to him.

She couldn't talk, couldn't function, couldn't think. Max. Her Max, his eyes half-closed in the same salacious haze that consumed her body from head to toe. She reached to take him in her hand, watching the pleasure play out on his face as she stroked him

Then he whispered in her ear, "You're up first, Ten."

Before she could finish processing his words, he scooped her into his arms, brushed the comforter and pretty lacy pillows aside, and again laid her on the bed. "Am I gonna have to get the handcuffs to keep you from sliding away?"

"I'm not going anywhere," she answered, laying her hand on the back of his neck and wrapping her fingers in the familiar dark curls. She pressed her fingers down, urging him toward her. He came willingly, closing his mouth on hers and then moving down, along her chin, her neck and between her breasts.

"I was kind of hoping…" She caught her breath as his tongue played with her nipples, coaxing them into hard points. "…um…for that guy I used to know who…um…" Max moved further down, his tongue circling her belly button, exploring her abdomen. "…liked to break the rules instead of…um…following them—" The last word disappeared in a soft squeal as he parted her legs and his tongue found its target.

Every Tupperware container in her brain popped its seal at once to spill its contents. "Oh my God," she moaned as he fondled the most sensitive parts of her with his tongue, with his fingers, over and over, until the building intensity turned her fog from red to purple. Her head thrashed from one side to another as she arched toward him, pleading for more.

Once she came, in a crescendo so strong she could have sworn she heard someone— probably her—hitting a glass-shattering note, it took a few minutes for her brain to clear. When it finally did, she focused in on Max lying beside her, his head propped up with his elbow. He appeared to be doing his best to give her a casual grin. And failing. The gleam in his eye and the way his body strained toward her without moving an inch said otherwise.

"Damn," he said.

"Damn," she agreed, closing her eyes.

She felt him lean in and then pull back. Her eyes flew open. "You're not done here."

"Ten, I can't—"

She looked down at his erect, ready-to-rock penis. "That's a lie."

"No." He shook his head. "You don't know—"

"I don't care." She reached for him.

He groaned, taking her in his arms and pressing their bodies together. "If it was anyone but you," he said, his whiskers rough against her cheek, his mouth hot on her body, his hands powerful and gentle at the same time.

She didn't give him time to finish the thought. When he entered her, she gasped at the roller-coaster ride of memories and feelings she'd thought long stored away. She smelled the freshly mown grass of the field, felt the caress of summer air on her face and reveled in the secrecy of it all, the danger they might be discovered making love.

She drove her fingers into his shoulders and then let them travel down his muscled arms, holding on tight as each thrust took her farther toward the edge. The man must have hacked into her fuck-me wish list and hit every single thing on it while throwing in a few extra—

Ohhhhhh hell...

They came together, in a joint, shared shudder, and collapsed into each other's arms, damp and spent. Tensley's throat was raw.

And Max, the man she'd never been able to forget because she'd never wanted to, was still deep inside her. In more ways than one.

This had been the best bad idea *ever*.

***

The birds woke her, trilling their songs directly outside the window. Tensley opened her eyes one at a time, luxuriating in the feeling of Max's naked body wrapped around hers. He'd held her all night.

She could hear his even breathing, feel it whispering across her shoulder. It had been a long time since she'd felt so relaxed, so a part of someone else.

Fifteen years and four months, to be exact.

She burrowed even closer.

"Mmmmm," she heard him say in her ear.

"You awake?" she whispered.

"No."

But she felt his grin against her hair.

"Too bad," she said, a playful lilt to her voice. Pressed against her back, his cock sprang into action. Always ready to answer the call of duty, that one. Now she grinned. "Get much sleep last night?"

"Almost none. It was great."

"It was," she agreed, her voice soft. She turned and as she did, caught sight of his gun on the nightstand. Somehow, he'd put it there during the night. Kate was right. There was something sexy about it.

She rolled onto her back, eyes on the ceiling, reveling in the feeling of his warm, strong arm across her. "So tell me about being a detective."

"Okay." He inhaled. "Haven't been one that long, though."

"A recent promotion?"

"Yes. I was a beat cop for several years. In northern California. And then here."

"What's the best part, chasing down bad guys and putting them in cuffs? Throwing them in the slammer?"

He chuckled. "You watch too much TV."

"Okay, then. Tell me what I don't know." She ran her fingers across the broad muscles of his chest.

He was quiet for a minute and then said, "Once in a while, I could get through to a kid. A kid who was heading somewhere he wasn't going to be able to climb back out of. I liked that. And I liked the idea that I was keeping people safe. Watching over them at night when they were asleep and there were creeps out there who might want to harm them."

"I can see that," she whispered.

He looked down at her, rubbing her shoulder with his hand.

"So why did you decide to be a detective, instead?"

His answer was quick this time. "Justice." Now he turned his gaze to the ceiling. "And puzzles. I like being smarter than the bad guys, figuring out what they're up to and making sure they don't get away with it."

"Great material. You should be writing about it. That life."

A self-conscious laugh as she heard his breathing quicken. "You said that before."

"You're a good writer."

"Haven't done anything in—a while."

She sat up. "Max Hunter. You're working on something, aren't you?"

He looked at her, then back at the ceiling. She could tell he didn't want anyone to know, but he wanted to tell her.

"You are. That's great!" She laid her hands on each side of his face, loving the feel of his morning whiskers against the tender skin of her palms.

"I didn't say that."

"You didn't have to. When will it be finished?"

He laughed as he pulled himself up, talking while his arms went around her and he began kissing her, teasing at her mouth. "It will be finished when I get it finished. When I figure out the ending. But right now I have something else to finish."

"Oh yeah? And what would that be, Detective Hunter?" Her heart began to beat faster, as her body pressed against his.

The sound of a ringing cell pierced the air.

Max abruptly pulled away, shaking his head. "Shit. What time is it?"

"I don't know." Tensley blinked and tried, but not that hard, to find a clock, or her cell, in the unfamiliar bedroom. "Don't answer it."

"Have to." He was up and across the room in a flash, locating his jacket on the floor and going through it until he found his phone. "Hunter."

As he stood, listening, Tensley put one arm behind her head and let her eyes travel up and down the back of his sculpted physique, from his broad shoulders to the hard mounds of his butt cheeks to his powerful legs and bare feet. She saw now a tan line she hadn't noticed last night, from swim trunks or shorts. That part of his skin was a few shades lighter than the rest.

Max had always loved the outdoors. She let her mind wander down a bunny trail of memories. She and Max would go swimming together. Somewhere remote, so they wouldn't need her bikini or his swim trunks. She smiled, remembering it. Then she looked down at her own body in the early morning sunlight. Pale, no tan at all.

Great. She was nocturnal, living in a strip club.

Ah, well. Nothing that couldn't be fixed. A little sunlight wouldn't hurt these new boobs. What were they going to do, melt?

After another curt response into the phone, Max turned. Tensley grinned. She flung the covers away from her body and dipped her chin, looking up at him through her lashes. Then she patted the spot next to her on the bed. "Come on back," she drawled. Right before she giggled.

"I have to go."

"What?" She scrambled upright. "Why?"

Max was already pulling on his clothes. First his jeans, then his shirt. By the time he'd finished strapping on his gun and shoving his arms into his jacket, he still hadn't looked at her.

"You can't," she sputtered, pulling the sheet from the bed to wrap it around herself.

He looked down at the floor, his jaw muscles working. From the other side of the door, Gemini yowled.

"I'm sorry about last night," he said to the floor. "I let things get out of hand."

"Out of hand?" she screeched, pulling the sheet tighter. "What are you talking about?"

"I have to leave." She heard a warning in his voice.

A warning she chose to ignore. "You're not going anywhere until you tell me what's going on."

"It shouldn't have happened, that's all. I'm sorry."

Icy fear crept over her. She began to tremble. "I don't understand."

"Let's just forget it, okay?"

"I can't forget it."

"You're going to have to."

"You're sorry that, what, you slept with me? A—a—" She couldn't say it. Damn him, anyway. *Ow.* She pressed her fist to her heart, forcing the words out. "A stripper?" If only he knew the truth. If only she could tell him, make him understand.

He still couldn't look at her. "I'm a cop." He turned away abruptly, striding toward the door. When he threw it open, Gemini hissed at him.

Good cat.

She followed Max, tripping and stumbling over the sheet. "I don't believe we did anything illegal, Detective," she snapped.

He turned back, right before reaching the door of her apartment. "Dammit, Tensley. You're a police department informant. Working with me. I don't know what I was thinking. Any kind of relationship between the two of us—" He broke off to rake a hand through his hair. "Could make it impossible to build a case against Gary."

"We're back to Gary." She began to jam all that had happened last night into a mental Tupperware container, but she couldn't find a lid to save her life. Where were the damn lids?

"Last night was amazing, wonderful. It was probably the best night of my entire life." This time, he let his eyes meet hers and she could see what looked like genuine anguish flash through them before it was replaced with something else. Resolve. "But it isn't going to happen again." He cupped her chin with his hand and gave her a quick peck on the cheek. "Next time, we'll meet at the diner. Apparently, I can't be trusted alone with you."

"So that's it. You're done." She knew she sounded bitter and she didn't care. This was Bryan-with-a-y-not-an-i on steroids. No. Scratch that. It was so much worse, there wasn't even a comparison. "Went back to high school to have a little fun and now you're done, out of here."

He straightened. "You know it's not like that."

"All I know is that you're making the decisions for both of us."

"Looks like I have to."

"I'm not like you. I can't just pretend it didn't happen."

"And what do you think Gary's going to do if he finds out you slept with a cop? You think he's going to let that go? You think Razor is?"

She opened her mouth and then shut it again, remembering Gary's fury over his stupid Maker's Mark. This could be a lot bigger deal.

"I can't let anything happen to you, Tensley, because of something I did. Not again."

Her eyes filled. She blinked hard. "Let's get this straight. It wasn't just you here last night."

His voice lowered. "I could have stopped it."

"*I* could have stopped it. But I didn't want to. And neither did you."

Gemini rubbed up against her bare leg, poking out from under the sheet. He meowed.

"Better feed him," Max said as he went to open the door.

"Don't go," she whispered.

He stopped, knuckles whitening as he gripped the knob. "Nothing happened last night, Tensley."

Pieces of her heart broke off and shattered, one by one. "Yes, it did." She lifted her chin. "Several times, as a matter of fact. Thanks for that, by the way."

He grimaced, closing his eyes. Then he opened them and turned the knob. "I'll be in touch."

When he had gone, Tensley leaned up against the closed door and slid on her back all the way down until she landed on the floor, the sheet in crumpled folds all around her. She didn't even care that her bruised backside screamed in pain. It could join the rest of her.

"Guess what, Max," she said as she stroked Gemini's fur. "I'm not a stripper. I'm vice president of Tanner, Inc. with a professionally decorated corner office. I have a beautiful condo and a gorgeous car and I vacation in fabulous, exclusive resorts where I swear they clean the sand every morning before I wake up."

The cat looked up at her and she went on, her voice cracking on some words and cutting out altogether on others. "This was all a huge, cruel mistake. I wouldn't have punched Rhonda. I *didn't* punch Rhonda. This isn't me. This is someone else's life."

She closed her eyes, leaning her head against the door. "And last night was the only time I was really me."

A single tear leaked out to roll down her face, followed by another. A few seconds later, she felt paws on her legs and her shoulder and then a sympathetic sandpaper tongue on her cheek.

At least someone understood.

CHAPTER SIXTEEN

Max got through the morning by focusing his complete and total attention on the city's hardware stores. Every time thoughts of Tensley nudged at his consciousness, he denied entry, slamming the door shut.

Except that only made him think about kicking the door to her bedroom open, sending everything flooding right back again.

"Hunter."

Max's chin flew up. His captain stood a few feet away.

"Yes, sir."

"You deaf? I said your name four times."

"No, sir. Sorry. I was just," he motioned toward the screen, "concentrating." Shit, what had he been thinking last night? Not about his job, that was for damn sure. Because he could kiss it goodbye if anybody found out he'd been with Tensley.

There were about four hundred rules and policies against that kind of thing and he'd probably broken every single fucking one of them. At least twice.

Make that three times.

"Uh-huh," said his captain, making it clear in two syllables that he didn't believe him. "Your CI come up with anything yet?"

"Uh, yeah." Max raked a hand through his hair. "Yeah, she did. She found out Gary Burns has a side business he doesn't want the police looking at." He squinted at his papers.

"What kind of a business?"

"Lane Family Hardware. Mr. Lane sold it to Gary Burns a couple of years ago, but Burns kept the name."

"Could be he wanted his own place to sell stripper poles."

"The place was on its last legs when Burns bought it. A Home Depot moved in a block away. My CI says the neighborhood hardware store doesn't have many customers."

"His club's got customers. The guy can probably afford a home improvement fetish if he wants one."

"Could be. But my gut's telling me there's something else." Max allowed himself a glance up, meeting his captain's eyes. "The people I told you about that I saw going into the back, they didn't even look at the dancers. My CI's telling me the girls— new girls, anyway— aren't allowed near Burns's office, not even to get supplies."

The other man's eyes narrowed in contemplation. "So what's the connection?"

Max looked back down, drumming his fingers on his desk. "Not sure yet. He's selling drugs, maybe. Or has a prostitution operation on the side. Or could be he's messing with the books. Running money through the club or the store. For a fee."

"A lot of maybes."

Max pulled his mouth in tight and nodded.

"Check it out, but don't spend time on dead ends." His captain's voice held a clear warning. "I need you on other cases."

"I understand."

"You at the club again tonight?"

Max jerked his head yes. If Tensley was on stage tonight—his dick stiffened at the possibility—it would take everything he had to concentrate on his job. "CI's going to get me something I can work with."

A pause. "Your CI's a good-looking woman."

Max heard the question. He shrugged, picking up his papers. "She's okay." *If you like smart, beautiful women who see straight through your bullshit and think there's actually something good there. If that's your type.*

"You've got a week. If you can't find anything going on at that club by then, you gotta get out of there."

There *was* something going on. He could feel it in his bones. "But—"

"You wanted a shot at this, so I gave it to you. But you spend too long at one place without anything to show for it, that's not going to look good."

Sleeping with his CI was going to look a hell of a lot worse. "Yes, sir."

His captain walked away, footsteps ringing on the floor like nails in the coffin of Max's law enforcement career.

***

Mid-day, Max got into his truck and drove to Rhonda's store. His cell showed she'd called him twice since he'd blown her off early this morning. He still felt like shit about doing that. As if she'd caught him cheating, which didn't even make sense.

But there wasn't a whole lot that *did* make sense right now.

Her store was in a once-crumbling area of town now considered up and coming, thanks to a group fascinated with the faded murals and stone archways. The fact that these structures had, in another century, housed the town's most profitable brothels apparently only added to the appeal.

The group had commissioned historical markers and a statue of one of the era's colorful madams at her most provocative self. The city's mayor, stepping in a beat too late, was now trying to put a stop to it all, saying it would give a whole new meaning to the term "bedroom community."

Big mistake. Rhonda, who had managed to get herself elected vice president of the group, had picked up that comment and run it up field for a marketing touchdown. The mayor was still trying to stammer his way out of a public fight with a police captain's daughter.

Max pulled into a parking spot in front of the store and cut the engine. Several bells clanged on the door when he entered the store, rising above the female conversation and sound of Lady GaGa singing in the background. Jammed with racks of women's clothing, the shop smelled of equal parts perfume, furniture polish and mothballs.

At an antique wooden counter, a young woman picked up the phone, announcing, "Rhonda's Rags to Bitches!" When she spotted Max, she waved hello and then pointed one long, orange fingernail toward another part of the store. "She's back there." Then she turned her attention back to the caller. "Yes, we have eve-en-ing gowns. You got a party to go to?" She grinned and wrinkled her sizeable nose at Max, causing the ring in its corner to disappear for a second.

He smiled, knowing it would only take a few seconds for Avril's attention to be diverted to—

It took less than that. "You *have* to try that on!" she screeched at a woman holding a dress with mirrored circles plastered to its front. They reflected in the light, casting rainbows on the walls and Max's shirt. "It's so *cute!*" Back to the caller. "You looking for glam or gorge?"

Max weaved through the racks toward the back of the store.

He found Rhonda sitting cross-legged on a table in the stockroom, surrounded by an explosion of clothing. She had paperwork in her lap, a pen in her mouth and a look of consternation on her face.

She hadn't seen him yet. For a few seconds, he thought about leaving. No good. Avril would only tell her he'd been here. He stepped around something sparkly on the floor. "Hi," he said.

Rhonda's chin flew up. "Hi." There was a streak of blue ink above her red lipstick. Her eyes, lined with black, were wide, anxious. "You didn't call me back."

"I was—working. Came as soon as I could." It was only a partial fib, so why did it leave such a bad taste in his mouth?

Rhonda slid off the table and began pacing back and forth before him like a wind-up toy at full speed. She'd always been able to go from zero to ninety in less than a minute.

In tight low-slung jeans that hugged her ass perfectly and a T-shirt that barely contained her generous tits, Rhonda had a body every man who saw her fantasized about being able to get into bed. Every man except Max.

Not anymore, anyway.

She stopped pacing and turned to face him, her arms crossed. Her lower lip quivered. "I needed you last night."

"I'm here now."

"But last night—" She broke off and raised her palms, appealing to the ceiling. Some kind of blue feather thing in her hair bobbed up and down. "I can't even tell you what a bad place I was in. It happened again. I started thinking about...you know...and it just still hu-hurts so much..." The last word disappeared as her eyes filled.

A familiar spot in his chest tightened. Yeah, he knew. But guilt had now taken up full-time residence in that spot because he'd moved on. Every time he wanted to tell her to quit living in the past, that guilt stepped up to figuratively punch him in the face.

She didn't call him as much anymore, though. Only on the occasional bad night. Maybe that was a good sign. He stepped forward and folded her in his arms. "Are you still going to that therapist?"

She shook her head and a blue feather flew in front of his face. Her words, mumbled into his shirt, weren't easy to understand, but he thought he could make out, "She didn't understand."

"You have to give her a chance to understand."

She lifted her head. "Only one person does." A loud sniff. "You." She tightened her grip on him. He winced as fingernails dug into his back.

Pretty much a replay of the conversation they'd had when she'd first found out he was back in town. He struggled for something to say that wouldn't make him sound like as much of a jerk as he felt. Couldn't come up with anything.

"I'm never going to be a mother."

"C'mon. That's not true."

She nodded so hard, the feather thing gave up and flew off her head, landing on the floor. "I haven't been able to get pregnant again since we—" An agonized hiccup. "I can't even s-say it."

So he did. "Lost the baby."

"The worst night of my life." Another hiccup. She closed her eyes, leaning her head against his chest. He breathed in the flowery scent of her hair and flashed back a million years.

To the warm, biting reassurance of a fifth of bourbon going down his throat after he'd lost Tensley. The jolt when he'd climbed out of his fog the next morning to find Rhonda in his bed. The aching regret when Rhonda told him a month later that she was pregnant. The sound of fall leaves crunching beneath their shoes as they made their way up the steps to the courthouse and a quickie marriage, Rhonda in a white, tight dress and Max in his only suit.

The judge hadn't looked at Max once during the brief ceremony. His eyes had been glued to Rhonda's chest.

Not many weeks later, the argument. Max had come home the next morning to apologize and found her curled in a ball, eyes puffy and one ankle wrapped. She'd told him she'd been crying so hard the night before, she hadn't seen the stairs. Until she'd tumbled down them.

It had been his fault. The fight, the miscarriage, the divorce after less than a year. The fact that he hadn't been ready to be a husband, let alone a parent. Ever since he'd come back to town, she hadn't let him forget it.

Not that he could have, no matter how much he'd moved on. She'd never let him. And neither would the guilt that twisted in him.

She sighed against his chest. "My sister-in-law told everybody at dinner that she's pregnant again, but this one's gonna be the last. My mother's so happy, she's asking, wouldn't it be nice to name this one after his grandfather? It's not like there's going to be any more grandchildren. She said that looking straight at me."

Max rolled his eyes, remembering his few encounters with Rhonda's mother. "You can't let her get to you."

"I would have been such a good mom, Max."

He put a hand up to touch her hair, but drew it back before making contact. "You will be." His voice was gruff; his feet already inching toward the door.

"You ever think about what he would have looked like?"

He couldn't let himself think about that.

"Bet he would've looked like you. Girls wouldn't have been able to keep their hands off him." A small choked sound. "We could have made it, you know. Been a family." Her warm tears soaked through his shirt and onto his skin.

One drunken night might make a kid, but it didn't make a family. Since he couldn't bring himself to say that, though, he just let his shirt get wetter.

"You know, I never would have come all the way over to your place last night unless I really needed you—"

What? "Hold on," he interrupted. He stepped back, putting his hands on her shoulders. "You went to my apartment last night?"

"You weren't there."

"I told you I had to work."

"You weren't there at four a.m."

"Rhonda." It took effort to keep his tone even. As usual, she was taking a hammer to his patience. "You can't just show up at my place. We aren't married anymore, remember?"

She threw her hands in the air. "You think I could forget? My husband doesn't even bother to tell me he's moved back to town. I have to find out from my father, like that wasn't uncomfortable. Real nice, Max."

"*Former* husband," he corrected. And then, because he was pissed off she'd gone to his apartment, he added, "First in a series."

"First, second, third, what difference does it make?" she bit out, jamming her hands on her hips. Then she seemed to think the better of it and when she spoke again, her tone had softened. "You're the only one who ever mattered. You know that."

He turned away, studying a necklace that looked as though it weighed as much as Rhonda. Where did she get this stuff, anyway? He picked it up and let it slip through his fingers to clatter onto a counter. "Husbands two and three might not agree."

"Oh, very funny. I don't even know where Jess is and Carl, well, you know what's up with that."

Unfortunately, he did. Carl, a more senior detective, had never gotten over the divorce and considered every male between the age of eighteen and eighty a rival for his ex-wife's affections.

"Jealous?" Rhonda purred.

Hell, if he could figure out how to get her back together with Carl, he would. Max changed the subject. "So, how's business?"

She brightened. "I have a blog."

He picked up a pile of clothing and dropped it onto a table to get to the wooden chair beneath. Shiny stuff—glitter or something like it—shot upward. He dragged the chair out of the danger zone and straddled it, crossing his arms over the back. "What's it about?"

"Fashion. How you can find great bargains and look amazing for not much money." She clasped her hands together. "I already have about a zillion followers. It's incredible."

"That's good." She needed something in her life besides serial marriage.

"And I gave it the perfect name." She paused, taking a deep breath, apparently to give the name a dramatic introduction. "Rhonda's RearView."

He covered his sudden, sharp laugh with a cough. "Nice," he managed.

She flashed a dimple at him. "You should see my photo. Everyone says my ass is my best feature." To illustrate her point, she thrust her hip toward him and turned, looking back over her shoulder. "Including you."

"It is, yeah," he said, "a good feature." It was getting hot in this stockroom and the musty smell coming from all these clothes was starting to get to him. He stood, pushing the chair aside. "But don't sell yourself short."

"You can't go." Rhonda rushed over and grabbed hold of his jacket. "You just got here."

He loosened her fingers. "Work to do."

"I was in such a bad place last night, I couldn't even trust myself. I was afraid of what what—I might do."

Alarm shot through him. "Go to the therapist, Rhonda."

"I told you. She doesn't underst—"

"Go. To the therapist. Call her."

She let go of him and stepped back, tipping her head and looking up through her lashes. "Take me to dinner and I'll think about it."

Not gonna happen.

She must have read the answer on his face because she answered before he did. "Forget it. You don't owe me anything. Even dinner."

"Rhonda." He stopped, not sure what to say.

She picked up a skirt, examining it. "Besides, I'm sure your girlfriend wouldn't like it."

He narrowed his eyes. "What?"

"Whoever she is. The one you were with at four a.m."

God help him if she ever found out. "Told you. I was working." He had been. At first.

"You can't fool a wife, Max Hunter."

"*Ex*—" He broke off. No point. "I've gotta go."

"Go on then." She fluttered her fingers, eyes still intent on the skirt. "I have to post on my blog. Today it's all about twenty things you can do with rhinestones."

He hesitated. Being with Rhonda felt like opening a window part way only to have it slam shut on your fingers without warning. Part of him felt obligated to keep trying to open it again, while the other part yelled that only an idiot got his fingers broken more than once.

He made for the door. "Have fun."

"Wait." A squeak of panic in her voice. "Max?"

He stopped and turned. "Yeah?"

"Still friends, right?" Her eyes were too bright, shiny.

As if he had a choice. He flexed his fingers. "Sure."

Relief crossed her face. "So then, go. Quit hanging around me so much." She adjusted her huge tits, shooting him a mischievous look. "You might be getting in the way of wedding number four."

"Oh God, Rhonda," he groaned. "You're not getting married again." He'd heard Carl hurling verbal bullets yesterday, so it couldn't be to him.

"Don't worry, baby." She flashed a grin and cooed, "There's time. You've still got a chance."

He couldn't get out of the shop fast enough. Avril only managed the first syllable of goodbye before he shot through the front door.

Rhonda. Of all the ex-wives, in all the towns, in all the world, she had to be his.

***

This time, when Tensley called Kate's office, she didn't have to make up an ill pet to talk with the vet. She gave her name and was put right through.

Her friend dispensed with the preliminaries. "I've been worried about you." In the background, a dog barked.

"Good. Because I'm worried about me, too."

"What happened?"

Tensley sighed. "Let's just say, he didn't put his gun on the nightstand right away. Don't think he had time, what with me ripping his clothes off and all."

"I *knew* you wouldn't be able to keep your hands off each other. I remember how you were in high school. Did I call it, or what?"

"You called it."

"So you slept with Max."

"There wasn't much sleeping involved."

Kate chuckled. "So that's how you decided you could help him. Did it work? And was it crazy amazing, with fireworks? A hallelujah chorus?"

Tensley sighed again and pressed a fist against her heart, remembering the way Max had left her. "For someone who's supposed to be my best friend, you ask a lot of questions."

"Oh." A pause. "So no fireworks?"

"No, it's not that." Tensley shook her head and sat down on the bed. She gazed down at the white sheet and spread her fingers across it, as though she could hold the memory of him there. "It was incredible. On the scale of the monster fireworks that aren't even legal."

"Okay." Kate's voice softened. "Then what's wrong?"

"He got a call and left."

"Cops do that. All the time."

"He turned into a different person when he answered his phone." Tensley curled her fingers into a ball, pressing it hard into the mattress. "Couldn't get out of here fast enough." Gemini hopped up onto the bed with a soft thump and sat, watching her. "He said last night was a big mistake."

The dog's shrill barking escalated until Tensley could barely hear Kate's sympathetic, "Oh, no."

"His case is more important."

"Then after the case is over—"

"Bullshit. He just doesn't want anyone to find out he was with a—stripper."

"You don't know that."

"I'm pretty sure I do. The irony, of course, is that I'm not a stripper. Or at least I wasn't until Madame Claire decided to screw with my life."

A voice in the background paged Kate to an exam room. "Listen, Ten—"

"You have to go."

"I do. I'm sorry. A very sick Great Dane. We'll talk more about this later, okay? I wish I knew what to say."

"It's okay. Not like I haven't been down this road before." Her attempt at sounding offhand fell to the floor with a splat.

"You don't know what's going on with him."

Tensley straightened. "Well, you know what? I don't care."

"Yes, you do."

"I can't afford to. So I won't."

Kate's voice was rueful. "Let me know how that goes."

"You'll know. Because I need a favor. Can I stay with you for a few days until I figure some things out?"

"Of course. Come by and I'll give you a key to my place. You can have the guest bedroom."

"Can Gemini come, too?" She couldn't just leave the cat.

"What do you think? Of course."

Relief surged through Tensley. "Thanks. I don't want to be here when Razor comes around. Or Max. Not that he—you know, *will*. But I want to make sure anything I do to help him is all business."

The overhead voice that paged Kate this time sounded less patient.

"I have to go," Kate said. "But think about one thing." She paused. "Maybe he's afraid of what he's feeling. And that's why he left."

Tensley's laugh was sharp. "Are you kidding me? Max Hunter," she said, "is a lot of things, but afraid is *never* one of them."

***

Max Hunter was, for the first time in his life, scared shitless. How could one guy screw up his life this bad in one night?

No matter how hard he tried, he couldn't shove aside the memory of Tensley's body against his, the feel of her mouth on him, the thrill of being inside her, the fierce need they'd shared. Like two people stuck in a desert who'd finally found a drink of cool water.

His mouth went dry and he broke into a sweat every time he thought about last night, which was… Every. Single. Minute.

"Hey, Hunter," an officer said as he walked by. "You okay?"

"Fine," Max said without looking up.

"Good," came the retort. "'Cause you look like crap."

Max zeroed in on his computer monitor, but the letters swam in front of him. Random, meaningless words about the hardware store Burns owned. He had to make sense of them. Fast.

And he had to stop thinking about her. Fast.

He'd call another woman. A cop never lacked for phone numbers; he had tons of them. Like maybe that cute little barista at the coffee shop who'd written her number on the side of his paper cup last week and slid it over to him with a smile, letting her fingers linger on his. That apron didn't begin to cover her sexy little ass, which he'd enjoyed watching as she'd walked away.

Her ass didn't come close to being as sexy as Tensley's, but still… *Fu-u-ck. Get your head in the game, Hunter.*

From the corner of his eye, he saw movement. He looked up. In front of his desk stood a hulking man in an expensive dirt-brown suit, with a scowl that took up every inch of real estate on his face.

You have got to be kidding me.

"Yeah. I'm just as happy to see you, sunshine," Rhonda's Husband Number Three, otherwise known as Detective Carl Cole, drawled. "But apparently you need help from someone who knows what the hell he's doing."

Seriously. This day just could not get any better.

CHAPTER SEVENTEEN

"I don't need help." Max stood and gathered his papers, shoving them into a file.

"That's where you're wrong," Carl said, scraping a chair's legs across the floor to pull it in front of Max's desk. He sat down hard, dwarfing the chair with his size. "Captain says you do. And then he tells me it's my lucky day. I'm the one who's gotta do the helping."

Max stopped, leveling a gaze at the detective, who worked in the investigations unit that handled fraud and forgery. "I've got it handled. You can leave."

The other man leaned back and templed his fingers. "It's not like I want to be here. I've got real work to do. Instead, I've gotta be wasting my time with some shit strip club. And you."

Asshole. Max narrowed his eyes. On the up side, Carl had more experience than Max did with this kind of thing. On the down side, he was Carl. Who still thought Rhonda was the love of his life and that any other guy, but especially one who had also been married to her, was an obstacle. "So get me somebody else."

The other man snorted. "Like we have a ton of guys sitting around waiting for—"

"Got it. You're the only one who has time on his hands."

Carl opened his mouth and paused, obviously confused. The scowl returned. "Listen," he said. "You don't get to disrespect an order. And neither do I. So sit your ass back down and tell me what you've got."

Max realized he wasn't going to get out of this. Shit. Why couldn't Rhonda marry outside the force? A fire fighter, for once.

He put both hands on the desk and leaned in toward Carl. "I respect orders, but I sure as hell don't take them from you. Are we clear on that much?"

"Crap." Carl scowled and adjusted his belt. "You could spend your whole life tryin' and not learn half of what I know—"

Max cut him off with, "You going to bitch all day or are you going to help?"

He took Carl's irritated grunt as assent.

***

Tensley picked up the key to Kate's place and then wove her way through traffic to arrive at a new high-rise not far from the downtown core. "Not bad," she said to herself, peering up at the endless bank of windows.

In Tensley's former life, Kate had bought a craftsman-style house in an older part of town. The two of them had had several debates about house versus apartment, but Kate had finally decided to take the homeowner plunge and ended up loving the place.

Tensley wondered why things were different now.

She followed the instructions her best friend had written out for parking and then lugged her suitcase to the entrance, plugging in the code she'd been given. After the door clicked open, she walked into a high-ceilinged lobby furnished with plush rugs, elegant chairs and sofas, and large mirrors edged in a subdued gold. Tensley stopped and closed her eyes, breathing in a scent of furniture polish mingled with vanilla.

This was more like it. So much nicer than the place she was living in.

The elevator came immediately when called, with the soft pinging sound of one that knew to announce its arrival quietly.

Tensley stepped into a mirrored car with gleaming gold rails, rolling her suitcase behind her, and pushed the button labeled 10. With a barely perceptible whoosh, she was delivered to Kate's floor.

She found the apartment halfway down the hall. Tensley fit the key into the lock and she and Gemini stepped into a haven of white walls bathed in natural light and leather furniture dotted with three bright pillows and two snoring dogs. Neither opened its eyes, even when she shut the door behind her.

She couldn't help but laugh, partially in relief. At least one thing hadn't changed. Kate still had her two senior citizen Yorkies—Stinky and Blinky.

"Hey, guys," she said, lifting her hand in greeting. Neither one stirred. Blinky, she knew, had trouble seeing and Stinky had trouble hearing. But both were champion sleepers. Gemini, wisely, didn't say anything.

She took her things to the guest room and sat on the edge of the large, comfy bed. While it was a relief to know Razor wouldn't come pounding on the door at any minute, Kate's place was also a poignant reminder of Tensley's previous life, where she'd had a similarly well-appointed apartment, tastefully designed and filled with luxuries large and small.

Flopping back against a comforter so soft, it felt like a cloud beneath her, she wondered who had taken her position as vice president of Tanner Industries and whether her mother listened to that person more than she had her own daughter. Not likely, she decided. Her mother didn't listen to anyone.

For a minute, Tensley thought about calling her office number, to see who would answer. But a knot in the pit of her stomach warned her off. It would only make her feel worse and even resent that person when she regained her life and rightful position with the company. She didn't want to know who had schemed his or her way into the job.

Especially if that person was better at doing it than she was.

It was quiet and peaceful in the apartment, with morning sun streaming through the windows. Thinking she'd just close her eyes briefly, Tensley didn't realize she'd drifted off to sleep until she woke to the sound of snoring dogs, now lying on each side of her on the bed. Gemini was sitting across the room, giving all three of them the stink eye.

She blinked and then rubbed her eyes, lifting her head to see the dogs that, once again, didn't budge from their slumber. "Stinky, I think you have asthma."

At that, Blinky opened his eyes, looking at her through the cloudiness she knew was caused by his cataracts.

"I don't suppose you remember me?" she ventured.

No response.

"Didn't think so." Tensley struggled to her feet, no easy undertaking with a dog on each side of her body. She found the bathroom and flipped on the light to see an expansive, gleaming Jacuzzi tub. "That is so calling my name."

Several minutes later, she'd filled it and was soaking in a relaxing bath, letting the scented steam fill her nostrils. With the exception of the Italian marble tile that lined the back of her tub, this one was so like the one she'd had that it sent pangs of homesickness through her. "I'm going to get my life back," she said to Stinky, who had padded his way into the bathroom. "No matter what it takes."

There was something else she didn't have in her former life. Max. But she wasn't going to think about him right now. Or maybe ever.

He very obviously wasn't thinking about her. And that's all she needed to know. What was that old saying? Fool me once, shame on you. Fool me twice—

Instead of finishing the thought, she ducked under the water and then shot back up again, letting it stream off her. She could figuratively, if not literally, wash away every trace of Max Hunter.

On the outside, anyway.

***

Max had to admit that Carl Cole knew his stuff. Within twenty-four hours, the detective had confirmed that not only did Gary Burns's hardware store seem to be doing extremely well when other independent hardware stores were struggling, but Burns also appeared to have an unexpected civic side.

Carl was following a trail that indicated Burns and his son might be behind two non-profit organizations—one called "Citizens for the Arts" and another called "Save our City"—that had recently donated to three political campaigns. "Somethin' must be goin' on," Carl said as he rifled through papers on his desk. "A guy like that doesn't give a shit about the city or the arts, unless he's gettin' some kind of cover charge for it."

Max felt anticipation ripple up his spine, the same feeling he always got when pieces of a puzzle began falling together. "Which political campaigns?"

"Too soon. Haven't connected all the dots yet."

Max leaned forward, pressing his hands hard into the wood of Carl's desk. "Don't care. Tell me."

Carl sat back, chewing on the end of his pen, his gaze cool and steady. "Moss for Mayor. Digman and Walker for City Council."

"Moss, Digman and Walker," Max repeated. "Interesting."

"I thought so." Carl took the pen out of his mouth, leaving an ink mark on his upper lip a lot like the one Rhonda had had. "But interesting doesn't get you very far in court."

"I saw a guy at the club," Max shook his head, thinking, "that I know I've seen before. High up somewhere. No way he should have been there. Maybe he's tied into this somehow."

"Name," Carl barked. "Gimme a name."

"Don't *have* one yet. Weren't you listening?"

Carl tapped his pen against his forehead. "I myself have a great memory. Most detectives do."

The guy was a dick and not just in the cop lingo way. What had Rhonda ever seen in him? "I'll remember who he is," Max muttered.

"Yeah, I'm not holdin' my breath."

Max stood. "Good. Never know what might happen, at your age."

Carl glared at him.

"I'm leaving." Max rapped his knuckles on the desk. "Work to do."

"Get outta here," Carl growled. "You're botherin' me."

Max stopped when he reached the door, curling his fingers around the jamb. He looked back over his shoulder. "Thanks."

"Yeah, yeah. Nothing we can pin on the weasel, yet."

Max's voice scraped gravel. "I'll get something."

The creases in Carl's face deepened. "What's your deal with him, anyway?"

Max's fingers gripped the door harder. "Just doing my job. That's all." He left before Carl could pick up anything on his face that said that wasn't the half of it.

***

Tensley dried her hair as Stinky watched and Blinky turned in circles, apparently trying to figure out where the whirring sound was coming from. Gemini had taken refuge in the guest bedroom.

The more she thought about who had taken her rightful place at Tanner, Inc., the more determined she was to find out. It was simple. She'd go see her mother, and ask.

Of course, nothing having to do with Esme Tanner had ever been simple. But somehow, the woman would have to see that Tensley belonged with the company. Whatever had happened between them would have to be forgiven.

Esme only had one child. And Tensley only had one mother. Blood will out. Or something like that.

She finished drying her hair and quickly applied her makeup, propelled by an urgency to be gone before Kate came home and tried talking sense to her. Tensley couldn't afford to be sensible right now.

She stepped into Kate's room and flipped through hanger after hanger of clothing until she found a tailored, conservative suit that Kate probably wore to veterinarian conferences. The shade of blue went well with Tensley's hair and the fit wasn't bad, given her altered body. She turned one way and then the other in the full-length mirror, hoping the unwritten best friend rule they'd always followed still applied—my clothes are your clothes until death, distance or unacceptable fashion taste do us part.

"Wish me luck," she told the dogs, who had followed her in. They looked as convinced as she was that this would be a good move. "Come on, you guys. She's my *mother*. How bad can it be?" Her pulse pounded out an answer.

Blinky turned and left, followed by Stinky, his nails clicking on the hardwood.

"Thanks for the support," Tensley called.

She turned back to the mirror, tugging on the jacket that was a little too big in the waist and a little too small in the chest. Her new boobs stretched the fabric into a gap. From the corner of her eye, she spied Kate's handbag collection and grabbed a large, flat Michael Kors bag to hold in front of her. "That'll work."

As long as she didn't lower it, she wouldn't have to see her mother's left eyebrow arch in displeasure.

Tensley had spent a lot of her life fending off that eyebrow arch. Even the *thought* of seeing it made her stomach turn over.

So she did the only thing she could. She shot out of the apartment before she could think any more about the wisdom of what she was about to do.

***

Tanner, Inc. had offices in a tall downtown building with a sweeping staircase below and a helicopter pad above. As a little girl, Tensley had been intimidated by it. As a woman, she found its size and seeming immobility somewhat comforting. Anything that large, with that much invested in it, would go on forever, wouldn't it?

But she knew better. Even if her mother didn't.

Now as she stood before the building, holding Kate's handbag tight against her chest in an attempt to slow the hammering of her heart, she could only think about the woman at the company's helm and what she would have to say to an estranged daughter. A daughter who quite possibly had brought unimaginable shame, in Esme's eyes, anyway, upon the storied family name.

One innocent visit to a psychic and everything's shot to hell.

Tensley cleared her throat, drew her shoulders back and held her chin high. Then she walked toward the building and through the wide glass doors that opened with a whoosh.

Once in the lobby, her heart lifted at the familiar sight of the gray-haired, grandfatherly security guard who'd come on board a few years ago. The two of them had a routine. Every morning, he'd greet her with a huge smile and a, "How are you today, Miss Tensley?" She'd say a cheery hello and lift her Starbucks cup in greeting. He'd tell her, with a grin, that too much coffee was bad for her. She'd reply that she could never have too much. He'd shake his head and then touch his finger to his head in a little salute.

And she'd know everything was going to be fine that day. One way or another.

But today, he didn't say anything to her. She lifted her hand, minus the cup of coffee, and called, "Good morning, Arthur!"

His brows drew together. "Good morning, Miss," he responded, his tone dutiful.

Arthur didn't recognize her. *Arthur*. Her heart sank. Despite the odds, she'd hoped he would.

She headed for the elevators. The security guard stepped in front of her. "Do you have an appointment, Miss?"

Tensley hesitated. "I—" She looked away, not meeting his eyes. "Don't need one."

"Can I have you check in with the young lady over here, please?" Arthur gestured toward a receptionist with a blond ponytail, who bounced to life at his direction.

"May I help you?"

"I'm here to see Esme Tanner."

The young woman picked up the phone. "Your name, please."

Once again, Tensley straightened her shoulders. "Tensley Tanner-Starbrook. Her daughter."

The receptionist blinked. "Her daughter?" It didn't seem to register with her.

Fear shivered through Tensley. It wasn't possible that Madame Claire could have erased her parentage, along with everything else…was it? *Oh God, oh God, oh—*

Arthur stepped over at that, indicating the receptionist should put the phone down. "I've got this," he said to her.

Of course, Tensley thought with relief. Esme's daughter wouldn't have to be announced.

Other people walked past them, heading toward the elevators with the cool confidence of those who belonged. One woman called out, "Hi, Arthur." He gave her a smile and the one-finger salute Tensley had thought belonged to her. Then his expression turned grave. He took Tensley's elbow.

For a second, she thought he was going to apologize, tell her it was all a mistake and how glad he was to see her back. The next second, she realized he was escorting her toward the front doors. "Wait a minute," she said. "What's going on?"

"Now, Miss," he replied, not unkindly. "Your mother's been pretty clear about this."

"About what?" Panic caused her voice to rise, waver.

"I'm not saying it's right she doesn't want you coming here." He kept his tone low, likely trying to save her from public embarrassment.

"Arthur. You're making a mistake." Though she tried her best to use her vice-president-in-charge-of-some-things voice, it didn't work. She sounded like a kid protesting being sent to her room.

"Yes, she is," he said with a sigh. "But let's not make this any harder than it has to be." The automatic door opened at their approach. "Take care, Miss. It looks like rain."

"Arthur," she pleaded.

He hesitated, but then turned away.

Tensley's eyes filled. The woman had given instructions not to let her past the front desk? She stepped through the door, head bent with the humiliation of a daughter rejected by her mother. Maybe she'd done something worse than become a stripper, with a record. At what point did a parent draw the line and disown a child? How bad did things have to be?

She felt ridiculous, dressed in Kate's suit that didn't fit her quite right. As though she were Julia Roberts in *Pretty Woman*, trying to get the snooty people on Rodeo Drive to wait on her when she knew they could see she didn't belong.

Maybe she was a hooker, too. Wouldn't that just figure.

With her head still bowed, she didn't see the woman who brushed into her until it had happened. She looked up to meet the startled eyes of Jen Joseph, a childhood acquaintance who had gone to work in Tanner Broadcasting's accounting department after high school. Though Tensley's office was on another floor, the two women had seen each other occasionally in the hallways. Neither had been happy about it.

"Tensley," Jen breathed. "What are you doing here?"

Irritation pushed humiliation to one side. "My family owns the place," was her terse reply.

"I know, but…"

"But what?"

"Your mother says you're not welcome here." Jen had never been known for her tact.

"So I hear."

"Well, you can't blame her," was Jen's reply.

"I think you can."

"Your lifestyle isn't exactly, you know, up to Tanner standards."

Prim little bitch. Anger took over from irritation, elbowing humiliation out of the way. "What do you know about it?"

Jen made a move toward the door. "I have to get to work."

"Wait!" Prim little bitch, or not, Jen might be the answer to what Tensley needed. A way to see her mother. Because no matter what order Esme Tanner might have given, there was now a principle involved. The principle that Tensley got to tell off her mother, face-to-face. For the first time ever.

Jen hesitated, creating enough of an opening for Tensley to stick a stiletto through. "I need your help," she said.

The other woman shook her head. "I can't help you."

"I have to see my mother."

"For God's sake, Tensley." Exasperation peppered Jen's voice. "I'm not an idiot. I'd like to keep my job."

She'd like to think Jen was overreacting, but Tensley knew her mother too well. Then inspiration struck. Could she do it? Probably not, normally, but after this kind of humiliation… "I have to see her. It might be the last time."

The other woman's expression turned doubtful. "You're going somewhere?"

"It's not me." She paused to let that sink in. "And don't you think a mother and daughter should at least have a chance to say a final goodbye, no matter what's happened between them?"

"I don't understand."

"Of course not. She wouldn't let on about something like that."

"She's *sold* the company?"

"No." Although that wouldn't have been a bad one to go with. "That wouldn't happen…until after."

Jen looked annoyed. "I don't have time for games. I have a job to get to."

Tensley curled her fingers into a fist, but she kept her voice cool. "I should never have said anything. She would hate for anyone to know all she's going through." She shook her head. "She's always been so strong, so healthy. It's not fair."

Understanding dawned on Jen's face. "She's sick?"

Tensley lifted a shoulder. "I can't speak for her."

"Oh my God. What will happen to—everyone's jobs?" Jen fell silent, the ramifications apparently too huge to talk about.

Tensley gritted her teeth. "I'm pretty sure the company will carry on."

"Maybe." Jen didn't sound convinced.

"I should have a chance to say goodbye to her, don't you think?" She touched Jen's arm in a plea. "She's the only mother I have. And once someone, you know…" she said, looking down, "you never get that chance again."

"Sick," Jen repeated. "She doesn't look like it. I'll bet she's never even had a cold."

Not to Tensley's knowledge. "With this—you wouldn't be able to tell. She'll look normal right up until the…you know. End."

Jen had never been the brightest. "Really?" She shuddered. "I hope the company doesn't go to some huge conglomerate that doesn't even know what we do."

Or the most compassionate. "Really. So will you help me?"

Jen's attention slid back to Tensley. "Help you?"

"Let me in the back entrance." It was locked twenty-four seven. Security didn't patrol there and even though there was a camera, she was pretty sure no one looked at it very often.

"Oh. I don't know about that."

"It's my last chance to tell the woman who gave birth to me how much she—" She stopped, then tried again. "How much I love her." *Cue the dramatic music.* Except that, unfortunately—for Tensley, anyway—it might be true.

Jen chewed her lower lip, but then appeared to make up her mind. Maybe she'd decided that if Esme Tanner had so little time left, this couldn't be a career-ender. Either that, or she'd finally sprouted a sympathetic side. "Fine," she said. "Meet me there in fifteen minutes. You know where it is?"

"I know where it is."

"I had nothing to do with this, though. You got it?"

Tensley nodded. "And you're not going to tell anyone about my mother, right?"

Jen slanted her gaze toward the door. "Of course not," she said before she turned on her heel and walked away.

So much for sympathy. Tensley knew two things about Jen. Not only was she born without the tact gene, she couldn't keep a secret to save her life.

Just wait until Esme Tanner found out that her employees thought she was taking her last breaths. This time her shiver went from head to toe.

Tensley hoped, really hoped, that the end justified the means. It could be that her mother would be relieved to see her only child, the daughter she'd smothered with hopes, dreams and expectations.

Or not.

CHAPTER EIGHTEEN

It took Jen twenty-five minutes, but she finally made it to the back entrance to open the door. Tensley could tell, by the other woman's flushed cheeks and bright eyes that she'd already begun spreading the word about Esme Tanner.

"You didn't say anything about my mother, did you?"

Jen looked away. "I don't even know why you would ask me that."

"Because you told Bobby Warner I liked him." *Talk about your third grade drama.*

Jen's mouth opened and closed, her eyes narrowing. "He had to get you out of his system."

Tensley's mind had already gone to the meeting with her mother. It took her a few seconds to return to the subject of Bobby. "He was eight years old. I would have been out of his system by recess."

Her mother's office was on the tenth floor. Would it be better to climb all those flights of stairs or follow Jen down the hallway and risk the elevator?

Jen's hand suddenly flashed in front of her face, a ring on her third finger catching the light. "Maybe you don't know my last name now," she said, a note of triumph in her voice. "It's Warner."

"Bobby's your husband?"

"He is."

So there had been a method to Jen's madness. Even at the age of eight. "Do you have little Bobbys?"

That seemed to ruffle Jen's calm, at least for a minute. "Not yet, but we will."

"Congratulations," Tensley said, because she couldn't think of anything else.

Jen nodded, folding her arms across her chest. "We're very happy."

"Great." Tensley wondered how this had never come up when they'd passed in the halls. In Tensley's real life. She motioned toward the stairs. "You don't have to worry about me, now. I'll just go up this way."

Jen's laugh echoed against the concrete. "Oh, believe me. I haven't worried about you for a long time."

Tensley didn't have time to figure out what that might mean. She had to get to her mother's office and make things right. Or at least not as bad as they apparently were. "Okay. Thanks, then." She grabbed the metal railing to begin the climb to the tenth floor.

Jen speed-walked toward the door, presumably to spread more gossip.

So far, not good.

By the time she scaled the sixth flight of stairs, Tensley was pleasantly surprised to find she wasn't even breathing hard. By the tenth floor, she was congratulating herself on being in such good shape. Who would have thought?

She wrapped her fingers around the door handle and pulled. Hard. And with defiance. Esme Tanner had issued orders to keep her daughter out of her own family's workplace. That was wrong on so many levels, Tensley couldn't even begin to count them.

The door opened so easily, she stumbled backward and had to catch herself. Not the most graceful way to make an entrance. She tugged her jacket down and pressed Kate's handbag in front of her chest. This meeting wasn't going to begin with a raised eyebrow, unless it was Tensley's.

Chin raised, she walked into the hushed reverence of the tenth floor, her shoes sinking into the carpet with each step. Her office was on the opposite side of the floor from her mother's, but she couldn't resist going by it first to see who had her position.

She kept a sharp watch for anyone who might spot her and alert security, but she didn't see anyone. Most people were likely at lunch. Chances were good her mother would be in her office, she knew. Esme Tanner preferred to spend the lunch hour alone.

Tensley tiptoed up and down the row, looking at the nameplate inscriptions. All of the same senior executives she knew, only one of them in his office, but with his eyes locked on his computer, he didn't see her. Just as well. She'd never liked Mark Dorlan. Maybe it was because of the way he looked at her, with that half-smirk that said he knew she only had a job because her last name was Tanner. Or maybe it was because her mother listened to every word he said.

Didn't matter. She was just sorry he hadn't been sucked into Madame Claire's psychic vacuum and ended up at some other company, smirking at someone else.

Then she came to her office. Except that it wasn't. Through the open door, she could see a clean, uncluttered desk and framed photos on the walls. Photos of exotic places, with the same brown-haired woman smiling front and center in each. In one, she held a fishing rod and a huge fish; in another, she smiled from the driver's seat of a sand-colored jeep, her arm draped across the steering wheel. In still another, she waved from the pilot's window of a small airplane.

Tensley peered at the nameplate next to the door. *Keira Knudsen, Vice President of Strategic Initiatives.*

Tensley's job.

The woman looked *way* too confident and competent. The only saving grace was that Mark Dorlan probably despised her. Unfortunately, that thought didn't help much right now. What the hell was some pilot-slash-fisherwoman-slash-jeep-driver doing in *her* job?

Tensley's breathing came so fast and her heart beat so hard, she could feel it thumping in her ears. With every step she took toward her mother's office, the pounding increased, until by the time she passed the desk of her mother's assistant, every part of her was trembling. But if she had to crawl in, she would.

"Hey!" she heard the assistant call. But the woman was no match for Tensley, who had already reached the door to Esme Tanner's office and turned the handle.

Tensley launched through the doorway, pulling up short at the sight of her mother, a smoldering volcano in a Marc Jacobs suit, rumbling to life at the center of the expansive desk. Their eyes caught and held as Esme Tanner shot to her feet.

"I'm sorry, Ms. Tanner," the assistant said from behind Tensley. "I tried to stop her."

"Leave us, Christine," Tensley's mother ordered.

The assistant did exactly that, meekly closing the door behind her.

Esme moved from behind the desk. "Sit."

"I'll stand." *For as long as I can.*

"As you wish." Her mother drew up a chair and sat down.

Tensley hesitated, and then dropped into the chair opposite her.

Esme crossed her legs, evaluating her daughter with a gaze on low boil. "I was given to understand you had left."

"I was given to understand you had ordered me to."

There went the eyebrow. A perfect arch, reaching toward the sky.

Tensley stood her ground. "Is that not correct?"

"You've lost weight."

"Must be the drugs."

At the look of shock that crossed her mother's face, Tensley backpedaled. "I'm kidding." She also crossed her legs, finding a new sense of freedom in saying whatever she liked to her mother.

Esme rose from her seat, gripping the back of her chair until her fingertips turned white. "I'm not so sure about that." Her words were coated in hot, rolling lava. "Which is why I said our relationship could resume only when you had put your life back together."

Tensley tipped her head. "What exactly is the criteria for that? Because I'm working, paying taxes. Earning my own way. *Not* on drugs."

"You take your clothes off for a living. I'd hardly call that an occupation a Tanner would be proud of."

Tensley splayed her fingers across her borrowed skirt, to keep them from making a fist. "At least I have a job. More than you would apparently give me."

"I do not give anything. People earn their way."

"People need a chance to show what they can do."

"They show that with the choices they make."

Her fingers clenched despite her best efforts. Tensley hid them by digging her fists into the upholstered chair. "You don't know anything about my choices or what I'm capable of. You don't know anything about me."

Her mother's smile was brittle. "Ah, but I do. You were bright enough, you could have gone to college, Tensley. You could have joined me here. To help carry on the family business I've worked so hard to build."

I did. Tensley swallowed a lump in her throat and tried to force out words that would redeem her. "I'm still bright."

"I think not or you wouldn't be here."

A slap of cold water across the face. Tensley put her fingers to her cheek. "I'm here because I want to talk to you. Like it or not, you are my mother."

"I cannot condone such a lifestyle. I raised you to use your brain, not your body." She gave a shiver of what looked like disgust.

This was not going at all as Tensley had planned. Her stomach squeezed into a knot of hurt and confusion. *Don't say it*, she told herself. *Don't go there*. And yet she did. "I'm your daughter. Your only child. You can throw me aside that easily?"

Esme Tanner turned her head, staring through her office window.

Silence. Pressing on her heart until she thought it would burst. "You can't even love me?" she rasped.

After a long minute, Esme spun around, meeting Tensley's eyes. "I loved you far too much to lower my expectations of you or compromise my principles."

Past tense. Tears stabbed at the backs of Tensley's eyes. She wished her mother would take her in her arms for one of those stiff hugs, with that hard pat on the back, to let her daughter know that it would all be okay, that she hadn't meant the things she'd just said, that of course she loved her. How could she not?

She wished— She wished she could make her understand what had happened, that this wasn't the life she lived, that she hadn't really grown up to disappoint her mother. Most of the time, anyway.

But a woman who couldn't understand how her daughter had fallen into the line of work she had would never understand about a psychic with too much power for her own screwed-up good.

The wail inside her was silent, only for Tensley's ears, just as it always had been. And it came from a baffled, wounded little girl. She struggled for control, for the mask that was effortless for Esme Tanner, but elusive for her daughter.

A knock at the door. Tensley took advantage of the interruption to turn away, pinching her leg to give herself another kind of pain to concentrate on.

Esme Tanner lifted her voice to say, "Come in."

Her assistant opened the door and took a nervous step inside. "Is everything all right, Ms. Tanner? Security is here." Arthur hovered behind her. Both of them cast wary glances at Tensley.

"No cause for alarm, Christine," Esme said smoothly, as though she and her daughter had been discussing nothing more than the weather. She turned to Tensley. "Arthur will see you out."

Clearly dismissed, Tensley rose from her chair, even less certain of herself than she had been when she'd come in. Christine backed out of the office, but Arthur stood waiting.

"One more thing," Esme said when Tensley reached the door.

Tensley stopped and then turned slowly. Carefully.

Her mother made a small circle with her finger, near the chest area. "A pin, my dear, would be a very good idea."

Tensley looked down and saw the gap where the fabric couldn't quite close over her boobs. Her pink bra winked up at her, matched, she was sure, by the pink flaming in her cheeks.

Without another word, on legs that felt as though they were made of rubber, she walked out of Esme Tanner's office. As she and Arthur neared the elevators, she thought she might have heard her mother call her name. But she kept going, the mirrored elevator doors taking less than a second to open and hasten her exit.

She kept her head down so that her hair would cover her face and pressed the small of her back against the elevator wall.

Arthur muttered, "It's not right."

Tensley couldn't trust her voice enough to reply.

"Kids take detours. Mine sure have."

She wondered why she hadn't ever thought about Arthur having a family. Tensley risked a sidelong look through her hair.

The older man shook his head. "You don't throw them out of your life when they need you the most."

Tensley lifted her head and swept her hair back, fingers brushing her still-warm cheeks. "She has standards."

Arthur made a sound of derision. "Maybe she should try following them herself."

Tensley couldn't remember anyone who knew Esme Tanner, even in passing, daring to suggest anything negative about her character. The woman was the standard everyone else was measured by. Anyone who worked for, associated with, or was related to her, anyway. She turned to Arthur. "I don't understand."

He opened his mouth to say something, but appeared to change his mind. "Forget it."

The doors opened to the lobby with a ping. "How many children do you have?" Tensley asked.

"Six. Four boys, two girls."

"Do they all live here?" They passed the receptionist, walking toward the front doors.

"Two of them do. The others are in Chicago, Toronto, San Francisco. With my grandchildren."

"Must be hard for you not to see them." She'd bet Arthur was a good dad. And grandpa.

They stopped in front of the doors. "Not as hard as it would have been on my wife."

Tensley glanced down to see a gold ring on the security guard's left hand. "Is she—aren't you married?"

Pain crossed his face. "She passed on last year."

"I'm sorry." She laid her fingers on the crisp sleeve of his shirt. "Was she sick?"

"Cancer got her."

Why hadn't she known this? She'd probably lifted her Starbucks cup to him every day, expecting her coffee lecture, while he was going through the pain of losing his wife. "I didn't know."

"No reason you would." He gave her a tight smile. "Look, your mama will come around someday."

She could tell he didn't believe that any more than she did. "I'm not holding my breath."

"You've gotta make your own way, then."

Impulsively, she leaned forward and gave him a quick, hard hug, catching a whiff of older man cologne.

"Go on, now," he said gruffly. "You don't need her."

If only that were true.

From the corner of her eye, she caught sight of a familiar figure. A tall man, impeccably dressed, with a stride and half-smirk that turned her stomach. Mark Dorlan, Tanner Cable's director of finance. She felt a brief panic that he would spot her, take pleasure in her humiliation, but instead, he looked straight through her and kept on walking.

He didn't recognize her. Sadness washed through her at yet another reminder she wasn't "in Kansas" anymore. What a time to be stuck without a Toto.

"Goodbye, Arthur. I hope you get to see your grandchildren soon." Tensley pushed her way out the building's front door and began walking, her heart numb. Whatever irrational hope she'd held that Esme Tanner would welcome her apparently prodigal daughter home and reinstate her in her old job had disappeared as fast as a stripper's bra.

Tensley would have to make her own way back. By helping the one man who had only ever proven to be her downfall.

The odds were not in her favor.

***

From his car half a block away, Detective Max Hunter watched Tensley walk out of the building, her head down, looking every bit as defeated as she had as a teen after a session with her mother. He still couldn't believe Esme Tanner would acknowledge a daughter in

Tensley's line of work. The woman had never been able to see farther than a business card.

He straightened and put his hand on the metal of his car handle, determined to go after Ten, to tell her yet again that nothing her mother said or did mattered. Yeah, he'd told himself he wouldn't get involved. To hell with that. This was Tensley and he wasn't about to see her get hurt by that evil bitch. Again.

Then he saw something else. The face he'd been wracking his brain to put a name to. The man who didn't belong in the strip club, but who had been there all the same. Max watched him stride past Tensley to greet a dark-haired woman carrying a leather briefcase.

With a building to link him to, the man's name came back to him. Mark Dorlan, a senior executive with Tanner Cable. Max had filled in for his boss at a City Club meeting several months ago where Dorlan had given a presentation. Afterward, Max had understood what the term "death by PowerPoint" meant. Probably why he had blocked out the guy's name; he didn't ever want to have to sit through something like that again.

So what the hell had Dorlan been doing sneaking into the back office of Gary's Gorgeous Grecians?

The woman Dorlan had greeted turned and began walking with him, away from the building. Their heads were close and a breeze pushed part of her hair over her face, but Max still recognized her. David Digman's campaign manager. The same David Digman who was running for reelection to City Council. And the same David Digman who had received a donation from an organization that may have been set up by Gary Burns.

To quote a character from a book he and Tensley had spent a teenage summer reading out loud to each other on a blanket spread over a field of summer grass…curiouser and curiouser.

Or maybe more appropriate, to quote Detective Max Hunter…holy shit.

CHAPTER NINETEEN

Tuesday must not be a big day for ogling naked women, Tensley decided as she wiped down the bar for the twentieth time that night. Better not be many more nights like this, when business and tips were practically nonexistent, or she'd never make enough money to get out of this place.

Only one possible upside to this little customer activity—Gary wasn't around. She hadn't seen him all night, which might give her an opportunity to make another run at his office.

She set the cloth down behind the counter and watched as the red-headed woman she'd talked to a few nights ago stepped onto the stage, in full Fiery Farrina costume. Tonight she carried a long black whip to accentuate the black leather and lace costume that made her pale skin glow in the blue spotlight. Her black boots had heels at least eight inches high.

The music pulsated as she moved forward on the stage, one long leg at a time, beckoning an invitation to the two lone men in the audience, each sprawled at a table of his own, drink in hand.

Fiery Farrina, aka Sarah, lifted her whip.

One man straightened; the other leaned forward. On the downbeat of the music, Sarah snapped the whip, causing both the men and Tensley to jump. She continued dancing to the music, wrapping her legs around a pole and teasing off the skimpy piece of leather that covered her breasts—all while never missing a downbeat and corresponding crack of the whip.

The two men were mesmerized. Tensley was fascinated. How did the woman manage to do so many things at once, while making every one of them look effortless? If Tensley were to try cracking a whip like that, she'd probably manage to snap off one of her own fingers.

Nothing like a dangling appendage to turn on a man. Tensley snorted at the thought and then put her hand to her mouth to cover for it, not that anyone could have heard over the pounding music.

Keeping one hand on the bar for balance, she began shadowing Sarah's steps. One leg forward, then curling it around a virtual pole and doing a half spin. Wrist up and a crack of the whip in time to the music. And another crack of the whip. Not *that* hard.

A full spin and she did it again. Kind of fun. She pictured Max's face, watching her on the stage, Tensley in full control—the take-charge woman she'd always wanted to be. Instead of the lovesick teenager she'd slipped back into as soon as he'd landed in her bed.

How pathetic. She'd been the only one to feel anything that night. As far as Max Hunter was concerned, she was a diversion. A game of woulda, coulda, don't.

Tensley dropped her chin, staring at the linoleum floor beneath the padded mat. She needed a new checklist. A short one. Get the dirt on Gary. Give it to Max. Get the hell outta here.

And if she never learned her lesson, then she never did. She was the only person she could rely on to change things. Even her best friend had let her down, putting her in a position where Madame Claire could wreak havoc on her life, without Tensley even realizing it.

Tensley raised her head, looking around Gary's Gorgeous Grecians with a new resolve. Even if she screwed things up trying to get out of this place, they couldn't get much worse than they already were.

Just ask her mother.

She spied Milo lumbering in her direction. "Hey!" she called over the sound of the two patrons clapping for Fiery Farrina. "I'm taking a break."

The big man frowned. "Who's going to watch the bar?"

"Who's drinking right now?" Tensley gestured at the men. "They've been nursing those beers for half an hour."

Milo twisted his mouth, clearly not happy. "Fine. Ten minutes."

"Twenty."

"Fifteen." He sounded injured by the negotiation.

"Great. Twenty, then." She gave him a quick smile that wasn't one. "Thanks."

"Damn, Lila. What am I going to say if Gary comes in?"

"Is he supposed to?"

"Hell if I know."

"Then don't worry about it." Tensley bolted from behind the bar and toward the back of the club before Milo could say anything more. She nearly slipped in liquid pooled on the floor. Someone's stale beer. Great. "Hey, Milo," she called. "Get someone to clean this up?" She pointed at the floor and then made sure she disappeared behind the curtain separating the employee area before he could say that it would be her cleaning it up.

She had enough trouble getting the smell of this place out of her clothes; she was pretty sure the combination of sweat, alcohol and lust was seeping out of her hair follicles now. No matter how hard she scrubbed in the shower, she could still smell it.

Once inside the dressing room, she sank into a chair, resting her head against its back and closing her eyes. Too bad she hadn't brought a drink with her. She could use one.

"Smoke?"

Tensley opened her eyes. Sarah, still in costume, had dropped into the chair next to her and was holding out a cigarette.

"No. But thanks." Tensley straightened.

"K." Sarah lit the cigarette and snapped the lighter shut. She took a long drag and blew out the smoke.

"The routine with the whip," Tensley ventured, "was really good. How long did it take you to learn to do that?"

"Thanks." Sarah inhaled again and blew the smoke out. "I grew up on a farm. Been playing with ropes and whips since I was a kid."

"I'd probably slice my arm off if I tried something like that."

Sarah flashed a smile. "You probably would." She crossed her legs and turned away.

After a few minutes of silence, Tensley ventured, "You're a long way from the farm."

"Yeah, well." A half-laugh. "You get knocked up at sixteen, get thrown out of your house, that's what happens." She tipped her head, thinking. "I used to compete in team roping. Was pretty damn good at it, too. Maybe I should change my costume. Use a rope instead of a whip in my act." She exhaled a stream of white smoke. "What do you think?"

"I like it. Tie up the guys in the audience until they cough up more tips."

"No shit. Cheap sons of bitches." The woman's mouth, carefully lined in red lipstick, made an "O" when she exhaled.

"Tough way to make a living." Tensley made it a statement, but meant it as a question.

"Only because, most of the time, it's too much money to leave."

"Right," Tensley was quick to agree. "Especially when you have a child, I'm guessing."

Sarah didn't answer.

"How old is your…" She took her best guess. "Daughter?"

The other woman's expression softened. "Eight already. I can't believe it."

Tensley did a rapid calculation. If she'd become pregnant at sixteen, Sarah was only twenty-three or twenty-four. Her cautious eyes and the set of her jaw made her seem older. "Do you ever wish she could grow up on a farm, like you did?"

Sarah eyed her.

"I mean—" Tensley struggled. "I don't know much about farm life." *Actually, I don't know anything about farm life.* "But it seems like it would be a nice way to, you know, grow up. Quiet. Peaceful. Safe," she finished lamely.

Sarah reached for an ashtray and stubbed out her cigarette. "I don't want Halley within fifty miles of a farm. Or a rodeo. Cowboys are dangerous."

"I think they're pretty cute. Great butts. You know, especially when they wear those…" She gestured at her legs, unable to think of the word.

"Chaps," Sarah supplied.

"That's it."

"Try a ripped cowboy wearing only his hat and a pair of tight, worn-in jeans."

Tensley pictured him. "I'd go for that."

"Yeah, me too. It's how I ended up pregnant at sixteen."

The chair next to them scraped against the floor. Tensley turned to see Terrible Tawny sit down, in full makeup, but dressed in jeans and a T-shirt with "#1 Bitch" written in green letters across it. Tawny shot her gaze toward Sarah. "Seriously. A cowboy?"

Sarah didn't say anything, just lifted her shoulder.

Something about the movement created a spark of sympathy in Tensley. "Are you still with him?" she asked.

Sarah gave another one of those half-laughs. "That's a good one." She paused. "I'm pretty sure he doesn't remember me. Wish I didn't remember *him*." She looked at the clock on the wall. "Gotta get dressed and out of here. Then I have to count up my tips and figure out if I have enough to pay for my kid's music lessons this month." She rose from her seat. As she passed by Tawny, she dropped her voice to add a question. "Do you know if I'm gonna get any extra time tomorrow?"

"Yeah, you will," the other woman answered. "Get that babysitter to stay."

Sarah hesitated, then nodded.

"Sarah," Tensley called.

The woman looked back over her shoulder.

"Would you be willing to teach me how to work a rope sometime?"

Sarah frowned. "Only need one cowgirl act."

"Oh. I wasn't thinking of it for the act. I just think it looks like fun. I didn't grow up on a farm. I grew up on a…city."

Sarah drew her fiery brows together in a perplexed frown. "Yeah, sure."

"Great. Thanks." *A little too much enthusiasm.* She tried a correction. "You know, because it just would be good to know."

Now Tawny was the one with the perplexed frown. "Girl, how do you get through life?" she wanted to know.

"I don't know what you're talking about," Tensley lied. But it was only *this* life she had trouble with. Mostly.

After Sarah had gone, Tensley asked Tawny, "How do you get extra time?" She didn't want to, God knows, she didn't want to. But it could help her get Max what he needed and help her save enough money to get out from under this place.

Just in case Madame Claire wasn't right about everything reversing.

Not going there.

Tawny shook her head. "That's not for you."

"How do you know?"

"You ask too many questions."

"If it means more money, I won't ask questions."

Tawny's laugh was short, hard. "Like that's gonna happen. Ever."

"You said yourself that I'm behind in my…" *What was it?* Oh. "…house rent."

The other woman got up and went to her locker. She paused, hand gripping the lock, and turned to Tensley. "You don't want to make money that way."

Tensley sat up straighter. "Why not?"

"Told you. Can't go ten seconds without asking stupid questions." Tawny jerked the lock open and slammed the door against its neighbor.

Tensley flinched at the sound of metal on metal and leaned back in the chair, closing her eyes. If Tawny thought she asked too many questions now, she hadn't seen anything yet. Getting the answers to those questions was the only thing that was going to get her out of here.

***

"You went to see your mother," Kate repeated. "Why?"

"Not only did I go see her, I spread a rumor around the company that she's dying."

Kate's chin dropped. "You did not. Be serious."

"Oh yes, I did." Tensley ran a hand through her hair. "Probably not the smartest thing I ever did, but I had a reason."

"What reason could you possibly have to—?" Words seemed to fail her best friend. "That woman will take you apart."

"Oh, don't worry. She already did that. And she hadn't even heard about the rumor yet." Much as she tried to keep it away, hurt wobbled through her voice.

Kate curled a piece of paper between her fingers. "That sucks. I'm sorry."

"Nothing I can do about it now."

The paper crumpled into a ball in Kate's fist. "The woman is evil."

"So I hear."

Her best friend looked at her long and hard. "You know, Max tried to see you after the whole thing with Rhonda. To explain."

Max. Tensley's stomach did a somersault. She picked up her own piece of paper, folding it first one way and then the other. "What does that have to do with my mother?"

"She sent Leo after him."

Tensley shuddered. Leo had been a sharp-toothed, muscular Rottweiler her mother insisted on getting when her daughter entered high school. Tensley had been scared to death of him. The dog had even slept in a military-ready position. "Leo would have made sure Max didn't get anywhere near me." Against her will, a spot in her heart warmed at the thought that he'd tried.

"Exactly. Max ended up in the emergency room."

Tensley froze. "What?"

"That dog bit him in the face."

The scar. She'd seen it that first night, when he'd driven her home from the club. She *knew* it hadn't been there before. She'd known and loved every inch of that man, and then some, in high school. "Along his jaw," she said.

Kate nodded. "It healed, but still. She didn't even call for help."

"I can't believe it." The problem was that she could. "I worked with my mother. Things weren't great, but we got along okay."

Stinky padded into the kitchen, followed by Blinky.

"Are you sure about that?" Kate asked.

Better not to answer. "At least I don't have to feel bad about what I did today."

"Just wait until she finds out how many people are already planning her funeral."

Tensley shook her head. "That won't be so bad. It's what she'll do when she finds out how many people are planning for *after* her funeral." For the fifth or fiftieth time in her life, beginning when she was a kid glued to the TV, she wondered why Elyse Keaton couldn't have been her mother instead. Strong, but compassionate. Driven, but still liked her kids.

And now that she thought about it, Tensley decided she would really like life to come with a pre-recorded laugh track.

For all those times when you just couldn't make it happen on your own.

***

When Tensley arrived at the club, Sarah was sitting at a table in the dancers' dressing room, a scowl on her face as she stared at a thick brochure.

"What's wrong?"

Sarah didn't answer. She pulled her red hair back with both hands, her eyes never leaving the piece in front of her.

Tensley leaned down and carefully picked up one end of the brochure. It was a catalog from the community college.

"Hey, leave it alone," the other woman was quick to say, grabbing the catalog away and tossing it in the trash. "I was bored. Needed something to look at."

"Are you thinking about going to school?"

"Nah, they asked me to teach a class," Sarah replied, sarcasm coating her words. "How to take off your clothes like you mean it. One-oh-one."

Tensley narrowed her eyes. "It's not as though you *wouldn't* have something to teach them. You're a self-employed businessperson."

Pink stained Sarah's cheeks as she looked away. "Yeah, right."

"This is like any other business. There's profit and loss. How much is your time worth? What expenses do you have? How do you make sure there are more nights when tips are good than there are nights with cheap sons of bitches?"

The other woman turned back, slowly raising her eyes to meet Tensley's. She opened her mouth to speak, then closed it again. After a moment, she said, "I haven't—you know. Thought of it like that."

"Maybe you should."

Silence. Then Sarah shook her head. "I'm a stripper. I don't know shit about business or I wouldn't be here. I'd be running a company or something."

"You are running a company. Your own."

Sarah pursed her lips and crossed her arms over her chest. "If I knew how to figure that stuff out, I would have done it a long time ago. Besides, all I'd find out is that Gary's the one making all the money. And I'm the one stuck here because I can't do anything else."

Tensley leaned forward in her chair. This could be it. The way she could help someone. Her ticket back home. Sarah had a problem that needed solving. Could there be a lesson in there somewhere for Tensley? God, she hoped so. She really, really hoped so.

"Listen to me," she said to Sarah, trying hard to keep the excitement from exploding out of her. "I hated business classes when I first started taking them. There was no way I was going to stay with that major. Where's the romance in a bunch of calculations? But it was the only way my mother was going to pay for college, so I stuck with it and it hasn't been that bad. I've even used it sometimes. Like now. I can help you figure out how much you're making. And how you can make more."

"Right." Sarah snorted and looked away, then back. "You're not serious."

"Oh, you have no idea how serious I am." *Get ready, Gary.* Tensley Tanner-Starbrook's business degree was finally going to get put to good use.

CHAPTER TWENTY

True to his word, the next time Max arranged for the two of them to meet, it was at Sol's diner. A public place. The front door squeaked when Tensley pushed it open and a rush of warm air followed her inside, ruffling her hair.

She wasn't sure about this. Not at all sure about this. But at least she was moving on to Plan B.

Plan B did not include Max Hunter.

Her bravado lasted until she saw him sitting at a table facing the door, in a navy T-shirt that stretched across the broad muscles of his chest and upper arms, his black hair tousled carelessly across his forehead and curling at the nape of his neck, blue eyes framed by dark brows and a day's growth of whiskers.

His gaze locked on hers. Hers wavered and then locked on his.

From the corner of her eye, she saw Sol set a plate down at the counter and stand silent. Watching.

Max slid from the booth and rose to his feet. "Ten."

The single syllable said everything and nothing. She could have melted in his arms and strangled him, all at the same time. Instead, she said only, "Max." And waited.

Her feet might as well have been dipped in glue, because they would not move from the diner's linoleum floor.

Sol, in an apparent bid to make sure his diner wasn't the scene of the world's most awkward reunion moment, lumbered to her side. He took her arm, loosening whatever had her feet locked, and steered her to Max's table. "Getcha some coffee?" he asked.

"Yes. Please." Tensley let him guide her into the booth.

Max sat down again, opposite her. He already had coffee in front of him.

Sol set a cup down in front of Tensley and splashed coffee into it. "What the hell did you do this time, Ace?" he muttered in Max's direction.

Max shot him a glare and then turned his attention back to Tensley. "I said I was sorry for leaving like that." His low voice caressed her across their steaming cups.

She took a long, slow sip of coffee. The china cup shuddered when she set it back down on the table. "Don't worry about it. I haven't," she lied.

"But if we want to get Gary—"

"Let's be clear. *You're* the one who wants to get Gary."

He leaned against the booth's high back. "You don't?"

"I'm not going to have to deal with him anymore. I'm getting out of there. I'm getting a different job." Oh, no. Now she was going to have to. And who exactly would hire a stripper with a record?

Max nodded, evaluating her with the deep blue gaze that turned her insides into a frothing, heated pool of pure want. Why, why had he come back into her life? Whichever life she was in. "I'm glad," he said. "You deserve better."

"Thanks." She looked away. "I'll finish the informant work, though."

He leaned forward, putting his hand on hers.

She wasn't prepared for his touch. Sparks shot through her. Alarmed, she drew her hand away. She didn't want to confuse his professional interest in her with his—fleeting personal interest. *Ow.* She clutched at her stomach, pushing her index finger in hard.

He didn't react for a minute. Then he nodded, back to cop mode, and looked down at the table. He drummed his fingers on its surface. "Speaking of that, do you have anything for me?"

"There's something about 'extra time.' One of the dancers asked Terrible Tawny if she'd be able to get it, so she would have enough money to pay her bills, and the answer was yes."

"Overtime."

"No." She raised her gaze, steeling herself for the physical reaction she knew would follow. And there it was. The memory of her and Max, naked, coming together—*bam*. *Throw it in the mental Tupperware.*

"Then what is it?"

Burp the lid. Store it on a shelf. Where it can't hurt anyone. "I'm not sure yet. But when I asked if I could get extra time, Tawny said I ask too many questions."

Max tilted his chin. "Keep going."

"She also said I didn't want to earn money that way."

He leaned forward again, pressing his forearms into the table. She watched his face tighten as he processed this information. Then he said, "We have to get into Gary's office."

Her. Max. On a dangerous mission. Together. She heard the Tupperware lid pop open. *Damn it.* "What do you mean...we?"

He grabbed her hand and held on tight. "This might be bigger than I thought and I'm not going to let you get in over your head. I have to be there with you."

Yes! No-o-o. So no.

"Don't you have to get a search warrant and all that? I don't."

He looked away and she knew she was right. "You've been watching too many episodes of *Law and Order*."

"Hey." She curled one of her fingers around one of his. "Don't worry about me. I can handle dangerous. I signed up for this thing, didn't I?" Why was her heartbeat speeding up? Just because his hand on hers made her remember the unimaginably good things those fingers had done to her when—

"I may have gotten you into this, but I'm not about to let you get hurt," he continued, his blue eyes locked on hers. Every virtual Tupperware container slid off the shelf in a tumble of plastic.

Seriously. Her heart, not to mention her imagination, might just explode if he didn't either let go of her or throw her into his bed. Right. Now. She clutched at his hand, hoping he didn't see. He should be the one to say why the hell didn't they leave the diner, the whole cop and CI thing, and go back to his place where they could shut the door on the world and—

"So this is who you've been spending time with."

It took a second, and Max's sudden release of her hand, for Tensley to realize the sharp female voice had come from just inches away. She whipped her gaze upward to see the last person on earth she ever wanted to see, in this life or any other.

Rhonda the Skank.

Her hand coiled into a fist. Tensley pulled it into her lap, out of sight, but not before she caught the narrowing of Rhonda's eyes.

"Rhonda," Max said. "What the hell."

The woman hadn't changed since high school. Still dressed in jeans so tight, it was debatable whether it was actually fabric or a denim-colored paint, and a T-shirt stretched across boobs so big, it was a miracle of nature she didn't fall over. And still with that all-knowing, I'm-so-a-bad-girl-by-birth-and-you're-so-not smile.

Tensley felt herself begin to shrink, inch by inch, into the booth.

"I had a craving for Sol's chili," Rhonda purred. She reached out to loop her finger through a curl of hair at the back of Max's neck. "So I had to get some."

Fury began a slow, rolling boil in the pit of Tensley's stomach. *Her* fingers had last been in Max's hair, not Rhonda's. That skanky woman had better remove her hand right now before Tensley did it for her.

Rhonda tipped her head and gave Tensley a cold smile.

Tensley's nails dug into her palm.

Max stiffened and pushed Rhonda's hand away.

Sol called from the counter, "Got your take-out chili right here."

"What are you doing now, Tensley?" Rhonda asked. "Bet you're a librarian somewhere, right?" Her eyes glittered.

Bitch. Tensley's mouth opened, but before she could say anything, not that it would have been the truth, Max jumped in with his cop voice. "Go get your food, Rhonda."

She didn't move. "So is this who you were with the other night, Max, when I needed you?"

What the—the other night? Max was still talking to Rhonda? How could he?

"We're having a private conversation," he replied, his voice terse. "Get your food and go home."

"A private conversation." Rhonda's laugh was harsh. "Nothing's private from a wife. Can't believe you haven't figured that out by now."

She'd just said—*no*. She couldn't have. But she had. Said—*wife*. Tensley couldn't breathe.

Steam was practically coming from Max's ears as every muscle in his body appeared to tense. Of course. He'd been found out. How could she have been so stupid? The phone call. Him leaving so fast. Worried about her. *Right.*

Rhonda's smile shot icicle daggers into Tensley.

"Get the hell out of here, Rhonda," Max ordered. Then he turned to Tensley, who had already dug her fist into the leather seat and was using it to push her numb body out of the booth. "She's not my wife anymore. Don't listen to her—"

Anymore. She wanted to have a great comeback, something worthy of a wronged heroine in a classic tale, but her fight-or-flight instincts took over instead, with flight asserting control. She was up on her wobbling legs now, pushing toward the door.

When she heard Max following, she made sure the door to Sol's diner banged on him. "Where are you going?" he demanded.

She didn't answer.

He caught up with her, grabbing her arm. "You know better than to listen to—"

Her voice returned, scraping like sandpaper against her throat. "You *married* Rhonda."

His hesitation told her everything she needed to know. "It's not that simple," he said.

"But it is." Tensley spun on her heel, unsteady as she was, and made for her car. She opened the door and hurtled inside, fumbling in her purse for her keys. This scenario was way too familiar for words.

That fast, Max was against the driver's side door, his arm on the roof as if he could stop her from driving away. He rapped on the window and gestured for her to roll it down.

She wouldn't. No way. She jammed the keys into the ignition.

Then she sat back against the seat and rolled the window down.

He leaned in through it, his face inches from hers. "Yes. Yes, I married her. But we're divorced."

"You still see her."

Again, he hesitated. "There's a reason for that."

Bryan-with-a-y-not-an-i all over again. It had to be in the male DNA. Tensley focused her gaze straight ahead. She turned on the ignition. "Step away from the car."

"Ten—"

"Step. Away. From the car," she growled.

He did.

There was some satisfaction in peeling out of the parking spot, leaving him standing in the exhaust. And relief in the fact that she hadn't decked Rhonda. Or Max.

This time.

No guarantees going forward.

***

Kate's neighborhood was a great place for a walk. Trees, flowers and a park not far away that bordered a city lake. People caught up in their everyday lives, shopping, working, taking care of kids. Not many who had enough time on their hands to stare into her face and wonder what was wrong.

Since her best friend wasn't home when Tensley arrived, she took the animals with her for a pounding, mind-clearing jaunt to the park. Blinky and Stinky weren't too sure about it and Gemini seemed alarmed, but they came, anyway.

Then again, they didn't have a choice. She held the leashes.

On the way to the park, she tried to sort out her feelings, which were racing through her at all different speeds and colliding in one pileup after another.

Stinky took the lead for their little group, acting as seeing eye dog for Blinky, who was close on his heels. Tensley followed, holding on as the leashes became taut from the dogs straining to go faster. Gemini brought up the rear, but kept enough of a distance to allow him to pretend he wasn't with them.

Max had married Rhonda. *Married* her. Even though he'd told her that whole kiss in high school had been staged so he could get Tensley to leave for college. Yeah, right. Since when did you marry someone you didn't care about? Tears pricked at the backs of her eyes as she visualized their wedding, Rhonda poured into a tight, white leather dress, showing cleavage so substantial, it needed its own zip code.

She couldn't help it; she glanced down at her own chest. A perfectly respectable C cup, but nowhere near Rhonda territory. Max must have felt like he needed a flashlight and a map to even find her boobs.

Stop it. Stop...it. She could not, would not, do this to herself again. This wasn't high school; she was a professional woman, even if her life didn't reflect it right now. She'd done fine without Max before and would do fine without him again.

One tear splashed downward, in the direction of an unsuspecting Blinky. That's when she realized how far she'd let her chin dip. Ridiculous. One night with the guy and she was back to being seventeen again.

But she had a much bigger problem, and she knew it. Pure nostalgia would be one thing. They'd have a good time in bed and say goodbye. Fun revisiting old times—see ya.

It wasn't that easy. Max the adult, the confident officer of the law, willing to do whatever it took to take down a bad guy...the man powerful enough, ripped enough, masculine enough to be gentle when it counted, was pulling her in with far greater force than a memory ever could. Old memories fade. It was the new ones you had to watch out for.

She'd tumbled into bed the other night with the shadow of a teenage boy. And ended up falling for the man who had taken his place. A man who had decided he had to draw the line between right and wrong in sleeping with her. It never should have happened, he'd said.

She both loved and hated him for that.

Tensley swiped at the tears with the back of her hand and threw her shoulders back. Her odd parade of animals had reached the park now. She steered them toward a bench that had been warmed by the sun and collapsed onto it, her legs sprawled in a tangle of leashes, eyes staring straight ahead at the lake.

She needed yet another mental checklist. First item, forget Max. She'd forget the club, too, if she hadn't promised Sarah she'd show up tonight to show her how to figure her profits and losses. The woman couldn't continue on not knowing how much she truly made. She had a child depending on her.

There was also the matter of Tensley making enough money to get out of that place for good.

So, second item, get another job. Where, she had no idea. But it had better be someplace that didn't do a background check.

Third item...um.... *Ummm.* Who was she kidding? She had no idea what was third on the list. She glanced down to see the two dogs sitting before her, faces turned upward. Even Blinky's blind eyes were filled with concern. From several feet away, Gemini also watched her, his tail swishing gently across the grass. When he saw her looking at him, he turned away. And then back again.

Her bruised heart melted a little. At least someone cared about her. So what if she had a two-item checklist. She'd get it finished that much faster.

"Come on, guys." Tensley stood, jiggling the leashes. "Let's go." Kate would be home before long. Bet she wouldn't be such a big fan of Max's once she found out he'd said "I do" to Rhonda the Skank, who could probably say "I did" about every guy in their high school.

Why did you have to go there, Max? Why Rhonda, of all people? It wasn't a question Tensley would likely get answered any time soon, or ever, since she was putting Max and his whole confidential-informant thing out of her mind for good. Let the police department sue her. She'd like to see them try.

She'd always been able to talk a good game, when it was confined to her own mind.

They turned onto the street leading to Kate's condo. The air smelled of cinnamon and freshly baked waffle cones. The legs of a wrought iron chair scraped against the sidewalk and an overhead umbrella creaked as a woman from a small café cleaned up the dishes of patrons who had left. Stinky led them around it.

The summer sun washed against Tensley's face. For a moment, she closed her eyes and imagined she was back in her old life, where she belonged. Where Max hadn't intruded and her worst problem was figuring out how to convince her mother to give her back her job after the Bryan debacle. Everything had been so much simpler then.

Stinky stopped, causing Blinky to run into the back of him and Tensley to stumble and step on Gemini's tail. Her eyes flew open at the cat's offended yowl. "Sorry," she apologized. "Stinky, what's the matter?"

Nothing, apparently, but a bowl with fresh water placed outside a red-bricked storefront. Stinky led Blinky to it, where they both lapped it up.

Tensley's gaze wandered to the store's wooden sign, "Fowler's Books and More." Her heart did the familiar coming-home leap it did whenever she saw a bookstore and longing spiraled through her for the smell of ink and feel of crisp pages beneath her fingers. All those stories she hadn't yet read, just waiting for her.

She dropped her hands to her sides, letting the leashes slacken. The dogs finished their drinks and backed away from the water bowl, waiting. "Come on, guys. We're going in," she said. She had to have her fix. Some people gambled, others drank, still others did drugs.

She bought books.

The black screen door creaked, announcing her arrival. The store was crowded, filled with tall bookcases of dark wood. A long table in the front, with a lamp on each end, held stacks of calendars, note cards and bookmarks.

All standard fare for a bookshop, but there was something not quite so standard about this one. Could have been the classical music, playing in leaps and bounds overhead. Or the smell of freshly baked cookies somewhere close by. Or the jaunty, bright curtains gracing the tops of the long, narrow windows.

Tensley's shoes made soft plodding sounds on the wood floor as she moved further into the store, followed by her faithful trio of animals, and faced a familiar dilemma—where to start. In romance? She craved it. Mystery? She wanted to figure it out. Self-help? She needed it.

Each shelf had a hand-lettered guide to the author's last names and all of them called to her. She wasn't sure how much money she had in her pocket, but she knew from experience she could hold eight paperbacks before she had to set them down at the register and get her second wind.

"Hello?" A woman with shoulder-length steel-gray hair, a well-worn pink sweater and smile wrinkles framing a sharp blue-eyed gaze appeared from behind a bookcase. "May I help you find something?"

Gemini answered before Tensley could. His meow bounced off the bookcases and landed in front of the older woman. "I wasn't asking you," she said to him, "but if you like, I'll show you where the cat section is."

Tensley smiled for what felt like the first time in months. "I hope it's okay they're with me. We were going for a walk and I saw your store and just..." She lifted a shoulder. "Had to come inside."

"Pets are welcome. As long as they mind their manners." The woman's attempt at a stern look didn't fool anyone, including the animals. Stinky began sniffing the floor, followed closely by Blinky, while Gemini adopted a bored look, flicking his gaze at the woman every few seconds to be sure she'd noticed.

"Thanks. I'll make sure they're on their best behavior." Her hands were itching to begin pulling books out and reading the back cover blurbs.

"If you need anything, let me know. I'm the only one here." She shook her head. "Was supposed to be with my grandchildren today, but my helper quit this morning."

Tensley paused with her hand on the top of a book in the mystery section. "Does that mean you might be hiring?"

"Do you know someone?"

"Uh, well, yes." She turned to face the woman square on and used her corporate voice. "Me. I'm dependable, good with customers, and I love to read." *Just don't ask why I can't work nights. Or what my customer service experience is.*

The woman was silent for a moment as she regarded Tensley. Then she extended her hand. "Patsy Fowler," she said.

"Tensley." She shook Patsy's hand. "Tensley Starbrook." No need to bring the Tanner part of her into it.

"All right, Tensley Starbrook. How about if you follow me back to the office. We can talk there." She gestured to the animals. "You, too. Come on."

Half an hour later, Tensley had learned that Patsy, who had opened the store twenty years earlier, didn't get to see nearly enough of her grandchildren. And she was not happy that she'd not been able to make the two-hour drive south to see them today.

The interview began with the store owner giving her a Q&A on the store's best-selling books—romance novels. Tensley passed with flying colors, especially when it came to the last question.

"Tell me a new writer you would recommend to one of my customers," Patsy challenged her. "And why."

"So many good ones to choose from. Depends on the kind of hero she wants to fall in love with." Tensley mused. "But okay, here are two. Marcella Burnard for sexy sci-fi romance. Takes you, literally, to a whole different world. Jami Davenport for passionate romance with the hot athlete you always knew had a tender side under all that testosterone."

"Good," Patsy nodded, jotting the names down on a piece of paper. "I'll order their books." Next, she moved the discussion to Austen, Hemingway and F. Scott Fitzgerald, along with a healthy rundown of mystery authors. Tensley held her own.

"Favorite quote from a book," Patsy challenged her.

"We all have a better guide in ourselves, if we would attend to it, than any other person can be."

"Jane Austen."

Tensley nodded and gazed over the other woman's shoulder, wondering why she hadn't reflected on the truth of that quote lately. "From *Mansfield Park*."

"I like it. I like you. When can you start?"

Her attention focused back on Patsy. "Right away."

"Good. Be here tomorrow, by nine a.m."

Tensley hesitated. "Do you want me to fill out an application?" She didn't want to, since she had no idea what references she would list, and she was terrified of a background check that would reveal the felony, but it would be worse to show up for work and be told she didn't meet the criteria.

Wait a minute. As Jane Austen had said…

"I'm not worried about it. You can do that tomorrow when you get here," Patsy said briskly, getting to her feet. "I can generally tell everything I need to know about a person from their favorite quote. "Now you'd better go finish your walk. That one," she pointed at Stinky, "is practically crossing his legs."

Tensley grinned. "Can I ask just one thing, Patsy?"

"Shoot."

"What's *your* favorite quote?"

With a smile of her own, Patsy replied, "I would always rather be happy than dignified."

"From *Jane Eyre*." She liked Patsy, she decided.

"See you tomorrow, Tensley Starbrook."

"See you tomorrow, Patsy Fowler."

She had a job. And in case the reverse spell didn't work, possibly the beginnings of a life AMC.

After Madame Claire.

CHAPTER TWENTY-ONE

The club was packed, but Gary wasn't there. At least Tensley hadn't seen him yet from her spot behind the bar. A perfect time, she decided, to make another run at getting into his office.

Because no matter what she might tell herself to the contrary, she was not a person who could run from an obligation. She'd told Max she would be his confidential informant and get him the information he needed to put Gary away.

And she would do that. Even if she would never be able to understand why he'd gone behind her back to marry Rhonda the Skank. Of all people.

She spotted her opportunity to try and get a look in Gary's office when Sarah came on stage, whip in hand, and her theme music began pounding in the background. Sarah commanded the attention of every person in the room, drunk or not. They all seemed transfixed.

Another woman was also behind the bar, helping with the rush. Tensley moved next to her. "I'm taking a break," she said, raising her voice to be heard over the music. "Is that okay with you?"

Without missing a beat, the woman motioned for her to go and Tensley worked her way through the crowd to the backstage area. She slipped behind the curtain and into the hallway with its now-familiar aroma of perfume, sweat, alcohol and burned coffee. Eau de nude.

No one was in the hall, but there were muffled female voices on the other side of the dressing room door. She hesitated for a moment when she heard what sounded like Tawny's voice and caught the words, "net profits." A grin stole over her face. Sarah must have started talking with the other women about their session to go over how much an individual dancer made, versus what Gary made.

Once Tensley had shown Sarah the basics of how to account for expenses and her time, it turned out the dancer wasn't making as much as she had thought. Gary might be in for a big surprise— women who were tired of being taken advantage of. Funny how that happened.

She walked past the restrooms, ignoring the hand-drawn enhancements to their signs. Still no one around. A turn around the corner and Gary's office was dead ahead, down the passageway.

Hold on. Was that a sound coming from further down the hall? She stopped, pressing her back to the wall and holding her breath, listening. She must have been mistaken. All she could clearly hear was the music accompanying Sarah's act.

She kept going until she reached the door to Gary's office. She put her hand on the knob and turned it, surprised to find it unlocked. The door opened easily and she slipped inside, hailed at once by the smell of dust, alcohol and men's cologne. *Ugh.* Not a great combination.

A massive oak desk dominated the room, with stacks of paper across its surface. Gary's chair, made of black leather, was also large, though the guest chair was narrow and small. In the corner, two gray metal filing cabinets stood side by side. Flyers advertising Gary's Gorgeous Grecians lined the walls, posted at haphazard angles.

There was also a framed photograph of Gary, standing proudly in front of his club, surrounded by dancers wearing bikinis. Tensley averted her eyes before she could see whether she was in the photo. She didn't want to know.

She didn't see a single photo of anyone else in the office, not even Razor. But then again, Gary couldn't be described as a family guy. She wondered what woman had been able to stand him long enough to produce his son. Tensley shuddered.

On tiptoe, she moved to the desk. One stack of papers appeared to be food and liquor receipts. Another had schedules, showing who was working when. She rifled through the first few papers in that stack and found that Gary had drawn a plus sign next to the names of four dancers, including Tawny and Sarah.

There wasn't a plus sign next to Lila's name. Nice. Rationally, she knew she shouldn't be irritated, since she didn't know what it meant, but *irrationally*, she was perturbed. Milo had said she was the best dancer out there, so why didn't she rate a plus sign? Damn Gary, anyway.

Still, she took one of the older schedules, figuring maybe he wouldn't miss one for dates that had already passed and, after folding it carefully, shoved it into a pocket in her skinny jeans. Next, she tried the drawers to Gary's desk. Locked. Disappointment ran through her.

She paused for a moment to make sure she didn't hear anyone approaching and then moved to one of the metal file cabinets. Very carefully, she pushed in the button on the handle of the top drawer, hoping against all reason that she'd find it unlocked.

No such luck. She gave it a pull, just in case it was only stuck, but it refused to budge. One by one, she tried the other drawers, finding the same thing. Each was locked. And she didn't have the first idea about how to break in. A definite speed bump in the path to her getting Max what he needed and getting out of this life. She sighed and then clapped her hand over her mouth, remembering, too late, that she could not make a sound in here.

In fact, she'd already been in Gary's office longer than was likely safe. Milo would come looking for her any minute. Tensley bent down to look under the desk, hoping Gary had a trashcan. People might lock their cabinets and desks, but they sometimes weren't very careful about what they put in the trash.

She spied his garbage can, the requisite round metal bin. Dropping to her knees, she crawled under the desk to go through it. Looked like receipts, mostly, for fast food. Wendy's, McDonald's, Burger King. And Gary didn't buy for others, she noted. They were all for one person.

There were a few crumpled notes, with phone numbers written on them. Good. She could have Max check them out. She smoothed and folded them as carefully as she had the schedule. Some discarded, used tissues. *Eww.* She withdrew her hand before she touched them. As she did, she heard a sound on the other side of the wall, to her left. Voices. Headed this way? *Nooo.*

Tensley straightened so fast, she bumped her head on the underside of the desk. She shot out from underneath it, rubbing the sore spot on her head with one hand and shoving the paper notes into her jeans pocket with the other. She had to get out of here before the people attached to those voices made the turn down this hallway.

On the tips of her toes, she propelled herself to the door, turning the handle and opening it without a sound. Then she sucked in a deep breath and poked her head out. No one. Yet. She was out that door, shutting it behind her, and down the opposite end of the hall so fast, she hadn't even yet allowed herself to breathe when she ducked, yet again, into the supply closet.

If someone found her, it would be better here than in Gary's office.

She let her breath out slowly and moved to the corner of the room, this time making sure she avoided the shelf where she now knew the liquid soap was kept. Just the thought of that soap sent her back to the time she'd spent in Max's arms, when he couldn't even hold on to her because of the soap clinging to her. And the adorable surprised look on his face, the way he'd run his hands along her body and made the most of the fact they'd ended up on the floor.

The passionate love they'd made, the hunger deep inside her he'd satisfied. A hunger she hadn't allowed herself to realize existed. Longing rippled through her, weakening her knees until she had to hold on to what felt like a stack of boxes against the wall. Some confidential informant she made, she decided. She couldn't even stand up when she thought about her…confidential cop.

The voices moved closer. Speaking in deep, low tones. Two males. She braced herself again, hoping she could hear from this vantage point when they went into Gary's office and hoping against all hope that they weren't headed to the supply room instead.

To her surprise, she heard them go past her door, further down the hall. Then she heard a door open and close somewhere on the other side of the supply room. In the darkness, she tiptoed across the floor and found the wall, pressing her fingertips and her ear against it. At first, she didn't hear anything. Then she heard muffled voices. A faraway tinkle of female laughter. And the rough voice of a man. The faint notes of music.

No one had said anything about another area, separate from the club. This she had to see. Could be something Max needed to know about.

She cracked the door to the supply room open and peered out. No detectable activity. She opened it a little more. Still nothing. Then she pulled it wide enough to let herself slip through it and closed the door behind her, all without making a sound.

The hall was unoccupied, no one in sight in either direction. A shiver of doubt went through her as she contemplated whether this was the smartest thing to do. Then she told her feet to get moving, before she could second-guess herself.

It grew darker the further down the hallway she moved. She hadn't realized it went back so far. Then it ended abruptly, with a pile of boxes in the corner, to her left. Strange, because she was pretty sure she could hear *something* coming from behind the wall to her right. That something sounded a lot like the murmur of voices and a faint hum of music. This was where the noise she'd heard earlier was coming from. But how did someone get in there?

Tensley put her hand up to the wall, feeling along the smooth, broad expanse of wood. *There*. A break in the wood. She let her fingers travel along it, halfway down, until it reached what felt like some kind of a handle. Her stomach fluttered. A hidden room in the back of the club. This could be it. Information she could give to Max that might actually help him.

Holding her breath, she slipped her fingers behind it and tentatively, gently pulled. Nothing. The door didn't open.

She exhaled and dropped her hand. Of course it was locked. If it was anything of significance, Gary wasn't going to let it be easily accessible.

Much as she hated to admit it, she wasn't like all those super hero crime fighter types on TV who knew how to slip a lock with a credit card. That kind of thing hadn't exactly been called for in her life. Until now.

A sound from further down the hall. Footsteps. Tensley's stomach dropped as she stood in the shadows, frozen in place. She couldn't get caught again where she wasn't supposed to be.

Before she had a chance to think about it, she dove for the boxes in the corner, pushing them forward just far enough to hide herself behind them. She curled up as small as she could, hands on her head, afraid to make a sound. And waited.

The footsteps came closer. Tensley peered through a tiny slit between the boxes to see two men. She couldn't tell for sure, but it looked as though one of them was Milo. Not many people were as large. His heavy step reverberated on the floor beneath her.

What would she do if they saw her? She could think of no good reason, none at all, that would explain why she was hiding behind a pile of boxes in an area of the club she'd been told to stay away from.

Her heart pounded so loud, she was sure they would hear.

Then she saw one person fumble with the door, possibly to unlock it, and it began to swing open. She nudged a box aside by half an inch and saw the two men disappear behind the door. It began to close.

Staying low to the floor, still in her crouched position, Tensley scooted out from behind the boxes to grab the bottom edge of the door before it shut. Then, after a quick look down the hallway to make sure no one was coming, she moved her fingers upward until she could peer around the edge of the door, careful to open it no more than an inch.

Inside, she saw muted lights in different colors and a flash of moving bodies. She snuck the door open a little further. There was a brown chair not far from the door, positioned sideways. In it sat a balding man with sweat glistening on his cheek and upper lip. His eyes were half-closed as one of the dancers from Gary's club, her back to the customer and her hands on his knees, moved her bottom in a figure eight above his lap. Though Tensley recognized her, she didn't know her name.

The topless woman appeared to be singing softly with the music in the background as she looked back over her shoulder at the man, hair brushing her bare back. He lifted his hands tentatively, questioning.

Tensley followed his gaze across the room and saw Milo standing, hands folded in front of him. He jerked his head in a nod and the man in the leather chair reached up to cup the dancer's breasts with his hands. His expression made him look like a kid who had just been handed the keys to a candy store. The dancer moaned. The customer moaned louder.

Whoa. So illegal, all this touching. And so…yeah, well. She wished she could try something like that out with, she'd go ahead and admit it, Max. She'd never done a lap dance, before, but it didn't look that difficult. Sort of a balance thing.

Tensley fanned her face with the hand that wasn't holding the door. Back to police business. What she wouldn't give to see Max in a uniform. And take it off him.

Further back in the room, she saw a table set up with bottles and glasses, of the good stuff. No wonder Gary had been so angry about his Maker's Mark. He used it to stock this little side business. As she watched, another dancer from Gary's poured a drink and moved toward the man, extending it with one hand while the index finger of her other hand pulled her bottom lip down in a pout.

It was Wild Windy, the dancer whose stage name Tensley thought sounded more like a weather report than an enticement. She seemed nice enough, though. She'd showed Tensley how to kick the vending machine the other night, to make it cough up her Diet Coke instead of keeping her money.

The man took the drink without taking his eyes off the dancer in his lap. Windy walked around to the back of him and began whispering in his ear, her bare breasts pressed against him. Then she reached down to unbutton his shirt. The customer now looked as though he'd died and gone to heaven.

Milo, arms folded across his chest and his mouth set in a tight line, didn't move. Tensley wondered where the boundaries were. If there were any.

She scanned the dim lighting for more customers. Just how many people were back here?

Bam. The door was pushed shut from above her, nearly catching her fingers. "Hey!" she protested as she pulled them away. Then she realized that whoever was above her, whoever had caught her and shut the door, just might be very pissed.

And confidential informant Tensley just might be in one hell of a lot of trouble.

CHAPTER TWENTY-TWO

Slowly, her heart pounding, Tensley sat back on the floor and let her eyes travel upward. Tawny glowered down, hands on her hips. "I cannot believe," the woman said, each word shot like a BB from a gun, "you are this stupid."

"I—" What? "Heard a noise. I came to see what it was." *And just who do you think you're calling stupid?*

"Uh-huh." Tawny's eyes narrowed. "From out at the bar, over the music playing, the people, and the clapping, you heard a noise. All the way back here."

"I wasn't at the bar. I was taking a break." She sounded, to her own ears, like a kid caught without a hall pass. She clenched her fists, as if that would help anything.

"Get up," Tawny ordered. "You're damn lucky I'm not calling Gary to tell him what you've been doing, but I'm only giving your skinny ass one chance. I catch you back here again and you'll be sorry. You understand me?"

Tensley unlocked her fists and fumbled her way to standing up. "Yes." She started to walk away, but stopped mid-step. She paused, then turned back. "Tawny."

The other woman had her hand on the door. "What the hell do you not understand about 'get out of here,'" she bit out.

"Would this sort of thing be considered extra time?"

Tawny's jaw muscles tightened. "I don't know what you're talking about."

Tensley steeled herself for one more try. "Sarah said she was getting extra time to help pay her bills. I have bills. I could use," she cleared her throat, trying to hide her nerves, "more time. I'll do whatever it takes." Her inner alarm bells began to clang so loud, she was sure Tawny could hear them.

"You're fucking crazy."

Tensley squared her shoulders and pretended her breathing was normal. "I saw what's going on in there and I'm pretty sure those guys are paying a nice premium for the extra service and that Gary pays more to girls who work that room and keep their mouths shut about it. *That's* what I'm talking about."

Tawny turned to face her, nostrils flaring. "You making a threat there, Pollyanna?"

Tensley's knees locked. "No," she hastened to say. Beads of sweat began trickling down the back of her neck.

"It sure as hell sounded like it."

It *had* sounded like that, which was damn brave, not to mention stupid, of her. "Just think about it. You know I'm one of the best dancers here. And I can do other things well, too."

Oh crap. She hadn't just said that. Yes, she had. "I mean, you wouldn't know that just from seeing me on stage, but I've had pretty good..." Stop her mouth. Stop it right now. "...feedback, so I'm pretty sure I could pick things up fast and—"

"Shut. Up. Just stop talking."

"But you'll think about—" She squeezed her eyes shut, pretty sure she didn't want to hear the answer. After a few seconds of silence, she opened one eye.

"Maybe I will, maybe I won't." Tawny pointed one long, daggered finger down the hall behind Tensley. "Get out."

"Okay." Tensley turned and began walking down the hall. "I'm going. You don't have to worry about me." Of course not. Only Tensley had to worry about Tensley.

How the hell did she know how far she would be expected to go in that room? But here she was, offering herself up like she was take-out dinner. She threw her hands up in the air as she teetered along at a fast clip. God help her, it had better be enough to tell Max this was going on.

She'd have to see him again to tell him this. And she'd have to manage that without demanding to know how Rhonda figured into his life. Or wishing she could fall back into Max's arms and into his bed.

Not going to be easy. But then nothing about this life was.

***

Max fought to keep his composure when he heard Tensley's voice on the other end of the line. He wanted to leap through the phone and pull her into his arms; he wanted to plead with her to understand what had happened with Rhonda; he wanted to make hot love to Tensley all night and all day, until neither one of them could remember Rhonda's name, much less find the strength to say it.

He did none of those things. Instead, he used his clipped cop voice to respond. He couldn't give Carl or anyone else in the police department even a hint of what had gone on between the two of them or he could kiss his job goodbye.

Tensley was his informant. That was it. End of story. So why the hell couldn't he shake the really bad idea that it could be the *beginning* of the story?

He had no desire to return to high school. Tons of guys did that kind of thing, screwing around on their wives with their old girlfriends, maybe to go back to their glory days, when they didn't have to worry about jobs or mortgages or kids or whatever it was that threw them back into the letterman's jacket. He wasn't one of those guys.

The teenage girl he'd loved and wronged had become a woman who turned his heart inside out and put his dick in a permanent flagpole position. He'd never come across any woman who could combine confidence with naiveté the way she did, turning lovemaking into one hell of a lot of explosive fun.

He'd also never met a stripper with as much raw courage as Tensley. Most of them had their defenses up so high, you'd have to have NASA's help to scale the walls. And they expected something in exchange for their trouble. Tensley didn't. All she'd wanted was for him to stay with her. Be with her.

The one thing he couldn't do.

Enough. He told Tensley to meet him at a coffee shop across town, instead of at Sol's. Last thing he needed right now was Rhonda showing up again unannounced.

He stood, shoving his phone into his pocket and pulling his jacket over his gun so it didn't show.

"Where you goin'?" Carl asked.

"Got a lead."

"Then hold on. I'm coming with you."

Max stopped, keys in hand, blinking at the detective. "I've got this."

"Sure you do, sunshine." The older man held up his own keys. "I'm driving."

"Seriously—"

"You seriously need your hearing checked." Carl's eyes narrowed. "You got a lead. We're checking it out together. Now get moving."

All Max could do was grunt his assent. And hope that whatever was still between him and Tensley wouldn't be apparent to the untrained eye.

Except—fuck it all. Carl's eye was highly trained.

***

Tensley was sitting in a corner of the coffee shop when Max strode in, Carl close on his heels. In spite of his size, the guy could move pretty fast when he wanted to. But you would always hear him coming. He had the footstep of an elephant.

Max didn't say anything to Tensley, just slid into a wooden chair across from her, beneath a poster shouting about a new kind of coffee.

The gaze she turned on him was cool and removed. "Detective Hunter," she said by way of hello.

He acknowledged her with a jerk of his head, then gestured at Carl. "This is Detective Cole."

Tensley nodded at Carl.

"You have something for me?" Max asked her.

She slid a piece of paper across the battered surface of the wooden table. "Found these phone numbers in Gary's office."

He smoothed the crumpled paper. "I'll check them out." He could feel Carl waiting by his side, his breath sounding uneven. Could just about read the guy's thoughts. He'd bet his life Carl had never seen a CI who looked like Tensley. They usually came with tracks, tattoos and sometimes missing teeth. "Anything else?"

"Yes."

Silence. He hesitated and then glanced up, realizing she'd been waiting for him to look her in the eye. The non-cop part of him took in everything, the shiny auburn hair brushing the shoulders he wanted to cradle, the tiny dip at the end of her nose, the green eyes, with flecks of hazel, that saw right through everything he was or had ever pretended to be. The woman who saw the secret dream he couldn't share with anyone else. And made him believe it could actually happen.

The cop part of him—right now he hated that guy—said, "So spill. Haven't got all day."

"There's another part of the club. In a room way at the back. Not sure about everything that's going on in there, but it looks like you can pay extra and get extra." Her eyes narrowed. "If you know what I mean."

Max's heart sped up. "You're kiddin' me."

"I am not."

Carl's grunt sounded skeptical. "How do you know?"

Max was one muscle flex away from knocking Carl off the chair he was torturing with his bulk. Instead, he took a deep breath and, his gaze never leaving Tensley's, attempted to reframe the question. "How do you know?" At least his tone was less obnoxious than Carl's. He hoped, anyway.

"I snuck back there and opened the door. There didn't seem to be any restrictions on touching the dancers in there, because there was a lot of it going on. From both sides."

Pride rippled through Max. He'd bet his ass Carl didn't have a CI this good. But the pride was fleeting; concern took over fast. "Anybody see you?"

Tensley looked away. "Not at first. But, well, yes."

He leaned forward. "Who? What happened?"

"One of the other dancers. Tawny. She pretty much runs the dancer side of things. And I think she either decides or helps decide who works that back room."

"You think or you know?" Carl growled.

Max shut him up with a look. The detective raised his palms and sat back against his chair, which protested with a squeak.

Tensley directed herself to him. "I said I *think*, which is what I meant." Then she turned back to Max. "I heard a dancer asking Tawny about working 'extra time' and when I asked Tawny whether the extra time involved working that back room, she was pissed I'd brought it up, but she didn't deny it. She just told me to get the hell out or she'd tell Gary I'd been back there."

Max clenched his fists at the mention of Gary's name. If that SOB ever laid a hand on Tensley, he'd slap him in jail so fast, the jerk would be somebody's girlfriend before his head had stopped spinning.

He stared at his hands, uncurling his fingers one by one, willing them to relax. He had to concentrate. "Get us some coffee, Carl," he said.

Muttering under his breath, the other detective got up from his chair to lumber toward the counter.

Max looked out the window and back at Tensley. "You okay?"

"I'm okay." Her chin lifted.

"I don't think you should keep going with this." *Too risky.* "We've got enough to go on. I'll take it from here." He'd screwed this up by getting involved with her again. The least he could do was back her out of the trouble he'd gotten her into.

"Forget it. I'm not getting this far just to quit now."

He knew that determined look. He'd rammed into it before. "Look, I'm the one who's running things here," he hissed, with a sidelong look at Carl. "If I say you're done, you're done."

"The hell you do." She leaned across the table. "You need to know how often this little side operation is open for business. I'm the one who can find that out."

"It's too dangerous." And he was no longer sure he could protect her.

"I can take care of myself. Besides, I already asked Tawny to let me work it. So I can get you what you need to shut Gary down." She shivered, then tried to pretend she hadn't.

What the—he didn't even want to think about some hammered, sweaty animal running his hands along her beautiful, soft body. "No," he shot back, more violently than he had intended. This was going too far, getting out of his control. Tensley was not the kind of woman who worked a room like that. Hell, she wasn't even the kind of woman who worked as a stripper. He still hadn't figured that one out.

Her brows drew together, forming a crease. "How else are you going to nail him?"

"You found out it was going on last night. So when you find out it's going on again, you call me and I'll move in. You don't go anywhere near it."

Her voice sounded like it was strung as tight as his. "I'm not sneaking back there again. Tawny will be watching for me. She'll kill me. If she doesn't, Gary will. And I don't want them finding out I'm an—an informant. People get out of jail, you know, and they go after people who told on them."

He tried to make light of it, despite his heart beginning to pound. *"Law and Order."*

"Damn right."

Max glanced over at Carl, who was trying to fit lids on three paper cups. He'd be back in a minute. Max kept his voice low, urgent. "I told you to stand down. I don't want you taking a chance like that."

She matched it. "How nice of you to be concerned, Detective. I'm touched."

Meaning she wasn't at all. She was furious with him; he could see it in her eyes. "What the hell. Is this still about Rhonda?" he demanded. "Because I already told you that wasn't what you thought." Carl was trying to push the cups into a carrier.

"It's about you not being able to get out of bed fast enough when she called you. Leaving me wondering what the hell was going on. Not that you cared."

His stomach dropped and he spoke before he thought. "How did you know it was her?"

"I didn't." She sat back, hurt and fury swirling in her green eyes. "Until now."

Carl plodded toward them, carrying the coffee.

"Nothing's changed with you, Max. She was always the one you really wanted. Not me."

"That is so fucking not true." Hard to say it convincingly from the side of his mouth, but Carl had set the carrier down hard on the table, slopping brown liquid out of the openings in the lids. "What's going on?" the detective demanded, pulling the cups from the grip of the cardboard container. "Here. You, you and me."

Max wasn't going to wait for Tensley to offer up an explanation. "She's not sure what she's supposed to do next," he said. "I'm setting her straight."

"The hell you are," Tensley answered smoothly, lifting her cup to take a sip. "I know exactly what I'm doing next. Next time I go in that room, it will be because I've been scheduled to work it. I'll let you know when that happens."

"Makes sense," Carl said.

"Who asked you?" Max snarled.

The detective's cool gaze went back and forth between the other two at the table. "You and I best be havin' a talk," he told Max.

"Later, Carl." Max looked down at the piece of paper with phone numbers written on it. "We can't get him on the back room stuff until we also have him on the money laundering."

Carl considered that. "We can if we prove they're connected."

"Which we can't. Yet."

"Not until we get in there. But if we have a witness who gives us enough for a warrant…"

"I want a better case against him first."

"And the judge is going to have to be convinced the witness is credible."

Tensely didn't lie. Ever. "She's credible," Max bit out.

The witness in question picked up her purse, apparently having had enough. "You two decide and let me know."

"You're leaving?" Max asked quickly. Too quickly.

"I have another job," she replied. "And I don't want to be late on my first day."

"Gary's gonna let you work at another club?" Carl asked. "Thought he made the dancers sign exclusives."

The look she gave him should have frozen Carl's thick eyebrows. "I'm working in a bookstore."

Relief washed over Max. She'd be out of that place. That life. And he couldn't get into trouble if—they could be together. "That's great," Max said. His breath sounded funny; his mouth was trying to smile, not smile, smile again.

Carl shifted in his chair. "It's not great if it means you'll be quitting Gary's before we're done."

Tensley stood. "Guess you'd better work fast."

Max clutched the piece of paper in his hand. "I'll check out these phone numbers. Carl will keep working on the hardware side of things."

"Fine." She pushed in her chair and took a step.

Don't go. "You need to check in with me tomorrow." He needed more than that, way more than that.

She didn't reply, just walked away.

Max kept his eyes locked on the paper with the phone numbers. "I'll check these out today. Should tell us something about Gary's associates."

He felt a punch in his upper arm. A hard one. "Hey. What the—?"

"You shit-for-brains," Carl accused. "How long you been sleepin' with your CI?"

CHAPTER TWENTY-THREE

"You've got it all wrong," Max said, knowing he sounded like every perp he'd ever come across. They were all innocent. Except they weren't.

"The hell I do." Carl gulped his coffee. "You know what something like that can do to your career?"

He had a pretty good idea. Max stared down at his untouched cup of coffee.

"End it," Carl said flatly. "Do not see her again. Have her report in to me from now on. I know better than to get involved with a CI."

Max looked up. "You got involved with a captain's daughter."

"I married her. Different story. She wasn't a stripper." The detective's eyes softened, a grin pulling at the edges of his mouth. "Though she could have been. Rhonda's got one fucking awesome body."

"And you divorced her."

"She divorced me." Carl's gaze turned cold. "And this ain't about me, sunshine. You're the one up shit creek."

"I can handle this."

Carl nodded. "Yeah, and I'm Brad Pitt." He downed the last of his coffee and smacked his lips. "Let's get out of here. You've got to get on those phone numbers and I've got to figure out how Gary's making money off hardware without selling any."

They got up to leave, Max picking up the used cups to toss them in the trash. "That's some hot wife you've got."

Thunderclouds formed on Carl's face. "What?"

"Could've sworn you said you were Brad Pitt." He shoved the glass door open hard.

***

Patsy Fowler had on running shoes today, Tensley noted, and a sweatshirt with "World's Best Grandma" written across the front. She wore wireless rimmed glasses with a smudge on the right lens. "Good. You're here," she said as soon as she saw Tensley.

"I'm here." Breathing in the subtle blend of ink, paper, old wood and dust, and feeling her heart lift.

"You know how to work a cash register?"

Tensley hesitated. "I've seen people do it." She doubted that counted, though.

She was right. It didn't. Patsy gave her a lesson, darting sharp glances in her direction to make sure she was paying attention. It wasn't that hard, Tensley was relieved to learn. Especially since the night job and day job scenario had her operating on little sleep.

"I'll be back before it's time to lock up. I've written my cell phone number down and put it there, on the counter." Patsy motioned toward the piece of paper. "You have plenty of change in the register and should be good to go."

"I'll be fine," Tensley assured her. "Go see your grandchildren."

"Can't get enough of those little buggars."

"They probably feel the same way about you."

Patsy grinned. "Wait until they see what I'm bringing them today." She lifted a cloth bag with a picture of the Space Needle on the front. It appeared to be filled to the brim with an assortment of books and toys.

Tensley leaned her elbows on the counter and returned the smile. "Have fun." Once the older woman had gone, she covered her face with her hands. She'd told Patsy she'd be fine. She wished she knew if that would be true. She wished she never had to go back to that awful strip club again. She wished she could be back in her corporate office, where she belonged. She wished Max had never come back into her life to turn it upside down even more than Madame Claire had.

She wished. More than a little irony there, since a wish had been what started this whole thing in the first place.

And as far as Max, did she *really* wish he hadn't come back into her life? If she only had the memory of that one night with him, of the shuddering out-of-body experience of their coming together, of his lips against her most tender places, of lying beside him, both of them spent, and curling up in his protective arms…could it be enough?

She sighed, from the top of her head to her toes. Like a heroine in one of her beloved Victorian novels, burdened by the tragic loss of her only love. Tensley felt as though she could understand the depths of that kind of loss, maybe for the first time in her life.

A tree next to the window rustled in the breeze; a car with a loud muffler drove by outside; a rafter in the old building creaked overhead.

One by one, Tensley opened each finger covering her eyes and straightened.

It wasn't enough, not even close. She'd started out wanting a piece of the past and wound up only able to see a future.

She was getting the hell out of this life. Whether she stumbled into the right lesson that changed the spell, convinced Madame Claire to figure out how to undo it, or she had to save every single penny she earned from the bookstore and the club to restart her life—she would do it.

When it all came down to it, she didn't have it in her to play the tragic heroine. Much as Tensley appreciated a good drama, she'd be the one behind the heroine, kicking her in her fictional ass.

A bell tinkled at the front of the store, signaling a customer's arrival. Tensley brushed her hair back and put on a smile, a real one this time. She moved out from behind the counter. "Hello. How may I help you?"

She stopped short, the words dying on her lips when she saw Max, his tall frame silhouetted in the door, shadows falling across his face. "You can give me another chance," he said.

Tensley looked down at her shoes, hoping he couldn't see the tsunami of emotion those six words had unleashed in her. Another chance. She turned away to straighten books that didn't need straightening. "How did you find me?"

"Detective. Remember?"

She lined up the corners of each book cover. "You followed me."

"I did."

"Let's just go on from here," she said, not daring to look at him. "Forget about that night. Pretend it didn't happen." Amazing how someone could say something they didn't at all mean. She stepped away from the shelf and made a sweeping motion with her trembling hand. "Done. Over."

He moved toward her. "Won't work."

Tensley's heart leaped into her throat. By the time she found her voice, he was standing inches from her, the heat of his body pulling her in. She couldn't do this. Couldn't risk it again. "Yes, it will. I've already forgotten about it."

His jaw muscles worked. "I haven't."

She watched the small scar move with the tension in his jaw. Her mother had done that to him. She tried to turn away again, but his arms folded around her, gently at first and then harder, with more urgency. His mouth closed in on hers and everything in her world blurred. Into a kaleidoscope of colors. A swirling torrent of colliding feelings.

She couldn't breathe for longing to be with him again, to feel his body on hers.

"Ten," he whispered in the brief second their lips were apart.

She lifted her arms around his neck, her fingers in his hair as he closed in again, harder this time, holding her as though nothing could ever part them again.

Through her haze, she heard a tingling, a bell. Angels applauding? No. The door.

Her arms came down to push him away and she stood back, trying to catch her breath. "You have to go," she managed to push out.

He shook his head. "No." He rubbed a hand across his face. "I'll wait."

Tensley turned away, focusing on a stack of bright covers in the romance section. A sliver of sunshine landed on the image of a man with his lips on a woman's neck. She closed her eyes. "Leave."

"Ten—"

"I have a customer. A job. A real one." What had she let herself do? He'd only break her heart again. She'd never asked him about kids. He probably had a whole family with Rhonda the Skank. One he'd be tied to for life. She snapped every last mental Tupperware container shut and stored it on a shelf so high she had to tiptoe to get to it. "Go."

"I'll be back."

"Yeah, well." Her fingers shook, but they waved him away. "I don't think so."

She straightened and took a deep breath. Max turned and left, the sound of his footsteps ringing on the wooden floor.

It wasn't until after she'd helped her customer find a stack of mysteries, and she was alone in the store again, that she let her tears fall onto the wooden counter, sliding off the edge to land on the floor.

***

Patsy returned, glowing from the time spent with her grandkids, in time for Tensley to go back to Kate's and get a few hours of sleep before she had to be back at the club.

As she opened her locker, steadfastly avoiding another flyer with her picture on it, she wondered if Max and his detective friend had come up with anything else to pin on Gary yet. The sooner they did, the sooner she was out of here. Gary was such a sleazebag, it didn't seem like it should take that much time.

She finished pulling on her costume, what there was of it, anyway, and shut the locker door, jumping in surprise when she saw Tawny standing behind it, staring at her. Hands on her leather-clad hips, the other dancer pinned Tensley to the wall with a single gaze. "You're up," Tawny said.

"What?"

"Half the damn world is out sick. I've got nobody to work the back room and two paying customers on the way. I said you're up, so move your ass."

Oh h-e-l-l no. Now that push had apparently come to shove, she didn't want to work that back room; she just wanted to get back there to see what went on. And call it in.

"Oh, okay. Great," Tensley said, her voice faint. She ran a hand through her hair, trying to think what to do.

"You said you wanted extra time."

"I did. Yes, I did. I said that."

Tawny's frown could have curdled milk. "Then get your ass back there so I can send them in."

"I will. Going right—" She pointed her finger at the dressing room door. "Now." She studied her finger, then let it drop. "Just have to make a quick call and I'll be right there."

"Uh-uh." Tawny shook her head. "No phone calls. No time." She narrowed her eyes, looking suspicious. "Milo's already back there. You want this or not?"

"Don't I maybe get a trainer? Get to watch somebody first, so that I, you know, am sure about what I'm supposed to do?" She sounded pathetic, even to her own ears.

Tawny closed the short distance between them in less than a second, her eyes blazing into Tensley's. "What do you think this is, McDonald's? No, you don't get a trainer. You get to tell me what the fuck is going on. And you get to tell me right now."

"Noth—nothing's going on." Tensley cleared her throat. "I just want to be sure I do a good job."

"Milo will tell me if you screw up." The dancer's index finger stopped less than an inch from Tensley's nose. "So don't screw up."

"Okay," Tensley whispered.

"Follow me."

Tensley had no choice but to do as ordered, leaving her cell, and the ability to call Max for help, in her locker. Oh God. What were these men expecting to get for their money? Olympic high divers began performing soaring plunges in her stomach as she followed Tawny out the door and down the hall.

She was a corporate executive. She didn't get paid for sexual favors. She didn't—*whoa*. A dive from the highest board. She clutched at her midsection.

"You're not gonna be sick," Tawny hissed. "So don't even think about it." She pulled a key from some nonexistent pocket in her leather pants and unlocked the door, pulling it open. "I'm doin' you a favor. You might start acting like it."

"Thank you." Tensley went through the door, spotting Milo right away. He was stationed against the wall, eyes straight ahead, hands locked in front of him.

"Bar's stocked," Tawny said. "Milo will keep anybody from getting out of line."

What constituted being out of line? Tensley screamed inside her head. Not surprisingly, there was no answer.

Tawny left, locking the door behind her.

Milo nodded toward the bar. "You want a drink, you'd better get it now."

A drink—or ten—might be a very good idea. Tensley went behind the small bar and grabbed a bottle of the first amber liquid she saw. She raised it to her lips. The alcohol burned going down, numbing her throat. Too bad it couldn't numb her brain. Yet, anyway.

"Put on one of those." Milo motioned toward a hook, where a few short silk robes hung. "They like to see it come off."

Of course "they" did. She obeyed, sliding her arms through the white fabric.

Max. She had to get to him, tell him. Somehow. Before she had to…ugh. Perform. For sleazy guys in polyester suits gripping money in their sweaty fists.

If only she'd had the chance to grab her cell. Hold on. "Milo!"

"Huh?"

"Give me your cell. Please."

He shook his head. "The customers are gonna be here any minute. You gotta get ready. Put on, you know, your face."

She frowned. "I have makeup on."

He swatted the air impatiently. "Nah, your face. You know. Like this." The big man closed his eyes halfway and pursed his lips, cocking his head to one side.

He was mimicking a woman being seductive. And he was serious. It was kind of sweet, in a twisted way. "Oh," Tensley said. "My face. Right." She nodded. "I will, and thank you for the reminder, but first I have to send a quick text. Really fast, I promise."

"No."

"Yes. Please."

"What the hell. They'll be here any minute. You don't send no texts from in here."

"Milo," she pleaded, walking to his side. "If you have ever liked me at all, please let me borrow your cell."

"Who you texting?"

She said the first thing that came into her mind. "My cat-sitter."

"What?"

"You know my cat. Gemini."

He shook his head, looking at her as if she were crazy. Which she probably was, all things considered.

"He has a—condition," she made up on the fly. "And if the cat-sitter doesn't give him his medicine as soon as she comes over, he could—well, you know. *Die*."

"Die?" He looked skeptical.

"Yes. Die." She moved her nose to within an inch of his. "You don't want that on your conscience. Trust me."

Milo hesitated, then reached inside his pocket to pull out an iPhone. "Didn't know you had a cat," he mumbled.

Tensley grabbed it. Thankfully, she had Max's number committed to memory. The numbers even sounded like him, strong eights and nines. No wimpy twos or zeroes.

She punched his number into text messaging, then typed out a cryptic note, praying he would understand. *Working extra time. Cat needs medicine. Right now. TT-S.*

Footsteps outside the door, the rattle of a key in the lock.

"Give it to me," Milo ordered, putting out his hand.

Tensley pressed "send" and handed over the phone, steeling herself for what was to come.

"Face," Milo hissed.

She put one hand on her hip and tried to adopt her best seductive expression, though she was pretty sure it looked more like "what-the-hell-am-I-doing-here" than "come-hither." From the corner of her eye, she saw Milo shoot her an alarmed look, which pretty much confirmed it.

Tawny opened the door, stepping back to allow two men to step inside. The first was a tall guy with a round, protruding stomach and a double chin. His thick, blond hair was faded with streaks of gray and he looked like someone who would laugh so loud, other people would be embarrassed for him. He raised one eyebrow at Tensley and said, "Now you know how to show a customer a good time, doncha?" over his shoulder to whoever was behind him.

Tensley froze.

Tawny glared at Tensley.

Tensley smiled, her upper lip trembling, at Big Blond Guy.

Seemingly oblivious, he lumbered toward her, eyeing her up and down. "Aren't you a fine-looking woman."

Tawny glided in from the back. "Have a seat, gentlemen," she said, gesturing at the leather chairs. "Tensley here is going to show you a *very* good time."

"Ah, now," Big Blond Guy complained with a skeezy smile. "We have to share?"

"There's plenty of her to go around," Tawny purred, arching her back. "I know you're both gonna enjoy yourselves."

The divers in Tensley's stomach performed synchronized flips.

"Why don't you stay, too, honey?"

"Can't, big guy. I've got a show to do." Tawny squeezed his arm. She pranced toward the door.

"Okay," he said, dropping into a chair and turning a hungry look upward at Tensley. "I'm ready."

She had just taken a deep breath when she saw the man with him, no longer blocked by the other's large frame. *N-o-o-o-o. It couldn't be.*

He gave that half-lidded, Cheshire-cat smile that showed his dimples.

It was. Bryan-with-a-y-not-an-i.

"All right, honey," said Big Blond Guy. "I'm ready for you."

Tensley heard a sound like him patting his knee, but couldn't tear her eyes away from Bryan. What was he *doing* here? Why didn't he look mortified that she'd found out he brought customers to a place like this?

"Hey." Bryan snapped his fingers at her. "He's first. Get going."

That was why. He didn't recognize her. Of course he didn't. They didn't know each other in this life.

Asshole. Thought he could snap his fingers at her, did he? She'd snap those fingers right off his hand and—hold on. She might have something better in mind for him.

She sauntered toward him, relying on her body's memory of how to do this kind of thing, which hadn't let her down yet. Thrusting her pelvis, one arm up in the air and then sliding down across her face, her breast, her hip. "You're first," she said, her voice low, sultry.

"What about me?" Big Blond Guy pouted.

"I always start with the amateurs," she replied easily, grabbing hold of Bryan's tie and raising a knee to his chest to push him into a leather chair. He stumbled and sat down hard. "See what I mean?" The look on Bryan's face said he didn't know whether to be pissed off or turned on.

"You're next, honey," she said to Big Blond Guy, "but if I don't take care of this one right away, it's going to be all over for him. Amateurs don't know how to hold themselves...*if* you know what I mean."

Big Blond Guy chortled. Bryan wasn't waffling any more. Now he looked pissed off.

She undid the belt of her robe, put her hands on the arms of the chair and leaned over him, her enhanced breasts inches away. She shook them.

"You'd better not be looking for a tip, saying that kind of shit."

Why had she never realized what a whiner he was? She leaned down to whisper in his ear. "Oh, I think you'll be giving me a great big, fat tip. Unless you want your wife to know where you're going on those business dinners. While she's sitting home in your pretty little house, taking care of the baby."

"Screw you." But he sounded nervous.

"Um, no, honey," she said sweetly. "I think we can do just about anything but that."

"I paid good money and it wasn't to have some—some stripper try to abuse me." He was now so furious, she could have sworn she felt spittle on her ear.

His words should have hurt, but oddly enough, they didn't. "Oh!" She stood up, putting a finger to her lower lip. "Abuse is in the other room. Is that what you wanted? 'Cause you're in the wrong place."

Big Blond Guy's laugh boomed. "What the hell?" he asked. "You need some woman to beat you up?"

Bryan's eyes flashed as he grabbed Tensley's arms. "I don't have to take this."

Oh, yes, you do.

Milo made a move toward them.

"It's okay," she said to Milo, waving him back. "We're just having a little fun. That's all."

And, sadly enough for Bryan, she was just getting started with that fun.

CHAPTER TWENTY-FOUR

Tensley had never been a person who enjoyed exacting revenge, but she could make an exception this one time. Really. She could.

She prevented Bryan from getting out of the chair by putting her boobs about an eighth of an inch from his face, where she could feel his hot breath on her skin. He was a boob guy and she knew he'd never be able to resist these girls.

Back a million years ago, right before she'd caught him in his lie, he'd casually wondered out loud whether she might want to have hers done. She'd been so eager to please him, she'd almost considered doing it.

She slid the robe off her shoulders. It fell on the floor.

His breath missed a step or three, and his hands began moving upward. She should have realized a lot earlier in their relationship that it had always been that way with Bryan. His penis ran the show. If he'd been a firefighter tasked with saving people from a burning building and he'd seen a pretty girl across the street, his penis would have shot up, knocked the axe out of his hand, and dragged him after the girl, burning house and people be damned. *Jerk.*

She loosened the tiny bit of string that barely encased her breasts in cloth and, in one exaggerated motion, took off her top, letting it also drop to the floor. "Come on, honey, don't you want to touch them?" she whispered.

Somehow, it didn't feel as bad as it would with a stranger. After all, Bryan had been with her naked body before, even if he didn't know it.

Oh, who was she kidding? It felt horrible.

He gurgled something unintelligible, but his hands closed in on her bare boobs, squeezing them like grapefruit. Large grapefruit, if one were to get technical about it.

"There you go, baby." She fought to suppress her nausea and began nibbling on his left ear, which she knew he loved.

"You're gorgeous," he choked out, eyes closed.

Uh-huh. And you're a cheat and a liar. "More gorgeous than Simone?" she murmured.

His eyes flew open at the mention of his wife's name. "Wh-a-at did you say?"

She loosened his tie and pulled it off, laying it across the arm of the chair. "I said, more gorgeous than you know."

"Oh." His voice was faint, his penis apparently shoving his cognitive processes into the background.

Next, she undid his buttons, but after two, gave up and ripped his shirt off. As in an actual tearing of fabric, which caused Big Blond Guy to get nervous. Tensley heard him call Milo over and ask, "Hey, we're not in that, you know, abuse room, are we?"

Milo loomed over Tensley long enough to shoot her some sort of warning look. She didn't care. She was too busy rubbing her crotch up against Bryan's bare chest while she finished tearing his shirt in half. That should be fun for him to try and explain to Simone. *I'd just left the meeting and was walking to the car when, out of nowhere, a crazed dog grabbed me by the shirt... Uh, no. I was running to catch a plane when my shirt got caught on that rolling walkway thing and... Hah.*

Wasn't easy to suppress both a giggle and vomit at the same time.

He put one of her nipples in his mouth and sucked noisily while grabbing her bottom and rubbing her hard against his lap.

Ugh. She steeled herself to stay, even though all she wanted to do was grind the heel of her stiletto into his nuts, and whispered, "You've been needing this release; I can tell, baby. Ed Cross being an ass to you again?"

"An ass," he agreed. This time, it took him a few seconds longer to surface from his haze. "Wait. Did you say—?"

"Your boss," she soothed. "He being an ass?" Convenient that his boss, Ed Cross, had a name that rhymed with his position. Now what else could she plant in his brain to pop up after his penis had expended itself and settled down for a quick nap....

She heard a commotion outside the door. Tawny's furious voice. And the voices of others. Male voices. Milo snapped to attention. Big Blond Guy fumbled with the zipper on his pants. *Eww.*

As for Bryan, Tensley wrapped her arms around his head and clasped him hard, determined to make sure he stayed right where he was, face in her boobs. The door sprung open and she looked up to see Max.

Shame washed over her, even as she held tight to a struggling Bryan. It was the worst in a series of nightmares. Max seeing her, like this, with a paying customer. She'd held as tight to the fantasy he didn't believe she was a stripper as she had to the one where she didn't believe it.

Guess they were both wrong.

Max jerked his head. "Get up," he ordered Bryan. "Hands behind your back."

Tensley scrambled off Bryan, retrieved the robe and pulled it on, cinching the belt tight. She couldn't meet Max's eyes.

"Officer," Bryan protested. "I had no idea. This girl told me to come with her. I didn't know what was going to happen. She must have slipped something in my drink—"

Tensley turned a disgusted look on him. "Nice try."

"Save it," Max ordered. He shoved Bryan up and out of the chair, jerking his arms behind his back to handcuff him. Then he grabbed Bryan's ripped shirt from the chair and tossed both pieces to another officer. "Evidence."

He looked over at Big Blond Guy. "What about him?" he asked Tensley.

She stared at Max's badge and shook her head. "He didn't do anything."

"I didn't, I swear! Nothing at all. I was trying to get out of here."

Again, she felt Max look at her. She shrugged and then shivered. It felt suddenly very cold in the room. "He probably was, I don't know."

"Paid your money, though, didn't you?' Max motioned to him. "Move it."

"He was the one who paid." The big guy pointed at Bryan.

Two officers led Bryan, who Tensley could swear she heard sniffling, and Big Blond Guy from the room. Milo followed. Outside the door, Tawny yelled something about calling Gary.

That should be a fun call. Tensley hoped she could miss it.

Max was saying something to her, but the sound of his voice twisted her insides into a knot of humiliation. He took a step closer and said it again. This time, she understood. "You, too. Let's go."

She nodded.

He leaned down and lowered his voice several notches, until only she could hear. "I have to put you in handcuffs."

"Can I get some clothes first?" she asked, keeping her head down.

He took her arm, leading her out the door. "Where's the dressing room?"

Tensley inclined her head down the hall, where Tawny stood, so furious she had already stomped off the heel of one shoe. "You're not closing this place down!" she told one of the officers. "You can't do that!"

"Yes, ma'am, we can," he answered. "Watch us."

Max steered Tensley down the hall and to the left, as she indicated. They passed Milo, being led away in handcuffs, his face stoic.

Halfway down the second hallway, Tensley stopped. "This is the dressing room."

Max nodded. He pounded on the door with his fist. "Police. Everybody out."

A squeal of alarm from the other side and a few minutes later, two dancers pushed past them. "What's going on?"

"Gary's is closed for the night. You need to leave."

"Lila?" said one of the women, the one who had helped her behind the bar a couple of times. "You okay?"

"Going to jail," she said, trying to sound offhand about it.

The woman glared at Max. "He'd better treat you right."

He had. That was part of the problem. "I'll be fine," she said, hoping it was true.

Max knocked again. No response. He opened the door to the dressing room. "Get your clothes on."

Tensley did as she'd been told, hurrying to her locker to pull on a T-shirt, jeans and flip-flops. She ran a brush through her hair and wiped off the worst of the over-the-top makeup. Jail. She couldn't even conceive of it. But that's what they did with women who traded sex for money. Even if she'd been the one to call the police.

Bile again rose in her throat. She ran to the bathroom, making it into a stall just in time. A few minutes later, she wiped her mouth with the back of her hand, brushing it across warm tears. She sat down hard on the tile, her head pressed against the metal of the stall divider, her eyes closed.

Had she ever felt worse, like such a failure, in her entire life?

Easy answer. No.

The voice of her fellow bartender sailed over the stall door. "What are you still doing here?" she demanded. "This is a women's dressing room. You some kind of perv, Cop?"

"I have a dancer in custody," was Max's calm reply. "Thought it would be nice to let her get her clothes on first."

"Yeah? Where is she? 'Cause I don't see anyone in here but you."

Tensley struggled to her feet, holding on to the side of the stall for support. "I'm here," she called, her voice thin. She made it to the sink and rinsed her mouth as best she could. A glance in the mirror showed her face was flushed and the front parts of her hair damp. Makeup she had tried to wipe off had smeared in a bluish-black streak to the side of her eye.

She looked the part. A stripper on her way to jail.

When she emerged from the bathroom a few minutes later, the other woman had gone. Only Max remained and he was staring at the mirror over her station, eyes locked on the Lila Delightful flyer.

She lifted her chin, desperately searching for a shred of dignity she might have overlooked. "May I request that another officer escort me to jail?"

"Funny thing," he snapped. "We don't take requests." Then he was at her side. "Hands behind your back."

She obeyed and felt the cool steel of the cuffs lock into place.

He held the dressing room door open, motioning for her to go through it. This place was even rattier than she'd first thought. With her head down, she saw the gum wrappers and other bits of trash kicked to the side of the carpet; the scuff marks against the puke-green walls.

Just as they arrived at the back entrance, the detective who had been with Max at the coffee shop came barreling through it. "Got the search warrant," he said.

Max jerked his head down the hall. "Gary's office is down there and to the left. Taylor and Baker can help. I'm taking her."

The other man barely glanced at Tensley before he took off in the direction of Gary's office. Alone again, Max and Tensley stepped into the summer night, where he opened the back of a black car and told her to watch her head when getting inside.

Though it had no markings on the outside, it was clearly a police car on the inside. The back seat was covered in plastic; she didn't want to think why. The handcuffs dug into her wrists and her shoulders protested at being held in such a position. And now she would have to either stare out the window at passing scenery, which would heighten her nausea, or look at the back of Max's head and contemplate all she'd lost. Great choices she had.

The worst part, though, was that for all she'd done, there had been no flash of light, no return to her real life. Madame Claire had either lied or Tensley had pinned her hopes on something entirely wrong. Frustration built until it spilled out in a tight question. "Did I help you?"

He turned his head to look in the rearview mirror, his expression quizzical. "You did a great job. We nailed him."

Tensley cast her eyes upward in a plea, as if someone, somewhere, should be able to hear her and send the flash that would shoot her out of the police car and back to her desk at Tanner Cable. She'd never take her job, her life, for granted again. She promised.

But nothing happened.

Max looked in the rearview mirror again. "You didn't have to do it. Thank you."

"In exchange, I get a cozy night in jail."

"What?" He looked baffled. "I'm just getting you far enough away to take the cuffs off. If they don't see you getting arrested, your confidential informant status isn't so confidential anymore."

"Oh." Her shoulders sagged in relief. "Thank God."

"Did you really think I would take you to jail?"

"Well, the handcuffs, the back of the police car...it all looked pretty real."

"You made a deal and you carried it out. I'll keep up my end."

A deal. That's all it was. "Thank you."

His gaze caught and held hers in the mirror. "You took some big chances. And you're probably still taking them. I can't promise they won't figure out you were working with the police."

"That's the least of my problems," she said, below her breath.

"What?"

"Nothing." She stared out the window. "Sorry."

"I don't want you to go back to your place. Razor could find you there and get suspicious."

Now he worried about her. "I'm staying with Kate." Her wrists were really beginning to hurt. "How long until you take these things off?"

"Hold on a couple of minutes more. I'll pull over."

True to his word, he did, bringing the car to a stop under an overhead light on a quiet side street. Relief washed over her as soon as he let her out of the back of the car. That lasted until he unlocked the handcuffs and his hands, rough, warm and gentle, brushed against hers.

She masked the shiver of excitement that shot up her spine with an exaggerated flexing of her arms and hands. "That's an experience I don't care to repeat," she said.

He contemplated her. "Which one?"

Let me name them, one by one. If you have an hour or ten. She changed the subject. "How much time will Gary do?"

Max shook his head. "Nothing for what was going on in the back. That'll just shut him down and result in one hell of a fine."

A fine? For all she'd had to resort to? "That's *it*?"

Max leaned against the car door, studying his hands. "But the other information you got could be a different story."

He kept talking, saying something about Gary and previous felonies, but she couldn't focus on his words. It mattered more that he wasn't looking at her. Probably couldn't stand to after what he'd seen her doing with Bryan.

She tried to pretend it didn't matter, looking down at her own hands, her feet. It didn't work. When he stopped talking, she said, "Glad I could help."

"Ten."

There was a jagged crack in the sidewalk, right next to her shoe. She did not want him to call her by her nickname; it reminded her of everything that had happened before he'd walked in on her with another man. A man who had paid for her services. Her throat went tight and all she could do was keep staring at that crack in the pavement

"One of those phone numbers you gave me. Turns out it belongs to someone who works with your mother."

That got her attention. She looked up. "What? Who?"

"Mark Dorlan. He's one of her senior—"

"I know who he is."

Max looked at her long and hard. "I think he's involved in some of the stuff Gary's doing. Outside of the club."

Tensley shook her head. "Mark Dorlan. I knew there was a reason I never liked him." She thought for a moment. "But I don't see him having anything to do with scum like Gary."

"Looks like there might be a connection to a couple of political campaigns."

Interesting. "Which ones?"

He hesitated. "It's still early in the investigation."

She shoved the toe of her shoe into the crack in the pavement. It was that big.

"The company that's making a serious run at Tanner Cable's franchise has a very good shot at getting it. They have support from key City Council members."

She frowned at the sudden switch in subject. "My mother prefers to handle the strategy on that herself."

Max opened his mouth and closed it again, looking confused. No wonder. *That was the old life, Tensley.* Her mother had shut her out of those discussions, even though Tensley was the director of strategic initiatives, likely because she hadn't thought her competent enough to handle something so important to the company.

Well, maybe her mother had been right. She cleared her throat. "I mean, that's what I heard, anyway." She shoved her hands into the pockets of her jeans as something else occurred to her. "Why are you talking about the franchise? Are you thinking my mother's involved somehow?"

"I don't know."

"Impossible. She'd never do anything to jeopardize the company. It's her whole life."

Max shrugged and looked away. "You never know what someone will do when everything they've worked for could be in trouble."

"The company isn't in trouble."

"You sure about that?"

"Yes." *No.*

"Okay, so say it isn't. Maybe it has nothing to do with Tanner Cable, but Dorlan's name keeps coming up when I try to connect the dots."

Mark Dorlan might be the poster child for self-righteous pricks in expertly tailored suits, but he wasn't a criminal. He flossed after every single meal and if he even had a snack. He'd told her that once. Not that she'd wanted to know. Now she was the one who shook her head. "I don't see it."

Max exhaled. "Like I said, it's still early, but if he's not involved in something, there are some pretty odd coincidences. I found out he's tight with Councilman Digman's campaign manager. That's a campaign Gary used his hardware business, and a political action organization that appears to have one member—Gary—to make a substantial donation to."

"Mark Dorlan can be friends with a campaign manager."

"He was in Gary's club."

Had he seen her? She wanted to throw up. Luckily, Max kept talking.

"The City Council votes on a lot of things. One will be the new club Gary has filed for permits to open. Another will be the city's cable franchise."

"Oh."

"Exactly." Max kicked at a pebble. "It's not all making sense, yet, but I keep going back to Mark Dorlan. I have a feeling the guy's in it up to his ears."

"Then trust your feeling." It wasn't as though Tanner Cable wouldn't be a better place without Mark Dorlan.

He didn't answer for a minute. "I used to trust my feelings. About a lot of things."

She tried to pull her shoe out of the crack in the sidewalk. Stuck. Nothing was going right. Nothing at all. And if she had to take a guess right now, it would be that nothing ever would again. She felt the heat in her cheeks begin to rise, her breath begin to come faster, like a train whistle signaling danger.

She didn't care. She didn't care about anything, maybe ever again. Least of all Max Hunter. Judger. What did he know about her life? About her circumstances? About how an innocent visit to a deranged psychic could take an absolutely normal life and flush it down the drain?

"If you knew me, really knew me, you would know that I would never have done *that*, in that room," she said, raising her index finger to point it at his nose, "if you hadn't asked for my help."

He looked startled. "Hold on—"

"You put me on his lap, you and your police department." She put both hands up and shoved his chest. "You hear me? You did it."

He said something. She didn't listen. Even her hair was sweating and she thought she might be having a heart attack.

His lips were moving, but her voice was shouting. It ratcheted up, to the scary hoarse place it only went to in an emergency. "You wouldn't have made me do that if you cared about me. At all."

"I told you not to." He put a hand on her wrist. She shook it off and shoved him again. He stumbled back. She jerked her leg hard until her foot pulled out of her shoe.

"You didn't mean it. All you care about is being a bad-ass cop."

His arms were crossed over his chest, his eyes turning dangerously dark.

"We doing a prostitute sting next? But you won't come in, gun blazing, until after the deed is done? Is that how it's gonna go?" Her voice was soaring off the charts now, hitting high notes she didn't know she had.

"I don't know what the hell you're talking about." His low growl penetrated her consciousness and she stopped, gulping for air.

"You." She jabbed him in the ribs with a forefinger. "Me." She turned the finger on herself. "And what's wrong with this picture." Her throat tightened. Here's where he would get it, where she would turn and leave him standing, all alone, drowning in the guilty truth of her words. The thought rose and swirled through her foggy brain until one tiny practical cell pointed out that she only had on one shoe, making a grand exit tough.

So instead, she hiccupped.

"Done?" he demanded.

"Haven't." Hiccup. "Even begun."

"You think it's smart to be shoving a cop?"

"Wasn't shoving a cop. I was shoving Max Hunter. Who needs to stop acting like a cop and try acting like a human being. What happened to you, anyway?"

"You want to know what happened to me, Tensley?" he demanded. "I grew up. I decided to be one of the good guys."

"You always *were* one of the good guys, Max," she shot back. "You just didn't believe it."

"Look who's talking."

She gulped.

"You think it didn't tear me apart to see you with that creep? You think I don't feel horrible for putting you in that situation? You think I don't know that wasn't really you? That none of what you did in there was you, but you did it because you have no fear, even when you should?"

"I have fear," she answered, her heart racing.

"You have more courage than most people could ever even think of. You have a stronger sense of right and wrong. You're smart, you're funny, you're loyal, hell, you're *kind*. And most people aren't, not when it matters."

She felt her chin tremble, her heart begin to pick up speed. "Max—"

He wasn't done. She could see his eyes begin to blaze, even in the harsh illumination of the streetlight. "But you let other people tell you what to think of yourself, Tensley. And even worse, you believe them."

"That's not true." *Was it?*

"Yeah? Then why do you think you ended up at Gary's?"

"Because I have a record. Maybe you didn't notice." She only realized she had yelled it when a window somewhere nearby slammed shut.

He took a step toward her. "Everyone has something they're not proud of."

"Not you. Look at you."

"I was the one responsible for you *getting* that record. If I hadn't come up with that stupid plan—" He broke off, raking a hand through his hair.

It was the guilt, the regret crossing his face that made her ask, "Is that why you went into police work, to make up for it?"

His answer was immediate, genuine. "I don't know. Maybe."

"Then maybe something good came of that whole thing." She tried to keep her voice light, but could tell she'd failed miserably.

"It doesn't matter what happened before or why. I don't want to live in the past. It only matters who we are right here, right now. And what we do with that."

He hadn't given up his past. A good job, an education, financial security. To live on what, tips tucked into a thong and minimum wage from a bookstore? With her only family a mother who couldn't stand the sight of her because of what she did?

"You don't understand," she whispered.

"You're the one who doesn't understand."

It happened so fast, she at first thought he grabbed her to push her against the car and throw shackles on her. But that wasn't it.

Not it at all.

CHAPTER TWENTY-FIVE

It was weird kissing an on-duty cop, some part of Tensley observed while the rest of her carried on, oblivious. The black jacket he wore over his T-shirt and the gun he had tucked into his waistband combined forces to assert a cold barrier of authority that tried to push her away even as she melted into him. Stay back, it warned.

He must have felt it, too, because he broke off the kiss and dropped his hands, looking down at her with a gaze that burned hot with questions she couldn't read, let alone answer.

She wanted to tell him how incredibly proud she was of him, that he'd overcome all that had happened when he was young to find a career, and a life, as a respected officer of the law. A detective, no less.

She wanted to tell him she loved the confident way he carried himself now. That he was stronger than he'd ever been because of how gentle he'd become, at just the right times. That the grown-up Max was so much sexier than the teenager she'd known, who'd had rough-edged promise, but unrealized dreams.

She wanted to tell him that she'd never been in so deep and she was scared to death she'd never be able to get out again, never be able to find another man who saw the parts of her she couldn't love herself. And accepted them.

That wasn't a part of the past. That was now.

She parted her lips, with no idea what would come spilling out from them, but didn't have a chance to say anything before she heard her name. Being shouted from a car across the street.

By her best friend, Kate. With the world's most horrible timing.

"Tensley!" she called again, leaning out of the driver's side. "We have to go!"

She turned back to Max.

He grasped her elbows. "What's she talking about?"

Damn. Those eyes. "I—I don't know." She tried to wave Kate away while she kept her gaze locked on Max. She had to know what had just happened here, what it meant.

Then she heard the slam of the car door. Kate was at her side before Tensley could summon the words to tell her to go away. Her friend pulled on her arm, still held by Max. "We have to *go*."

"Why?" she and Max asked at the same time.

Kate addressed herself to Tensley. "Trust me."

"I do, but—"

"We have an appointment." Kate's eyes widened, obviously trying to convey some meaning Tensley wasn't getting. "With someone named *Claire*?"

Ow. It actually hurt a little when your heart skipped. "Are you kidding me?"

"How can you have an appointment with somebody at this time of night?" Max demanded.

Kate turned to him. "Good to see you again, Max. This has nothing to do with you."

"The hell it doesn't. We're not done here, Tensley."

Oh God. Oh God. Oh God. She didn't want to be done here. She didn't want to leave him, not now, not when this streetlight was bringing out things she'd never heard before.

"*Claire*, Tensley. Remember you asked her about doing something for you? She says she will, but it has to be now."

"Now?" Tensley asked, faintly.

"Right now."

"You need to tell me what's going on." Max's voice was terse.

"I can't." Tensley tried to swallow past the lump in her throat. She pushed him away from her, heading blindly for the car. "I have to go."

"Again with pushing a cop," she heard him call. "I could put you in jail for that."

"You won't," Tensley said.

"He won't," Kate agreed.

Tensley got in the car, then whispered, "Wait. How did you find me?"

Kate whispered back. "She told me where you'd be."

Tensley widened her eyes as Max raised his voice to be heard over the engine of Kate's car. "If I put you in jail, at least I'd know where you were."

Kate and Tensley stared straight ahead, neither saying a word. Kate steered the car out into the street and flicked on her turn signal. They had someplace to be, a psychic to see.

* * *

Madame Claire's hands shook. "We must proceed immediately," the woman said. "It is not all night I have."

"Not so fast," Tensley said. "Kate said all you told her was that you figured out the right spell. How do you know for sure it's the right one?"

Madame Claire adopted what might have been a serene expression if it hadn't wobbled around the edges like a facelift about to fall. "My mother's writings. I went through them." She pursed her lips. "There was a notebook I found. She had perhaps forgotten to mention it."

"Seems as though there's a lot she didn't tell you," Kate muttered.

Madame Claire narrowed her heavily lined eyes.

Tensley leaned forward. "How do you know for sure what's going to happen this time? I can think of all kinds of possibilities." And the more she did, the more worried she became. "I'm floating back and forth between two lives, never sure which one I'm in. Or I'm in some kind of horrible *Groundhog Day* situation." She turned to Kate. "Have you seen that movie?"

Her friend shuddered. "That would be terrible."

"Point is," Tensley told Madame Claire, "this is my life you're messing with. You've already screwed it up once. How do I know this emergency spell won't screw it up again?"

The psychic shifted in her chair, not meeting the eyes of either woman. "There are indeed things that must be considered."

"What things?" Tensley and Kate exchanged alarmed looks.

"Your life will be as it was before. But with this spell, the one of my mother's writings, it is not only your life that will change. It will apply to both do-over spells. This you must think of. There is no going back. After."

"Not just my life," Tensley repeated, trying her best to absorb it. "You mean," a quick glance at her best friend, "Kate, too?"

A nod, then Madame Claire stared down at her lap. "I have only performed this do-over twice." She pointed, without looking up. "You and you."

"Kate." Tensley grabbed her friend's hand. "I can't do that to you."

Her friend's eyes had filled with tears, which she tried blinking away. "What, are you kidding? Look what I did to you. This whole thing is my fault."

"You were trying to help me."

"The way things were going, I thought you'd never trust yourself enough to get over everything that's happened, to be who you should be."

"So I'll make sure I do this time."

Tensley turned to Madame Claire. "Will I remember this happened?" she demanded. "Will Kate?"

"Remember? Well—" The woman avoided their eyes. "No," she said finally.

"You're sure."

"It is as sure I am as one can be," the psychic huffed.

That's comforting. Tensley stood and began pacing back and forth, the wooden floorboards creaking beneath her. What about Max? If everything was undone, he might have kept going down the path in life he'd been on. Who knew what he would end up as? But it probably wouldn't be good. "This is crazy. It's an impossible choice." To get her real life back, she'd have to potentially ruin two others. The lives of people who meant everything to her.

"There isn't a choice, Tensley," Kate said. "You just have her undo it. That's all."

"It's not that simple." Why, oh why, couldn't anything be simple anymore? Why couldn't somebody else make this decision? Kate was right. Max was right. She couldn't trust herself to know what to do; she never had been able to. For God's sake, she'd thought she was in love with Bryan-with-a-y-not-a-i. When given half a chance, she'd punched Rhonda the Skank and then tried to run from the cops.

She was a walking train wreck when it came to making good decisions.

Just ask her mother.

Tensley walked to a window, laying her fingers on the glass, and staring out into the sleeping city. When Patsy the bookstore owner had asked her favorite quote, she hadn't hesitated, coming right up with the words of heroine Fanny Price in *Mansfield Park*: "We all have a better guide in ourselves, if we would attend to it, than any other person can be."

Fanny had said the words with such certainty. Tensley wondered now if the reason she loved that quote so much was because she hadn't ever lived it. It must be wonderful to know you could rely on yourself to do the right thing, to get through life, if not unscathed, at least not totally undone.

Max had told her she had a strong sense of right and wrong. She did, especially when it came to other people. But when it came to herself, things were a lot less clear. Every time she thought she knew what to do, and went after it, she spent all her time second-guessing herself. By the time she'd done the thing, she'd be telling herself how wrong she'd been. Before anyone else could say it.

"Tensley?" Kate asked from across the room.

"It is not all night I have," Madame Claire repeated.

Tensley turned, letting her gaze go from Kate to Madame Claire and back again. "We're not doing this." *What?*

"Wha-at?" Kate stuttered.

"What?" the psychic demanded. "It was not a pleasant task, that going through my mother's things."

Tensley nearly didn't recognize her voice when she heard it, level, confident, leaving no room for argument. "Something tells me you'll need an emergency spell again," she said to Madame Claire. "So you had to do it." To Kate, she said, "If you're okay with it, I'm going to stay with you a little longer. Until I save enough money to get my own apartment."

Kate looked stricken. "You're going back to that place?"

"Not to Gary's, no. Never again. But I do have another job. At a bookstore."

"You don't know what you're doing…" Kate's voice trailed off.

"I think I do, actually," Tensley disagreed. "Maybe for the first time ever." She pulled the business card Max had given her from her pocket and clutched it in her hand.

Madame Claire's eyebrows rose to the ceiling. "My fee, if you please," she shot at Kate.

"Do not give her a penny." Tensley strode to the door. "I'll be in the car." Her heart pounded; her mouth had gone dry. This had been the biggest decision of her life. Either one.

Her inner guide, now unleashed, had better not let her down.

CHAPTER TWENTY-SIX

As Tensley stepped through the door of Madame Claire's, a blinding explosion of light caused her to cover her eyes. A second later, a powerful gust of wind swept her hair backward.

She barely had time to register it as a repeat experience before she shot up in bed, gripping a pillow to her chest and struggling to catch her breath. It took a few minutes to regain a shaky hold on her composure before she could brave looking down. Her favorite Victoria's Secret pajamas, silky smooth on her skin. Her 1500-thread count Egyptian cotton bed sheets, soft and reassuring. The king-sized bed she'd spent months picking out.

She was in her condo.

Slowly, she pulled the pillow away from her chest. *Hello! Ye-e-s-s.* Her smaller, unenhanced, all-hers, one-hundred-percent original boobs.

She flopped back down on the bed in relief and stared up at the ceiling, giggling. Must have all been a dream. A crazy, wild dream. Wait until she told Kate.

Then she realized she held something in one hand, clutched in her fist, as though afraid to let it go. She opened her fingers one by one and stared at the business card that floated from her open, outstretched hand onto her chest. Didn't even have to look at it. She saw the police department logo, knew whose card it was.

There was only one reason she would have the card. She'd held it in her hand when she went through the door of Madame Claire's shop. All of this insane crap had actually happened. Her giggle dried up and disappeared, replaced by a knot of panic. What had happened to Max, to Kate? Had Madame Claire ignored what she'd said—because she wouldn't put it past the bitch—and done the emergency spell, anyway, without permission?

Oh no, oh no…. Please, no. She fumbled for her cell, lying on the nightstand next to her, and began dialing. She knew Max's office number by heart, had memorized it as soon as he'd first given it to her. The phone began to ring. She'd caught a flash of the time on her cell display. Three a.m.

The ringing stopped. Voicemail clicked on. Tensley held her breath. A male voice. "You've reached Detective Carl Cole in the midtown precinct," the man growled in her ear. "Leave a message and I'll get back to you."

Tensley's heart sank as she pushed the button to end the call. No Max. She stumbled out of bed to find her laptop. The few seconds it took to wake up felt like an eternity. With trembling fingers, she went to the police department's site and did a search for "Detective Max Hunter." Nothing.

She put her head in her hands. It was all her fault.

This time, she crept back to bed, trying to make as little noise as possible with her presence in the world, and pulled the sheet over her head. Max could be anywhere, doing anything. She'd never looked for him before because she had been afraid of how hard she might fall again. Now she was afraid to look for him for an entirely different reason.

After several minutes, she used both hands to uncover her eyes, then her chin. There was someone else she needed to call.

She picked up the phone and dialed another number. A sleepy female voice answered. "Ten?"

"Kate."

Her best friend mumbled something indistinguishable.

"Please tell me you're a vet."

A sleep-laden sigh on the other end. "How much have you had to drink?"

"Tell me."

"Of course I'm a vet. What's wrong with you?" The words were clearer now, and so was the irritation.

"Madame Claire." She couldn't say any more than that, for fear recounting the story somehow made it more real.

"Oh." She had Kate's attention now. She heard the covers rustle as Kate apparently tried to shake off her sleep. "Did you go? How was it?"

"I don't—don't think so. I'll call you in the morning. Go back to sleep. Sorry for waking you up."

Kate yawned. "Fine. Bye."

The phone clicked off.

So they were back at the beginning, where Tensley must not have made the mistake of going to see the psychic in the first place. At the word "mistake" her mouth twisted into a grim smile. She lay back against her luxurious pillowcase, eyes wide open. She might as well get up and get some coffee. There was no going back to sleep now.

The new life gone. The old one back.

Madame Claire hadn't invoked the emergency spell, after all. Tensley had learned her lesson. Her…lesson.

For once in her life, she hadn't second-guessed herself; she'd listened to herself and what she thought was the right thing to do. She'd stood up for herself, despite what other people thought.

She'd followed Jane Austen's advice and listened to her inner guide.

While the love she'd thought impossible to find had crumbled as fast as Madame Claire's alleged psychic abilities.

She finally knew what learning a lesson the hard way meant. With a sob, she pulled the sheet back over her face.

***

Tensley matched her mother's stare with an unblinking one of her own; a move so unusual she could tell it caught her mother by surprise.

"You are clearly mistaken," Esme Tanner said. "It never serves one well to repeat gossip. I would have thought you, of all people, would be aware of that."

Verbal knife stick to the ribs. Yes, Tensley was aware of that. The office gossip had apparently run rampant about her taking time off after she found out the truth about Bryan. The latest story she'd heard had her pregnant and running away so the baby would have Canadian citizenship.

"This is not gossip," she said firmly. "Mark Dorlan is either mixed up with fixing City Council votes for our franchise or he's about to be. Either way, you need to be asking him about his association with Digman's campaign manager."

"Really, Tensley. I know you don't like him, but you're taking things a bit far, don't you think—"

"I think you'd better not be in on it with him, Mother."

Esme Tanner's face froze, her eyes huge. "I cannot believe you would say such a thing." She hurled the words at her daughter one by one.

"I'm asking. Warning. Whichever one is appropriate." Tensley kept her voice level. "The police know about it or they will soon and if you're in it with him, this company will come down around your ears."

The door opened with a creak. "Ms. Tanner—"

"Not now, Christine!" Esme thundered.

The door closed with a thud.

Esme directed her attention back to her daughter. "You may say goodbye to your position here."

"I already said goodbye to my position here."

Her mother looked taken aback. "I had assumed you were here to ask for your job back after behaving so foolishly going after that—that man."

Tensley nodded. "It was foolish going after Bryan, but it would be even more foolish to ask for my job back."

"So you're hoping for another position. Mark Dorlan's, perhaps."

"Seriously?" Tensley laughed. "I have no interest in Mark Dorlan's job. Trust me. You need to look into what Mark's doing and if what I told you is true, you'd better get someone else in there." She rose from her chair. "But it isn't going to be me, Mother. That's one thing I'm sure of. Me and my inner guide."

"Your what?" Esme also rose, looking confused. "I don't understand."

"It's simple. This isn't for me."

Esme's entire body began to shake in fury. "What do you mean, 'it isn't for you'? This company is your legacy and without it, you don't have anything. You'd damn well better come crawling back in here asking for your job back."

Tensley put a finger to her chin, pretending to give it thought for a moment. "No," she said. "I have a much better idea."

"Don't be an imbecile. There is nothing better."

"But there is." Tensley grinned. "I'm buying a bookstore. Talked to the owner today and it turns out she wants to spend more time with her grandkids than she does working in the store."

"A bookstore." Esme made it sound like a porn shop.

"Yes. A bookstore." Tensley had her hand on the door now, ready to leave.

"Wait!"

She did.

Esme's mouth worked for several seconds, as though she had to force words from her mouth. "Come back. Please."

Though her heart melted at the request and what she knew it had cost her mother to make it, her instincts told her that would be the worst thing she could possibly do. "I can't, Mother. But thank you." She hesitated, then suggested, "Dinner next week?"

Esme sat down hard. "I'll have to think about it," she said.

"Good. I'll call you with a time." She couldn't pinpoint the feeling she had, the lift in her soul, the cheery jump in her outlook. Oh, wait. She'd never before left any kind of meeting with her mother without feeling like a bug squashed under designer heels.

She loved her mother, but with this new approach, she might also find some things to *like* about her. There was always hope.

With a smile, Tensley left. She called a greeting to everyone she passed on the way to the elevator and once she'd reached the lobby, she made sure to seek out Arthur, the security guard. He put a finger to his forehead when he saw her, ready to begin the casual banter.

"How are the kids, Arthur?" she asked.

He looked surprised by the question, but recovered quickly. "Doing fine, thank you."

"And your grandchildren?"

Pride spread across his wrinkled face. "The oldest one just made the Dean's List. His first year in college."

"That's great. You must be so proud of him."

The older man's eyes sparkled. "That's for sure. Though I don't know where he got his smarts from."

"I have a pretty good idea." She squeezed his arm. "Take care."

"Yes, ma'am. Good to have you back."

"I'm not coming back to work," she explained. "I'm buying myself a business."

"No kidding. Good for you!" The guard put his hand out to shake hers.

"Thanks. Here's the name of the place. Come see me, okay?"

"I sure will."

"I'll still come in once in a while to visit my mother. Make her go out to lunch."

Arthur chortled. "That woman doesn't like anyone trying to take care of her."

"All the more reason to do it." Tensley lifted her hand. "See you soon, Arthur."

***

Patsy had agreed to let the woman in the expensive tailored clothing watch the store for her while she drove off for a visit with her grandkids. Due diligence, Tensley Starbrook had called it. More like a trial run, Patsy figured.

Patsy was still mystified how the woman had known she was thinking of selling the bookstore; Patsy had not even quite come to the conclusion herself.

But it had sounded like such a good idea, now she couldn't let go of it. Time with those little ones that she hadn't been able to have with their mothers because she'd always been running the store. Time was one thing you couldn't get back, Patsy decided.

You only got one chance to do things right, so you'd better make the most of it. Retirement was sounding better and better all the time. Good thing, since Tensley Starbrook's offer had been made and accepted so fast, Patsy's head was still spinning.

The woman's certainty and clear love of books, though, made Patsy think the store would be in good hands.

She started up the Buick, checked behind her, and drove off, the passenger seat piled with books for her grandkids.

***

Tensley had finished going through Patsy's records for the last year and was walking through the bookstore's aisles, jotting down her ideas for changes, when she heard the front door open. A customer. She put on her best smile and turned.

Then she saw him. Standing before her. "Max." Her knees turned to jelly at the same time a thrill of excitement shot up her spine.

"Tensley." His voice caressed her as his smile washed over her, wrapping her tight with its warmth and visible relief. "I wasn't sure you'd remember me."

"Not remember you." She walked to him, laying a hand on his arm. "I don't know how you could even think that." Then she realized that, as far as Max knew, he hadn't seen her since high school. "You're back in town," she said.

His blue eyes held hers. "I'm back in town."

She became lost in his gaze, the scent of his cologne, the nearness of him. Neither one of them said anything for a minute. Then the coal-black cat Tensley had just adopted from the pound brushed up against her legs with a meow, startling her. "Oh!" She pulled away from Max.

He looked down. "Yours?"

"Yes. Um." She felt awkward all of a sudden. Possibly because she was remembering that amazing, incredible night they'd had. The one he *didn't* remember. Because to him, it hadn't happened. "His name is Gemini Too."

Max tipped his chin, then looked back at Tensley. "Split personality?"

"It made sense at the time."

He nodded. He looked hotter than ever, Tensley decided, dressed in a blue T-shirt and jeans, with sunglasses tucked into the neck. The kind of self-confident, gorgeous, dangerous guy women would turn to look at. And lust after.

What he didn't look like...was a cop.

"So what are you doing now?" she asked casually, leaning on the wide wooden counter for support, since her knees continued to betray her. She leaned in too far, though, sending papers and pens scattering.

"Let me help," he said easily.

They kneeled at the same time, knocking their heads together.

He laughed, rubbing his head. "And here I was trying so hard to be super cool."

"You don't have to try," she said softly, picking each pen up carefully and trying, but not too hard, to hide her grin. "Comes naturally to you."

"Must be the cop side."

She straightened too quickly and fell on her butt on the wood floor. "You're a cop?"

"Was a cop," he explained, "for several years. Then I went on to something different."

Tensley scrambled to her feet. He put out a hand to help her. And left his hand in hers, warm, strong, gentle.

She could hardly think, but managed to put together a question. "What's the something different?"

"That's why I'm here," he said. "I went to see you at the Tanner Cable office, but the security guard told me you'd moved on. That I could find you here."

Arthur. Thank God she'd given him that card.

"I have something to show you," Max said. He moved away from her and toward one of the front bookshelves. He grabbed a hardcover book and brought it back, handing it to her. The title read *Nine-One-Done.* The author's name, in tall red letters, was M. T. Hunter.

"Max," she breathed, staring at it. "Hold on. Are you serious? You're M. T. Hunter."

"That's me." He gave a small bow. "Author of the Detective Will Fox series."

"That's amazing!" She wanted to burst with pride, relief, and fourteen other emotions she couldn't name or decipher.

"Here's what I wanted to show you." He opened the book to the dedication page. It read, *"With love and gratitude to Tensley, who always knew I could do this. Even when I didn't."*

Her eyes filled. "Max."

"I'm here for a book tour. Decided to start it in my hometown."

She shook her head. "I can't believe it."

"Neither can I. Keep thinking somebody's going to pull it all back, say they found out I don't really know what I'm doing." At the edges of his smile, she saw a distinct wobble.

"You're a wonderful writer," she burst out.

"And that's why I couldn't wait to see you." He paused. "Was wondering if you might like to go to dinner with me tonight."

"Dinner? With you?" she echoed. She still couldn't believe he was standing here, in front of her, in her living, breathing *real* life.

"Seems like the least you could do, since I put your name in print, and all."

"In print," she repeated, wondering if there was any possible way he could remember the night they'd spent together. How could that much passion be wiped away, with a murmur of a Madame Claire spell?

He misinterpreted her hesitation. "Hey, sorry. I didn't even ask if you were—with someone."

"No!" She took a deep breath. "Not with anyone." An even deeper breath. "You?"

He shook his head.

"Great!" she said brightly. "I'd love to have dinner with you. On one condition." She didn't want to give up being with him, but if he couldn't accept this...

His eyes narrowed. He looked skeptical. "What's that?"

"I don't want to talk about high school. At all. This isn't about the past."

Relief spread across his face. "Don't want to. I just ran into Rhonda Reardon. Purely by accident. That's all the going back to high school I can take."

"Rhonda the Skank?" It was out before she realized it. "Oh. Sorry."

He laughed. "I think her skanky days are behind her. She's married to a police detective and they have four children. She's a soccer mom now."

"Sure she isn't sticking those soccer balls under her shirt?"

Max laughed. Tensley did, too, but then she added, "Sorry. She didn't deserve that. I'm glad she's happy."

"So about dinner."

Her heart had begun beating way too hard for its own good. She pointed at the book's dedication page. "If this isn't about the past, what is it?"

"I did that a while ago. At the time, it was about thanking you. For believing in me. But now…" He shook his head, putting a hand up to scratch behind one ear. "You're going to think I'm crazy, but for the last few weeks, I haven't been able to stop thinking about you."

It wasn't as crazy as he might think.

"It's like all day and all night long."

"Really." *Go on.*

"Not about high school, though. I swear I must have seen your picture somewhere, because I pictured you just like this." He swept his hand up and down. "And I felt as though I knew something about your life now. Almost doesn't make sense."

Her heart soared. Hallelujah for another possible Madame Claire screw-up, in the right direction this time. "Oh, it does." She nodded, grinning from ear to ear. "To me." They would be great together, her and Max. Her inner guide said so. In a flash that felt a lot like a vision, she saw children. With deep blue eyes. Oh God. The damn psychic must have rubbed off on her.

She cleared her throat, willing herself back to the present. "Dinner," she croaked. "Pick me up here. At six." Patsy would be back by then.

His entire face, a face minus a certain small scar, was wreathed in smiles. "I'll be here."

She didn't want him to leave, even for that short amount of time, and he didn't seem to want to, either. He grabbed both of her hands and held on.

After a few minutes, and more prodding from the cat, they broke away from each other. "I'll see you at six," he said, walking backward toward the door.

"Six," she promised. "Oh, and Max?"

He stopped.

"I've started working on my own book."

"Really? That's great!"

"It's called *Tips for the Self-Employed: Stripping Down to the Basics.*"

"Love it."

"You have no idea." But give her a few days and he would.

After he left, Tensley started humming as she put a hand lightly on the counter for balance. She put one leg forward, then curled it around a virtual pole and executed a spin. Perfect.

Oh, yeah. I still have it.

Wait until Max saw her use it.

THE END

ABOUT THE AUTHOR

A native of the Pacific Northwest, Jane and her family recently moved to Ohio. She loves reading and writing books with feel-good endings, rescuing dogs in need of a home, feeding a shameless addiction to both reality TV and PBS, exploring the country with her husband, and being a mom.

She is also the author of *Grab the Brass Ring* and *Say It Again, Sam.*

Did you enjoy this book? Drop us a line and say so! We love to hear from readers, and so do our authors. To connect, visit www.boroughspublishinggroup.com online, send comments directly to info@boroughspublishinggroup.com, or friend us on Facebook and Twitter. And be sure to check back regularly for contests and new releases in your favorite subgenres of romance!

Are you an aspiring writer? Check out www.boroughspublishinggroup.com/submit and see if we can help you make your dreams come true.

40279496R00181

Made in the USA
Lexington, KY
04 April 2015